The Trouble With Some People

A GUSSIE SPILSBURY MYSTERY

by Laura Haferkorn

To Shirley
Happy Reading!
Laura

Produced by:

FriesenPress
Suite 300 – 852 Fort Street
Victoria, BC, Canada V8W 1H8
www.friesenpress.com

Distributed to the trade by The Ingram Book Company

DEDICATION

Lovingly dedicated to my husband, Canute, without whose
daily expertise in the kitchen this book might never
have been written. And to my four beautiful 'roses'.

ACKNOWLEDGEMENTS

Thank you to Florence Chatten and Doris Potts, both former teachers, who kindly took the time to read an early draft and offer suggestions and support.

Thank you to Joshua Augustin, who was in on it from the beginning and kept the secret.

Thank you to my dear family for bringing so much colour and excitement into my life.

And lastly, a belated thank you to my Grade Six teacher, Miss Jean Broatch for giving me such a good grounding in English grammar and encouraging me to explore it further.

The Trouble With Some People

A GUSSIE SPILSBURY MYSTERY

Laura Haferkorn

1

MISSING POP

Jesse scuffed his way along the narrow trail that would take him deep into the woods beside the Old Barge Canal Road. It wasn't really a trail. More like an animal track. Made by deer. Or raccoons. If Adam hadn't shown him where it was, he never would have found it. The wind, which had been blowing steadily since suppertime last night, had filled it in with leaves, making it even harder to follow. Jesse had tried to get in this way once before, but that was way back last May. Hungry mosquitos had driven him out before he could get down as far as the swamp.

His friend Adam had shown him how to look for trails in the woods. He'd spent a lot of time showing him how to find animal tracks. Adam was so good at spotting even the faintest impressions of hooves that the local hunters liked to take him out with them before the start of Hunting Week to help them figure out where the best places were for them to hunker down and watch and wait for deer. How Adam got off school, Jesse didn't know. Adam split his time between his Dad over on the Reserve and his Mom in town. He went to the same Junior School as Jesse in Bickerton. Maybe Adam went to two schools. *That would be neat*, Jesse thought. *Each school would think you were at the other one and you could take off and nobody would know.* The hunters didn't pay Adam for helping them. But they did treat him to two double cheeseburgers and a Coke. Every time, Adam said. He'd made Jesse promise not to tell anyone. He'd get in heck with his mom, for sure. She didn't like him hanging around the kind of guys who roared up and down the back roads in their pickups during Hunting Week. Making their tires squeal. Throwing up clouds of dust. All hot to find something to kill.

The wind wasn't blowing quite so hard now, but every once in a while a sharp gust would sweep over the piles of fallen leaves, making them swirl up into Jesse's face. Shoving his hands in his pockets, he squinted up through the swaying trees at a dull gray sky flecked with wispy white clouds. The way the colours ran together reminded him of Pop's old plaid bush jacket that was still hanging in the back kitchen. Pop left it behind when he took off last month. Seemed like lately everything reminded him of Pop. *Wish I could take off like him,* Jesse muttered to himself. He aimed a kick at a huge clump of dry weeds. And another at a broken branch that lay across his path. *Boy, I wish it would snow soon. I wish it would snow and snow ... bury the school ... bury that old bag teacher ... bury those rotten kids that are always making fun – bury them all!* Just because his skin was darker than theirs.

"*I'm not black!*" he'd told his mother angrily after storming his way home from school that first day, "I'm brown. I'm *brown*. Why do they call me *black* ? Miss Snelgrove didn't even try to stop them and I know she heard them, she was standing right there. Snelgrove, Smellgrove, *I hate her!*"

Nothing his mother could say would calm him down.

"Why'd Pop leave, why did he have to go with Christmas coming?" he'd hurled at her. She just looked at him, her eyes filling with tears. He felt like crying himself, but that day he'd been too angry to cry.

Snow. Snow would turn everything white. White Christmas. Dreaming of a White Christmas. *Whoever thought up that crap. Why not a Brown Christmas? Everything covered in brown. Brown. Like chocolate.* Chocolate reminded him of Pop again. Pop loved chocolate. He said it helped him keep his tan all winter. Jesse knew it wasn't really a tan, but he went along with the joke. Pop always kept a big slab of bitter dark chocolate around somewhere. He used to break off chunks and feed them to Jesse like he was a baby bird. They made a game of it.

Pop loved birds. He taught Jesse their names, how to tell a downy woodpecker from a hairy woodpecker. When to watch for robins. Where to look for their nests. He'd made two big bird feeders and hung them in the maple tree behind the house. He bought sacks of black sunflower seeds from the Co-op and laughed with Jesse when the blue jays dive-bombed the woodpeckers, chasing the mourning doves and the house finches away from the trays and scattering seeds everywhere. Pop said blue jays were really bully birds, easily scared off. But those little chickadees, now, you could train them to eat out of your hand.

After Pop left, Mom said they were going to have to get used to Pop not being there all the time. He would tell them when he might be back, she said with a sigh.

"Pop doesn't love us any more," Jesse had said over and over to his mother, "he doesn't love us or he'd still be here."

"Not true," his mother said. "Not true. He just can't stay here right now."

"But why?" Jesse asked, "Why, why, *why?*"

His mother stopped talking then and turned back to her desk.

"I've got to get this done tonight, Jess," she said. "Go find a book or something."

Since Pop left, Mom spent more and more time at her desk. She did freelancing, as she called it, for a big company in the city. It looked boring to Jesse when she showed him, all numbers, pages and pages of numbers. Numbers meant math and Jesse hated math. He liked words better. Words told you stories.

Jesse loved stories. No matter how late Pop came home, he'd find Jesse still waiting up for a story. Pop was real good at it, too. He could do all the voices of the people so it made them seem alive, like they were right there in the room. He'd turn Jesse's little lamp off, lean back on his heels with his hands on his hips and open his eyes until the whites showed and say, w'aal now, what'll it be tonight, Soldier? Pop always called him Soldier. Jesse didn't know when he'd started doing that. He guessed it had been forever. What'll it be tonight, Pop'd say again. Cowboys and Injuns? Pirates? Politicians?

Then, he'd laugh and laugh in his booming voice that seemed to come from the bottom of a well. Jesse's favourite was about the boy who got lost in the woods and wandered around for hours and hours and finally crawled in under the branches of an old pine tree and fell asleep. In the morning, the boy was wakened by a little black dog licking his face. He always asked for that one first. Pop would say, not that old chestnut, why do you always want to hear that old chestnut? Pop knew the answer, but he always asked anyway. He knew Jesse was dying for a dog. Jesse knew just exactly what kind of dog he wanted. One small enough to tuck under his arm and carry upstairs and sneak into his bed without Mom noticing.

His mom didn't want a dog in the house. She told him when she was Jesse's age, she'd had a dog, a brown and white terrier that she loved better than anything in the whole wide world. It was okay as a little pup, but when it got older, it found its voice and yapped and whined. Whined and yapped. All night long, his mom said. Keeping the whole family awake. One day, when she came home from school, the dog was gone. Her father had taken it away, she never found out where and her mother just said good riddance, maybe now we can get some sleep. His mom told Jesse all this one day when he had been pestering her to let him have a dog. If we get one that turns out like that, well, I don't want to have to go through that again, she'd said.

But Jesse wasn't to be put off. When he asked his father that night could they get a dog, Pop said, maybe. Maybe one of these days, when my ship comes in. What ship, Pop? But Pop just laughed again and said, you've got to have patience, Soldier. Got to have patience. Then he lowered himself down into the squeaky old rocker by the bed, stretched out his legs, gave a big sigh, and said, w'aal now, it was like this, you see, there once was this kid named Jake who ... Jesse snuggled down under the well-worn green quilt Pop's Great Auntie Kate had made years and years ago and stared up at the shadowy ceiling, trying to imagine what it would be like to be lost in the woods, all alone, all in the dark full of scary sounds, all cold and shivery. Pop's musical voice rose ... and fell, rose ... and fell, like waves coming in on the beach. Jesse had a hard time staying awake until the end. Then Pop leaned down, brushed his lips lightly across Jesse's forehead and whispered, sleep, my good little Soldier Boy.

Just thinking about Pop made his throat feel tight. Jesse stumbled over a rock as he felt hot tears coming again. "Big baby," he said aloud. Crying made him think of the time he came home and found Pop standing by the stove, slicing up a mess of onions for his own special chili, wiping his eyes with the back of his hand every few minutes, the tears streaming down his face. Imagine a vegetable making a grown man cry, a *vegetable*, he'd said when he saw Jesse standing in the doorway. Pop was a real good cook. Better than Mom, who'd open a can of beans, slap some cheese slices on bread and call that dinner. He knew Mom loved him, she was always telling him she did, but he wished she'd spend more time with him. Especially now with Pop gone.

The sky was a charcoal grey now and the scudding clouds seemed to be sinking down lower and lower and closing in on him. Jesse picked up a long stick from the path and switched it through the piles of leaves as he walked along. He hoped to get in to where the swamp was supposed to be before it got dark. Adam said it was called the Hidden Swamp because it was so hard to find. Ha, ha. That was a good name for sure. Adam said there used to be an easy trail into the swamp, but someone had dumped a huge pile of old truck tires across the entrance. Now the trail was a jungle of poison ivy mixed in with wild grapevines that tripped you up. The only other good way in was through private property. You had to know the people or they'd send their two big dogs after you. Adam said he tried it once, but didn't get far. The monsters nearly caught him before he could hoist himself back up over the massive iron gates where a big sign said **KEEP OUT**. Sure, Jesse loved dogs but not that much.

When he dropped by the library at noon hour, Miss Roxton, the nice lady at the desk, told Jesse a Great Blue Heron had been seen in the swamp the day before. He didn't have the nerve to ask her how she knew. He thought about it all afternoon and couldn't wait for school to be over. What if he told old Smellgrove he had to go to the washroom or something and then snuck out? No. It wasn't worth the punishment of 'staying in' after school for a whole week. Anyway, his mom would be real mad at him. Wading birds, especially herons, were his favourites, the way they could stand still for so long, waiting for a fish to come close and then *pow!* They'd make a sudden lunge and nail the fish before it knew what was happening. As soon as the school bell had rung, he'd rushed home, grabbed Pop's old army field glasses and taken off for the swamp.

He wished Miss Roxton, not that old Smellgrove, were his teacher. *I wouldn't want her to get buried. She's nice. Gee, better hurry or it'll be too dark to see anything.* He started to run. Giving the stick a heave into the woods, he startled a grouse, which flew up with loud flapping of its wings, scaring him into running faster. The narrow track, which was getting harder to see, suddenly veered off to the right. Rounding the bend, he tripped over something and, before he could stop himself, found himself sprawled on the ground. Something was sticking out of a pile of leaves right in the path. In the dimming light, it looked like a stump. Jesse crawled over and scraped the leaves away to take a closer look. As he pulled at the stump, a flash of something bright caught his eye, like the colour of a Hallowe'en pumpkin. But it wasn't a stump. It was a boot. A big old work boot. He squatted down and hoisted the boot up to take a closer look. The boot had something bright orange at one end of it. Another instant and Jesse dropped the boot like it was red hot.

Scrambling to his feet, Jesse took off as if a hundred demons were chasing him, back the way he had come. In his panic, he forgot all about the track and ran blindly through the undergrowth, the twigs and thorns scratching his face and snatching at his clothes, Pop's field glasses thumping madly against his chest.

It seemed like forever before he broke through the underbrush and found himself back on the Canal Road. Dragging his bike out of the ditch, he made straight for home, slammed into the house, ran upstairs and threw himself face down on his bed, panting for breath and trying to muffle his sobs in his pillow.

His mother found him there when it was time for supper.

2

WHERE IS HINKY?

From somewhere behind her, a faint scrunching sound began invading CeeCee's dream. She was lying on a beach somewhere lovely and warm and Hinky was blowing gently in her ear. Mmmm. He hadn't done that for a long time. She didn't want him to stop. The scrunching got louder. Then it was joined by another louder sound, like bells ringing. *What the heck are bells doing on a beach?* CeeCee's eyelids fluttered and then opened as the dream faded. Darn. *Just when things were getting interesting .* But the bells were still ringing. Drat. She'd forgotten to put the cat in the basement. Reluctantly, she eased herself off the sofa. The morning paper, which had served as a temporary blanket, slid off with a swoosh. *Yep. There he is, the little dickens, chewing on the needles he's yanked off the Christmas tree. So that's what's making the decorations jangle. Now I'll just bet he'll start that awful yowling sound he makes before he throws up. Yep! There he goes. Darn it all anyway!*

They went through this every year. Why couldn't Hinky see they needed an artificial tree? And why did he insist on putting up the tree so darned early? It'll look awful by the time Christmas gets here, she thought. Says it's too gloomy after we've gone back on Standard Time and he can't stand it. Not bright here like it was in the City. Says we need the tree up good and early to make things cheerful. Outside lights are too much of a bother to string up and anyway who's around to see them. No. Hink had insisted that Christmas lights belonged inside the house. And on the tree. A real tree.

Maybe I should leave the mess for him to clean up, she thought. Ugh! She might step in it if she waited for that. Drying her hands on her hips, she realized she was still wearing her good grey skirt. And her good blouse. Darn it all again. Now they were both creased. She hated ironing. *Oh well. So I forgot to change. So what?*

Rinsing the rag out in the sink, she saw that it was starting to get dark. Drat these shorter days! The kitchen clock told her it was not quite four. Four! *A whole half hour past tea time!* Better plug the kettle in.

"Hey Hinky! Time for tea," she shouted up the stairs. No answer. "Hink?" she frowned into the gloom of the basement stairs. She flicked the light switch. Rats. Hink'd forgotten to replace the burnt out bulb. Another reminder for his job list. *Where the heck is he? He loves his tea, especially with those short-bread cookies he's been fussing over.* The kettle began whistling at her. She filled her teapot, hesitated, then pulled out the plug and set the kettle aside. Hinky didn't like it if she made his tea without asking him what kind he wanted. They'd gone off coffee since Hink'd had some trouble with his heart last spring, and in no time they'd amassed a huge collection of teas in brightly-coloured tins sitting on their own shelf near the window. Hinky usually preferred the mixture his Granny Hinchcliffe used to brew for him when he visited her in Newfoundland. CeeCee thought it looked like tar. To her it smelled horribly like tobacco and old rope. *But you never know,* she thought, *maybe today he'll be in the mood for some Darjeeling.* Drinking that other stuff depressed him, especially this time of year.

Stifling a yawn, CeeCee tuned the radio to CBC and half-listened to a report about the rising popularity of René Lévesque and his Parti Québecois. She sat down at the pine table by the kitchen window with her tea mug. If this had been the old days in the City, he'd have left her a note. The day after he retired, Hinky had presented her with some new rules. He wasn't going to account for his every move any more, he told her. That was finished. If he felt like going somewhere, he'd go and come back when he bloody well felt like it. The one exception he'd made was teatime. As far as he was concerned that was an immoveable feast, as her mother used to say. Maybe that was because his Gran was always waiting in the kitchen with a mug of tea for him after school. Probably trying to make up for him having no parents around. CeeCee still couldn't get used to the change in him. He'd always been so considerate of her when he was working.

She sighed and stared moodily into her mug. What the heck could have happened to him? When she left the house right after breakfast, he'd been busily chopping up meat and vegetables for a stew for their supper. That was another new rule. Hink was going to be the cook from now on. He'd always wanted to try it and there wasn't room for two in the kitchen, he'd said. CeeCee said that was fine with her, she'd never liked cooking all that much anyway and if that was the case he could do the grocery shopping too, since she wouldn't likely buy what he wanted and she'd never liked that job either. Fine, he'd said, and so that was what they did. Her friends were envious. They couldn't get their husbands to boil water, they said. *Helpless Hannahs,* she thought. *Or was it Johnnies?* And useless to boot. At least Hink had never been that. He'd always pitched in, even when the kids were little, done his share of the picking up and wiping noses and bottoms. Not like some husbands she'd heard about, who thought such chores beneath them. So if Hink wanted a little freedom now and then, she guessed he'd earned it.

Still, she couldn't help wondering where he'd got to. She'd been so exhausted from looking through a ton of old books at the library in town, as soon as she got in the door she slapped a sandwich together, grabbed a tin of pop from the fridge and collapsed on the sofa with the newspaper. Never even noticed he wasn't there. The next thing she'd heard was the cat's scrunching. Her sandwich lay forgotten on the coffee table, the edges curling. She wrinkled her nose and let out a sneeze. An odd smell was coming from somewhere. *Wow! Something's burning!*

She jumped up and dragged the stewpot off the burner. Funny. She hadn't noticed that either. *Must be getting senile,* she thought. She chuckled to herself. Hinky and his cooking. Not like him to put something on the stove and forget about it though. He'd sure changed a lot since he'd retired. No more suits. No more shirts and ties either. He'd thrown them out before they moved. At least, he thought he had. CeeCee had sneaked his best suit out of the rag bag when he wasn't looking. She was sure he'd need it sometime or other. Not wearing that stuff any more, he'd said. Bloody uniform. All the guys looked the same, he'd said. Clones. That's all we were, bloody clones. CeeCee winced every time he said things like bloody this and bloody that. He'd picked up that kind of language when he was still a kid. His Uncle George had come back from the War with a new vocabulary. Hink quit the habit after they were married, because he knew she didn't like it, but he must have been thinking those words all along.

The other thing CeeCee couldn't get used to was Hinky being so crazy about birds. In the City, he'd never noticed them unless they pooped on his car. He was always complaining about 'those dirty old pigeons' on the windowsill outside their bedroom. Said they woke him up too early in the morning. Wanted to call in an exterminator and get some peace, he'd said. She'd managed to talk him out of it. Then a couple of weeks after they moved out here to Bickerton, he went on a nature hike one Sunday down near The Landing and bang! Now all he talked about day and night was adding to his bird list. CeeCee couldn't see the sense in it. Who cares which birds you've seen? It wasn't long before Hinky met others like himself, all mad for birding, and had gone rushing off with them more than once to look for some bird that someone said they saw. How did he know it would still be there? Birds have wings, you know and they scare easily, she said. Hinky had ignored her. Went to the City, bought the most expensive binoculars he could find, said she wasn't to touch them. As if she would. Didn't need them anyway, her eyesight was so good she could see any old birds plain enough without.

Gulping down the last of her tea, CeeCee sighed again, remembering how she'd looked forward so eagerly to Hinky retiring and them doing things together. He'd never had time for much besides his job. It was his idea to move to the country. Better for us, he'd said. Cheaper too. You could even eat out once in a while and not break the bank. Since when had they eaten out? No really decent restaurants. Anyway CeeCee coughed a lot in the City. Bad air, he'd said. Need to get out of it. Bickerton was where an old aunt of his lived when Hink first came to Ontario. Used to invite him down for a couple of weeks every summer. Knew everyone. Took him around with her. She was an avid gardener, taught him a lot about plants. But never birds. Thought birding was a waste of time and birders were crazy. CeeCee wished she'd known the old gal. They would have had a lot in common.

Leaving Toronto hadn't worked out the way she'd hoped. They'd been here over a year now. Hink had gotten into the bird thing, cooked the meals, did the shopping, worked on things around the house, didn't want to go with her anywhere much. He was making his own friends. CeeCee felt left out. She didn't make friends as easily as Hinky. The country's okay, but you need somebody to talk to and something to talk about. She missed listening to Gordon Sinclair at CFRB. He could always be counted on to say something outrageous. She and her neighbours would huddle over morning coffees to listen to his gravelly voice.

Now, their nearest neighbours were even out of shouting distance. Her one new friend lived in the next village. You could run around naked and no one would know, he said once. *As if we'd do such a thing,* she chuckled to herself. Anyway, it wouldn't matter how long they were here, they'd always be outsiders. When someone told her you had to be here fifty years before you'd be accepted. CeeCee had just laughed. At this rate, she doubted she'd last five. If it hadn't been for the library and her hobby researching local history, she'd have gone mad.

Retirement was supposed to be enjoyed. At least that's what everyone said. CeeCee thought it was just like childbirth. You can take all the prenatal classes you like, practise the breathing, do Lamaze, or whatever they do now. But nothing prepares you for the real thing. Retirement. She'd heard you could even take classes in that too. In the City. Wouldn't do much good to study that either. *You don't know what you're in for until you do it.* Anyway, CeeCee suspected those classes were being given by all those new money management companies just trying to grab new clients.

She jumped when the telephone rang. Someone for Hinky. Wanted him to join the Rotary Club. Don't you have to be working to belong, she wanted to ask but didn't. She took the message. Twenty to five. Still no Hinky. Trying not to get panicky, CeeCee found the phone list and started calling the few people they did know. No luck. No one seemed to be home yet. *Better get out and look for him.* Yanking her old blue ski jacket off the hook by the back door, she remembered to shove a flashlight in her pocket. Just in case. *Need a hat too, there's a nip in the air.* She jammed a wool cap over her greying hair, which to her regret was getting thin on top.

Outside, a faint trace of wood smoke hung in the dusky air. *Smells like applewood. Must be coming from the orchard down the road.* Halfway down the drive she stopped. What had Hink been wearing? She'd better check so she could tell the police. If it came to that, God forbid. She shivered as she backed the car up to the house. Yep. Usual stuff. Beige jacket. Khakis. Cap. The old boots he wore birding were gone from their usual place by the back door.

Omigosh, better get a wiggle on, it's almost dark!

3
ORANGE SOCKS

Halfway down the main road that led to The Landing, CeeCee put on the brakes. Where were the places Hinky said he'd seen birds? The beach ... the lighthouse ... the back pasture ... the whole darn place! She switched on the headlights. *Getting too dark to look for birds now. Or for anyone.* What on earth made her think he'd be down here? For that matter, how could he have gotten here? *I had the car in town ... someone must have picked him up ... must have left in an awful hurry or he'd have remembered the stew.* She struggled to think of the names of his birding friends, besides the ones she had already called. No good. She couldn't remember. Was she having 'a bit of an empty space' as her new friend Dottie Kibbidge jokingly called forgetfulness. Or hadn't she been paying attention when Hink told her. Lately she'd developed the habit of tuning him out. Especially on the subject of birds.

Turning off and driving slowly down the Shore Road, not a soul, not a car was to be seen. Only a few deer clustered close to the edge of the road in the gloom. *Better be careful I don't hit any of them...those Bambi lovers'll be after me for sure.* A rabbit suddenly appeared in her headlights, and then was gone. *This is crazy. He can't be here.* She drove around the hairpin curve at the lighthouse and headed back up the Straight Road. Still nothing. She remembered there was a sort of café place just off the Straight Road. *Yep, there it is. The Quick Bite.* Two people were just getting into their car. The Wychwoods. Maggie and Pete. Well. That much she did remember. More birders. Well, Pete was anyway. CeeCee tooted her horn as she turned into the tiny parking lot and pulled up beside them. Rolling her window down, she asked if they'd seen Hink anywhere about. Pete said no. Not today. Sorry. They were in an awful hurry, he said. Maggie ignored her. Well, thanks anyway, she said. They took off, their rear wheels throwing up a spray of gravel. Some of it hit CeeCee's car. Thanks for nothing, she said to their disappearing taillights. Wonder what's eating them?

She sat for a moment, trying to get up the courage to go into the café. She hated going in places like this without Hinky. Always got stared at. People would stop talking and stare. *Newcomer.* She could almost hear their thoughts. The wind made the door hard to open and followed her through when she finally managed it. She tried not to let it slam behind her.

Inside, there was only one table with anyone at it. Not much of a place. The air was rank with the smell of fried fish. She recognized the voice before she saw him. *Nick...Nick Fearnley, that's his name.* Nick, the birding guide from The Landing, was sharing a platter of French fries with a young couple in matching yellow jackets. They looked cold. He was regaling them with some bird story, talking in a loud voice. *The centre of attention as usual.* Nick thinks he's God's gift, Hinky had said only last week. But he knows his birds. Goes down to the Lake every single day. Weekends too. Has his name in the bird sightings book more than anyone else, he'd said. Well bully for him, CeeCee'd said. Who'd read a book like that anyway? Everyone who goes down looking for birds, he'd said. How do you know for sure what they put in the book is true? Hinky had puffed out his cheeks in disgust. They just do, he'd said scornfully. Nick has a terrific reputation among the birders. *Double wow,* she remembered thinking. She didn't dare say any more on the subject. She wondered what Nick did for a living. Could you live on what bird guiding paid? Or did he have another job somewhere? She'd been afraid to ask Hinky. Nick's skill at finding birds was all that mattered to him.

When he saw who it was that had let in the draft, Nick's tone changed. He started lecturing the young couple. *Poor kids. Don't have a clue what they're in for,* thought CeeCee, fingering a menu that felt greasy. Nick was in full sail. Their clothes were all wrong for a birding expedition, he was saying. The colour was too bright. They should be wearing beiges, browns, greens. Stuff like that. Turning slightly in his chair, he aimed his next remark at CeeCee, who'd decided to break the no-coffee rule and was ordering a mug from Joe, the café's owner, who appeared at her elbow. Nick told them all about the new guy who wears the loud socks, so loud they scare the birds away. Started laughing. The young couple looked uncomfortable and didn't join in the merriment.

Ignoring his jibe, CeeCee asked Nick if he'd seen Hinky that afternoon. No, he said. Not today. Definitely not today. He laughed again, turned his back on her and started boasting about some of the places he'd taken birders. Places like Costa Rica, Panama and Cape St. Mary's, Newfoundland where the gannets are so noisy you can't hear yourself think.

CeeCee paid for her coffee. It left an oily taste in her mouth. She was getting up to leave just as Nick started name-dropping. Going on about all the well-known people he'd guided. *What a bore. How does Hink stand him?* She was glad to escape into her car. *Not fair about the socks though.* But it was kind of odd when you thought about it. Hink Denton, who for the last thirty-four years had worn navy blue suits with white shirts and dull ties, since his retirement had taken to wearing bright orange socks. His other outdoor clothes were the correct shades of green and brown. *Must have taken lessons from Nick.* CeeCee chuckled to herself at the idea.

What to do now. She decided to head home. Maybe Hink would be back. She stopped by the liquor store to pick up some Screech, that Newfie rum that Hinky liked to mix with milk and maple syrup on cold nights. Booze was on his forbidden list, but Hinky said the stuff wasn't real booze, just what was left in the barrel after the good stuff was poured off. *I'll bet,* she wanted to say, but kept quiet. Tried it herself one night without telling him. Slept like a baby. Like a baby. Whoever made up that expression didn't know what they were talking about. Babies don't sleep all that soundly. She remembered the nights she'd gotten up with their second child. Night after night after night. Hinky never heard a thing once he was asleep. There'd been a bad house fire in their old neighbourhood and he'd slept right through all the excitement. Boy, was he ever cross with her in the morning when he found out. He said she should have wakened him. She'd sure tried hard enough. Good thing it wasn't their house. She'd have lost him for sure.

She looked around her as she stepped out of the store, clutch- ing the brown-bagged bottle. Funny how there was no snow. And with Christmas only weeks away. It had been a glorious fall with the brilliant colours of the leaves lasting long past their normal time. No rain. Lots of sunshine. Didn't even need our heavy coats yet. We'll pay for this, sure as shootin', everyone said when the subject of the weather came up, as it always did. Global warming, Hinky said. Changes everything. He'd been reading about it in some science magazine. Good for birding anyway, he'd said. The annual Christmas Bird Count would be done next week. Hink would be gone all day until late at night. Driving around with his friends counting birds. How do you count birds? she'd asked. Not hard once you know how, he'd said.

Hink and his birding friends would stay down at the old lodge near The Landing after all the counters had come back and compared notes, turned in their reports. He wanted her to make a triple batch of her raisin tea biscuits for him to take down. Someone would be bringing a huge pot of baked beans. Someone else was bringing apple pie. He'd be dog tired when he got back. CeeCee couldn't understand it. What did it matter whether the birds got counted? How did you count a huge flock of, say, ducks? What if you count the same ones as somebody else? He said it was all organized. Divided up into areas with team leaders. Those fellows know what they're doing, he'd said. Been doing it for years. CeeCee just shook her head. It was all a mystery to her.

Driving slowly back up their lane through the darkness, an uneasy feeling began to take hold of her. As soon as she got safely inside the door, she started calling Hinky's name. Her voice seemed to echo, mocking her. The cat came out of the basement, yawned, stretched, sat down and began licking a paw. There was a draft coming from somewhere. CeeCee went through to the old back kitchen where they kept the wood for the fireplace.

The glass from the only window in the room was lying in pieces on the floor.

4

TOWNS AND VILLAGES

If you stay on the road through Bickerton and cross the high bridge over the Old Barge Canal, a few minutes farther along you'll find yourself in the Village of East Thorne. Once upon a time, on the Bickerton side of the Canal, there was a West Thorne. Descended from a small group of hardy souls who settled there in the previous century, its male inhabitants went away to work at the lumber company up in the Great Forest, while their wives and children had to be content to manage alone. Things went along fine until one evening in late November, just after the end of the Second World War, one of the women was burning brush when the fire got out of hand. Driven by the sharp gusts of a north wind that had come up, it swept through the village and engulfed the houses, which had been built from logs by the original settlers. Most people escaped with nothing but the clothes on their backs. The only thing left standing was a weatherbeaten sign reading WEST THORNE Pop. 37, which no-one had the heart to take down. Two small children died in their beds that awful night and their devastated mother killed herself the next day.

Nobody wanted to live there after that. People who knew what had happened there didn't linger as they passed through the area. Three families moved across the Canal to a place that became known as East Thorne. The others left the area for good.

The few larger houses that eventually appeared in the new village were never as grand as the ones built by the well-to-do in Bickerton, but they faced onto the Canal and had wide front porches where on hot summer evenings you could sit back, enjoy a cool drink and watch the boats go by.

More recently, East Tee, as the locals called it, was gradually turning into a retirement community for people escaping the City. Its own residents were fast disappearing. Some moved into the new retirement home up in Cooley's Mills. Others went to live with their children in the much larger town of Dunhampton down the highway past Bickerton, or in Bickerton itself. Its young people left as soon as they could. The tiny village didn't offer them much excitement and they weren't exactly welcome in Bickerton either. Too many fights had been breaking out in the parking lot behind the Snake Pit, Bickerton's only bar. Especially on Saturday nights. Noses were bloodied and sometimes broken. Sunday mornings would reveal a litter of smashed bottles, or deflated car tires and other damage for which no witnesses could be found.

This situation was a constant aggravation to Constable Gussie who wished she could lay her hands on the culprits. Bickerton people whispered among themselves that it was 'those no-goods from over the Canal' that were to blame. Some said it was the fault of the Town Council for not providing activities for young people. Council members scoffed when they heard this and said it wasn't *their* problem, those kids should be put to work. Trouble was, there were never enough jobs to go around. East Tee'ers were glad the Snake Pit wasn't on their side of the Canal, but they were powerless to keep their young people in line.

People in East Thorne had other complaints. They weren't at all happy watching strangers taking over the big old homes or finding unfamiliar cars parked on their streets. They were used to knowing everyone. Newcomers made them feel threatened. Those city folk might as well have come from the moon as far as East Tee was concerned. They had different experiences, different expectations. Rab Kibbidge, who owned the little grocery store on the main road through the village, told Sherry Roxton that one of them even had the nerve to ask for some kind of European rye bread he'd never heard of. Another wanted some weird-sounding Oriental spices. If they want that stuff, they should've stayed in the City, Rab said as he parceled up Sherry's weekly order. Can't stock everythin'. Sherry murmured her thanks and smiled to herself as she left the store. She much preferred shopping at Rab's than at the tired old Smales Market in Bickerton. Secretly, she welcomed the new arrivals. They brought the excitement of the unknown to the dreary little village. Many of them had lived lives and traveled to places she could only read about in the books she ordered for the library.

Typical of the newcomers were the Otterleys. They liked their new home on the Canal much better than the cramped little shoebox they'd left behind in the City suburb, where the houses were so close together that if you sneezed, your neighbour might be tempted to wish you Gesundheit. Besides, with their past history, which they had so far managed to keep a secret, East Thorne was a good place for them to bury themselves.

On the afternoon Hink Denton failed to come home in time for tea, the Otterleys were sitting in the breakfast nook of their colonial style kitchen, enjoying coffee and some of Francy Otterley's homemade doughnuts. They were arguing in a friendly sort of way about whether to sign up for the Listers Day birding expedition down at The Landing. That was right after New Year's when you started a new bird list for the year. Ferd was all for it, maybe he'd do better this year than last, maybe even catch up with Hink Denton, he said. But Francy wanted to go into Toronto to visit her daughter from her first marriage. Listers Day was always the second of January and Francy knew Marlene had that day off.

Lately it seemed to Ferd that Francy complained at least once a day about being too far from the City. He thought they'd gotten that all sorted out when they'd decided to move here. Besides, Ferd didn't approve of Marlene's lifestyle, said if that was the way she wanted to live, fine, but he didn't have to have anything to do with it. Marlene lived in a run-down rooming house in the Inner City that was always a mess and which she shared with an ever-changing crowd of rough looking young people. They disgusted Ferd who told Francy they could all use a good scrubbing and some clean clothes. Once when he asked Marlene how she could stand it, she just laughed and said, "hey y'know, it's real handy to work, and the rent's real cheap and anyways, it's only 'til I can afford my own place." Ferd doubted *that* would ever happen. Marlene was nearly forty.

In the middle of the discussion that was getting less friendly as it went along and during which Ferd had to struggle to keep from losing his temper, the telephone rang. Francy hurried out to the front hall to answer it. She was gone for so long Ferd finally went out to see what was keeping her. As he stepped into the hall, she plumped the phone back on its cradle and turned around with a frightened look on her face.

"That was CeeCee Denton. She was so excited, I could hardly make out a word! Hink's disappeared!"

"Aw, he's probably off somewhere birding," Ferd said, unsympathetically. "You know how he is. The guy's gone crazy on the subject."

"Just about as bad as you," retorted Francy.

Ferd glared at her. "I've never been *that* bad and you know it," he said.

The Dentons were the first people the Otterleys met after coming to East Thorne. They met one afternoon when they went down to The Landing to watch for shorebirds. Francy and CeeCee took to each other right away, but the two men were rivals from the beginning, trying to top each other in the number of bird sightings. That's what happens when you really get into it, Francy told CeeCee. Francy liked birding only because it gave her a good excuse to get away from housework. One thing she hadn't realized when they bought the house in East Tee, as she was already calling it, was how much more work those big old places were. They seemed to attract more dust and dirt than smaller ones. Even out here where the air's supposed to be cleaner, and we're not even using all the rooms, but Ferd says I have to keep the whole house up, she'd grumbled to CeeCee, who thought to herself, then why doesn't he pitch in and help with the cleaning? CeeCee suggested they paint the woodwork off white, especially those big wide baseboards and then the dust wouldn't show. And put in some wall-to-wall carpeting with a busy pattern on it. But Ferd thought those were silly ideas and anyway it would be too much work to strip the ancient varnish off all that wood. And he'd never liked wall-to-wall, said it was a waste of money and what was wrong with good old hardwood anyway. Francy knew what was wrong with it all right, it had to be kept waxed and polished all the time. Why couldn't they get the floors refinished with that new stuff that never needs waxing, she'd asked. But Ferd said no, another waste of money and anyway that new stuff stinks for weeks after you put it on. Ferd was full of allergies. Just talking about things like that could start his nose dripping.

Sometimes Francy wondered if leaving the City had been a mistake. Not just for her but for Ferd. He seemed so restless, never able to settle to anything. The other men in their neighbourhood joined the golf club, played darts at the Legion over in Bickerton once a week, went fishing at the Canal, with a few beers after. Not Ferd. He'd never been a joiner, he said. She guessed that wouldn't change. As far as she knew, the only person he'd gotten the least bit friendly with, other than Hink Denton, was Syd Spilsbury, the owner of the *Bickerton Bugler*, the town's weekly newspaper. He'd disappear over to Syd's and be gone for hours. He never told Francy what they did and she didn't dare to ask. Ferd had worked as a community news reporter in the City years ago, but he couldn't handle the long hours. Or what he considered being nosey when you had to poke around in other people's business. Anyway it had been his Dad's idea. Right after his Dad died, he'd quit the newspaper, gone to college and gotten his degree to teach high school mathematics. If he'd hated the newspaper business so much, Francy wondered what he and Syd found to talk about.

"We'd better get over to Dentons' and see what's going on," Ferd said, carefully wiping the sugar from the doughnut off his moustache and then folding his napkin. Ferd was neat, if nothing else. Not much mess to clean up after him, Francy thought. I should be grateful for that at least.

Ferd's suggestion surprised Francy who thought he wouldn't have cared if Hink was gone for good. But she was worried about CeeCee. Out there in that big house. All alone. So, she rinsed off their mugs and plates and stacked them in the sink and they drove off, across the Canal Bridge and along the main road out to the far side of Bickerton. By now it was quite dark and getting colder by the minute. As the old Buick laboured up the steep hill to the Dentons' lane, the beams of their headlights bounced off low lying, fast moving clouds.

"Wow, would you look at that!" Francy said, peering at the clouds through the windshield. "That looks like snow coming for sure. Well, it's about time." She shivered and hunched down into her old fur jacket.

Ferd didn't comment, but tightened his grip on the steering wheel. He hated to think of the long winter coming on them again. Cold days and colder nights. Tons of snow to shovel. He didn't let on to Francy that was how he felt, but nonetheless he shuddered at the thought.

He guided the car carefully between the towering pine trees that hugged the edges of the Dentons' narrow lane, making it look like an endless black tunnel.

Francy was glad it had been daylight when they'd been out here before. It would have seemed much scarier if they hadn't. As they got closer to the house, they could see a solitary figure silhouetted against the light that was coming from the living room windows. Francy heard Ferd mutter something about 'still got no outside lights' as he stopped the car up by the side of the house. CeeCee came running out to meet them, trying in vain to control her full skirt in the strong wind.

"So glad you could come," she said, when she could catch her breath, giving them each a hug. "I'm at my wits'end. Don't know what to do. Hink's never done anything like this before." They went through the side hall into the kitchen and stood there awkwardly, not sure whether they should sit down.

"Have you called Constable Spilsbury yet?" Francy asked. "I think they call her Gussie, isn't that right, Ferd? Surely you must have called Gussie by now," she said without waiting for Ferd to agree.

CeeCee shook her head. "Hated to do that. Still hoping he'll show up. Would you like something hot to drink? Won't take a minute."

But the Otterleys both said no, no thank you, not to bother, they had just had coffee and were up to their gills in it. Ferd moved to the table and said that maybe they'd better just sit down and try to figure out what to do, it was getting late and he didn't want to get caught way out here on the back roads if it was going to storm, which it certainly looked like it might.

"I still think you should call Gussie," Francy urged, draping her jacket over the back of her chair. She wrinkled her nose. Was that the smell of burnt meat? And, the kitchen wasn't all that warm, it seemed to her.

"We hear she's very efficient, isn't that right, Ferd?" Francy went on. She looked around her again. She could never get over what a large kitchen it was. Much larger than hers. And CeeCee didn't even cook. Now, if this was her kitchen...

"Oh, no, no," CeeCee said slowly. "At least, not yet. Hink would never forgive me if he found out I'd gotten the police involved. Besides, he could turn up at any minute. Then what? No. No police." She leaned back in her chair and sighed.

Francy thought she'd never seen CeeCee so agitated. Her short grey hair was standing on end she'd run her fingers through it so often. It gave her a startled look, as if she'd seen a ghost. The skin around her eyes, which were a watery blue, looked puffy and wrinkled. She kept clasping and unclasping her hands. She was wearing what looked like an old shirt of her husband's under a garish purple and orange striped shawl that she'd knotted across her chest.

Being a newcomer to Bickerton, CeeCee couldn't possibly have known that Constable Augusta Spilsbury, better known as Gussie, would have been gratified to think she gave the impression of being efficient. Still fairly new on the job, Gussie felt she had yet to prove herself. She was that rare individual, a strikingly beautiful and intelligent policewoman. Rail thin, with hair down to her waist that gleamed like polished mahogany, and velvety brown eyes, she looked more like a fashion magazine's idea of a lady cop than a real one. But as more than one person had discovered to his regret, those looks could be deceiving. Gussie could be tough when the situation demanded and had broken up more than one fight singlehandedly, had hauled men twice her size off to the town jail, even stopped the Watson twins dead in their tracks when they held up the Central Bank. But CeeCee was still unaware of that terrible event.

Once upon a time she'd been Mrs. Syd Spilsbury. Gussie and Syd had been so crazy about each other, everyone thought their romance would last forever. But less than a year after the wedding, a habit of hers began grating on Syd's nerves so badly it ended their marriage. When they first started going together, Syd thought it was cute, but after a while it started to annoy him. Finally, he couldn't take it any longer. They'd stayed friendly and still saw each other occasionally, but Gussie's heart was broken and she'd buried herself in her work. To get rid of her frustration, she'd taken up karate and in no time had earned her black belt. Now she was learning how to lift weights at the gym up in Cooley's Mills. That is, when she could find the time.

"Don't you think you should close the drapes, you're awfully exposed here. Like a fish in a bowl," suggested Francy, in a shaky voice.

"Hadn't thought about it. Been so distracted. And I think … someone … broke into the house when I … I … when I went down to The Landing." CeeCee's eyes filled and she turned away from them and pretended to search for something in the pocket of her skirt.

"What makes you think that?" asked Ferd, itching to tell her to stop being silly. It made him nervous when women cried. It reminded him of his mother, who burst into tears over nothing that he could ever figure out. Tears were a sign of weakness, didn't solve anything.

"Back window was broken. Sure it was okay when I left. Was scared to look upstairs in case someone was there. Made myself go up. Couldn't tell if anything was missing, though."

CeeCee was crying openly now. She left the table and went across the hall to the living room to close the drapes.

"Oh no!" she said in dismay, "it's snowing!"

Ferd left the kitchen to have a look for himself. "That settles it," he said grimly. "We've got to call Gussie. Now!"

But when CeeCee phoned the police station, they told her Constable Spilsbury was out on a call and could they take a message. She was too upset to carry on. Wordlessly, she handed the phone to Ferd who repeated the telephone number and added tersely, "Have the constable call Mrs. Denton. Her husband's missing."

5
JESSE'S STORY

"You've got to tell me what's wrong! Jesse Woodcock! Sit up and look at me," Kitty ordered. She'd been trying for ages to get Jesse to talk to her, but he just lay like a lump on his bed, clutching his quilt and staring up at the ceiling. He'd been soundly asleep and groaned when she woke him for supper. She'd been feeling a bit guilty lately and had made them a proper meal of macaroni and hamburger casserole with a spicy tomato and cheese sauce. When she asked if he felt sick, he shook his head. Wasn't he hungry then, she asked.

"I've made your favourite," she said, to coax him.

Jesse kept his eyes shut. He groaned again. Exasperated, Kitty sat down in the old rocker.

"Oh Jess, I just don't know what to do with you. I wish your Pop was here," she said, starting to rock vigorously, making the old chair squeak in protest. That set Jesse off to crying again.

"Oh Pop, Pop," he sobbed and pulled the quilt up over his head.

"Is it something to do with Pop, then? Did he call or what?" Kitty leaned over and tugged gently at the quilt. "Jesse, please tell me."

"Oh Mom, I saw ... I saw ... something bad!"

"Something bad?" she repeated. "Where was it?"

"Bad. Real bad, real *real* bad!"

"Where? Where was it? Jesse, you've got tell me!"

She was glad to be getting something out of him at last, but beginning to worry what he was going to say next.

"I was trying to go in ... in to ... you know ... to the Hidden Swamp ... I told you about it before ... to see ... see a bird Miss Roxton said was there, but, but ..." his voice was muffled under the heavy quilt. He started to shiver, rocking himself back and forth. Kitty moved over to the bed and lay down beside him.

"Oh Jess honey, if you don't tell me what happened, how can I help you?"

She put her arms around what she could reach of him and began softly humming an old lullaby from his babyhood. He calmed down then and gradually his shaking stopped. After a few minutes, he lowered the quilt, pulled her head closer to his and whispered something in her ear. She sat up abruptly.

"You sure about this?"

"Oh Mom, oh Mom," was all he could say.

Kitty sprang to her feet and ran downstairs. In less than a minute, she was talking excitedly to someone on the phone. Jesse wrapped his quilt around him and shuffled to the top of the stairs.

"It's okay," Kitty called up the stairs, "Constable Spilsbury's coming right over."

When she got the call, Gussie had been staring out the window watching the flakes of snow swirling around the lights outside the station. *This'll mean more work tonight, people have to learn how handle the first snow of the season, they'll be sliding off the road and I'll have to stay here late.* She'd been hoping for a few quiet hours and a chance to get reading that new book on bones that Sherry over at the library had gotten for her through the Interloan Service. Some scientist had written this really neat stuff on how you could tell from bones how long someone had been dead. And how they'd died. And it didn't matter how old the bones were. Gussie doubted she'd ever have a case where she'd need to find out, but it was fascinating all the same. She loved anything to do with the science of forensics and was always looking for more things to learn about crime.

Gussie had been ecstatic when her father supported her decision to go into police work. When she was in Bickerton Public School, the kids used to call her Guts, Guts Noble, because she was always reading murder mysteries. When she got to high school, fiction began to bore her so she switched to books about murders and other true life crimes. It wasn't who did it or how it was solved that interested her, but why. Why would a person kill another person? Nothing she'd read so far had fully answered that question, maybe nothing ever would, but she kept on reading every book on crime and detective work that she could get her hands on.

After graduation, Gussie had gone to Toronto, supposedly to take up modelling. Everyone said she had the looks for it. They still remembered her mother, who had been the Prom Queen in her last year in High School. But sadly, Gussie never knew her mother, who'd died in childbirth. She had only photographs to give her some idea of how her mother looked. Her father, Mac, who by then was a popular Town Councillor, sold his highly profitable hardware business and devoted all his energy towards improving life for the residents of his beloved Bickerton. He adored his only child, so when she told him the only career she'd ever wanted was to be a cop, he offered to pay her way. It wasn't that they didn't think she would do well they made up the modelling story, it was just that the town was so full of idle gossip, which had a way sometimes of turning nasty. Mac thought it was better if they kept Gussie's activities in the City to themselves until she passed all her courses and field tests. Which she did with flying colours.

After finishing her training, Gussie stayed on in Toronto for a year to complete her probation and took extra courses in criminology and psychology at the university. No one in Bickerton was any the wiser. By the time she came back to town, Mac Noble was already the Mayor. It wasn't hard for him to convince the Town Council to retire old Constable Gerald Finch, who'd had the job forever, it seemed. When Gerald's wife died after months of suffering with cancer, he'd gotten careless with his drinking. Finally, after he wrecked two cruisers in a month, the Council decided unanimously that, even though his mother had been a Bickerton, which counted for a lot, they couldn't afford him any more. Two weeks later, Gerald left town to live with his sister Up North. Gussie came home and took Gerald's place. On a temporary basis of course, until they could find another male constable. But Mac had no intention of searching for one. He was sure his Gussie was up to the job.

Once everyone had gotten over the shock of seeing the glamorous Augusta Spilsbury in uniform, with her beautiful hair hidden under a cap, and certainly after the way she handled the Watson twins, there was no more talk of a replacement. Gussie was appointed to the job of policing the Town of Bickerton, with a five-year contract, which up until then was unheard of for anyone, let alone a woman. The only thing that bothered Mac was Gussie's tendency to be impulsive. Sometimes she bypassed the rules of procedure and went her own way, blithely ignoring anyone's efforts to restrain her, slow her down, to make her see that she had to think things through. He tried not to remember how close she came to getting herself shot when she went after the Watson twins.

When Gussie showed up at the Woodcocks' house down past the Public School, she found Kitty and Jesse in the tiny kitchen eating ice cream and butter tarts. Stamping the snow off her boots in the back kitchen, she seemed to tower over Jesse's mom, who took her wet jacket and hung it by the stove. An enticing odour of tomatoes and onions lingered in the air, reminding Gussie that she hadn't stopped for lunch that day.

"Now, what's all this about, young man, what's all this about a boot in the woods, I mean a boot in the woods?" she asked, after refusing a cup of coffee.

Still huddled inside the old quilt, Jesse stared down at his plate and concentrated on scraping the last of the ice cream into his spoon.

"Don't do that Jess, please. Just answer Constable Spilsbury," Kitty said, taking his plate away to the sink.

Jesse pulled the quilt tighter around his shoulders.

"I'm cold, Mom, can I have some coffee?" he asked, ignoring Gussie's question.

"We shouldn't have eaten the ice cream, it's going to be real cold tonight, and no you certainly can *not* have coffee at this hour, you'll never get to sleep. How about a nice hot chocolate?"

"It sure is getting colder and snowing like the devil, I mean like the devil," Gussie agreed. "Hot chocolate sounds real good, I mean real good. I'd love a cup if you're making some."

"Sure thing," said Kitty getting out the milk and tin of cocoa. "Three hot chocolates coming right up."

"Now, Jesse," said Gussie, sitting down across from him, "tell me. Where did you see the boot?"

Jesse rolled his eyes back in his head and muttered something about the Old Barge Canal.

"The thing is, you see," said Kitty waiting for the milk to heat, "he thinks it might be his Pop."

When she said this, Jesse put his head down on the table and started to cry.

"If you want to cry, that's okay with me," said Gussie, patting him gently on the head, "but I have to know more than that, I mean more than that."

Jesse kept his head where it was.

"The thing is, you see," said Kitty again, "Albie, that's my husband, Jesse's Pop, well, Albie left us a month ago and Jess has been pretty upset ever since. We haven't heard a thing from him."

She sighed as she poured the steaming cocoa into three big blue mugs.

Gussie tried another tack.

"What were you doing over by the Canal, just messing around, I mean just messing around?" she asked, gently.

Jesse sat up and said indignantly, "No, ma'am, I was trying to get in to the Hidden Swamp. To see a bird."

Gussie noticed he had enormous brown eyes ringed with long sweeping lashes. Be a heart breaker some day for sure.Gussie laced her long thin fingers around her mug and said, "Boy this feels good, I mean this feels good. Let's drink up while it's hot and then we'll take a little drive down to the Canal before the snow gets any worse. They sure didn't predict this storm."

"It's not on the road, it's way along this track I found ... uh, that Adam showed me. Maybe I won't be able to find it again." Jesse blew on his mug of cocoa and took a few sips. He was looking better now. Some colour had come back into his sallow cheeks. His curly black hair glowed reddish in the light of the lamp that hung over the table.

Gussie had to restrain herself to keep from touching his head again.

"Then I guess we'll have to wait 'til tomorrow, it's too dark now, I mean too dark now. We'll need to see where we're going. I better get back to the station, there's bound to be trouble on the highway tonight." She swallowed the last of her cocoa and stood up, just as her beeper went off, startling her. Kitty looked up.

"Sorry," Gussie said, sheepishly. "I can't seem to get used to this thing. Makes me jump every time, I mean every time. We'll go first thing tomorrow, Jesse. That is, if it's okay with your mom. May I use your phone, Mrs. Woodcock?"

The two women disappeared into the living room. After a few minutes, they were back where Jesse sat. He could tell by the expression on her face that she had agreed to let him guide the constable to what he'd seen.

"Oh boy! Does that mean I get to stay home from school?" Jesse asked, sitting up straighter.

"Oh yes of course, I'll need your help, I mean I'll need your help. Thanks for the cocoa, Mrs. Woodcock, good night to you both." Gussie grabbed her coat, pulled on her boots and was gone out the door in a flurry of snow.

"Boy, she's real neat," Jesse said, as he tried to stand up and keep the quilt from falling off. "She believed me, she really did." He yawned.

"Off you go now Jess, I'll be up in a minute to tuck you in," Kitty said, still holding her half-empty mug. She stayed at the kitchen table for a few minutes, her fingers twiddling and twisting the ends of her hair, which was the colour of bleached straw and which she habitually wore in a long thick braid over one shoulder. Was it safe to let Jess go with the cop? Sooner or later, he'd have to face up to the unpleasant things in life. Now was as good a time as any. After all, his twelfth birthday was coming up soon. He was no baby any more.

Something else had been niggling away at her all the time Gussie was talking. Maybe she should have told the nice young lady cop about the stranger who kept calling Albie at all hours the week before he disappeared.

6

THE BODY IN THE WOODS

Jesse was almost asleep when Kitty came upstairs to say a proper goodnight. He'd wrapped himself up in his quilt like a mummy.

"What if I can't find the place again, Mom, then what?" he murmured sleepily, keeping his eyes shut as she bent down for a kiss. She said, "Now Jess, don't get to thinking about that now, let it wait 'til morning."

She crossed the landing to her own room and went over to the window. The wind had picked up again and was rhythmically buffeting a dangling section of eavestrough against the side of the house. *Trying to peer through blowing snow is like trying to see through a closely worked lace curtain,* Kitty thought. She could barely make out the squat shapes of the darkened houses across the road. Crawling wearily into bed, she slid down under the blankets and lay listening to snowflakes beating against the window, sounding like a hundred tiny fingers trying to get her attention. *Jesse's a good kid, he wouldn't have made up a story like that. God, Albie, I hope and pray it isn't you out there.* She quickly shut off that thought, and being a person who had learned a long time ago to take things as they came, switched her mind over to thinking about the complicated project she was working on. Which was as good as taking a sleeping pill.

Somewhere around three in the morning, the wind dropped and the temperature rose, but the snow kept on falling, piling itself up in drifts everywhere, obliterating the sharp edges of the houses, blanketing the trees, transforming the landscape. As she'd predicted, Gussie had been up all night trying to cope with the results of the season's first snowstorm. Several cars had slid off the roads and had to be hauled out. Gussie was relieved no one had been hurt in those mishaps. Her biggest problem was more serious. A transport loaded with scrap metal had skidded and jackknifed, blocking the main highway north of Bickerton, so she'd had to set up a detour through the centre of town. She was sure to hear about *that* in the morning. People living along the detour route never failed to jam the police switchboard with complaints when heavy truck traffic rumbled past their homes all night long, making sleep impossible. Well, it wasn't the first time that had happened. And it wouldn't be the last.

Finally, just before seven o'clock, she called up to Cooley's Mills to a couple of Auxiliary Police she knew to ask if they could come down and relieve her for a few hours. Being so much farther north of the Lake, they hadn't been hit quite so hard by the storm, which had swept in from the south. They said sure thing, they thought they could make it down to Bickerton in less than an hour.

She just had time to grab a quick coffee at Jimmie's Variety across from the station and get out her own car before leaving for the Woodcocks'. She thought it would be better not to take the cruiser. It always attracted attention and she was afraid this might turn out to be a wild goose chase. Still, that call about Hink Denton being missing had come in while she was at the Woodcocks', and although Myrna reported that CeeCee Denton was on the edge of hysteria, it was probably just another case of a husband staying out later than his wife thought he should. Gussie had returned the call as soon as she got back to the station and taken down the details from a calmer Mrs. Denton, who sounded more in control of herself. Gussie had been fooled by this sort of situation before and wanted to wait the usual forty-eight hours before getting serious about looking for what would most likely turn out to be a husband who just needed some fresh air. *Dumb time to have a disagreement though,* Gussie thought. That was usually what set them off.

Bickerton's brand new snowplow had already cleared a strip down the middle of each street and was making a second round. Mac would be having a fit. He'd just hired a new driver who would need to be trained in better than that or they'd be in trouble with their snow clearing budget. The Town would find themselves having to pay overtime and this was just the start of the plowing season.

Jesse was waiting outside the little house for her, stomping up and down the front steps. He had on a bright red jacket and an enormous pair of snow boots that must have belonged to his father. She wondered how he would get through the deep snow in those things. At least he was wearing mitts and a woolly cap. Most kids seemed to run around in as little as possible in winter. Gussie remembered being in trouble with Mac more than once for going to school bareheaded when it was below zero.

Kitty appeared in the front window and waved when she saw Gussie. She was still in her housecoat. Gussie felt a little twinge of envy. Imagine being able to take your time in the morning. When he spotted the car, Jesse pushed his way through the deep snow and clambered into the front seat beside Gussie, mumbling a shy hello in response to her greeting.

"Some snow, eh kid? I was up all night, I mean all night," Gussie said, struggling to make conversation. She wasn't used to being with kids by themselves. She never knew what to say. Jesse nodded, but sat quietly without fidgeting, staring straight ahead as they drove slowly through the falling snow on the narrow road that came to a T end at the Old Barge Canal Road. When they'd gone along there for about five minutes, he suddenly said,

"There, over there! By that big tree, that looks like it! Where I got into the woods, I mean!"

Gussie thought for a moment, then decided to leave the car where it was. In the middle of the road. So few people lived over this way, it was always the last road to be plowed out. With an effort, they pushed their doors open and climbed out into snow up over their knees.

"Wow, this isn't going to be easy," Gussie said, turning up the collar of her jacket and squinting through the snow into the dense brush that bordered the woods, "but let's give it a try, I mean give it a try. You lead the way."

But Jesse was off before she could get her balance, lifting his feet as high as his boots would let him. Gussie floundered along behind him, his bright jacket acting as a beacon against the black-green of the woods. She was relieved to see there was an opening in the brush that led into a sort of path. When they got into the woods, the going was a bit easier. The trees were taking the brunt of the snowfall. Their topmost branches were already weighted down and some were hanging dangerously low. Twice Gussie slipped and fell. She hoped that Jesse, who was ahead of her, hadn't seen her tumble. Her wool pea jacket was plastered with snow, making her wish she'd worn her leather one, which shrugged off snow like a sled dog's fur. After the second fall, she was out of breath, but dragged herself to her feet again, determined not to let a mere child outdo her.

Half an hour later, after a few wrong turns, just when Gussie was beginning to think they should forget the whole thing, Jesse stopped abruptly.

"There! Over there, there's where I think the grouse flew up," he said excitedly, as Gussie struggled to catch up with him. He pointed to a small clearing ringed with white birches. The snow had drifted in such a way that the surface of the track was slightly depressed around the bend where Jesse had started to run the night before, which made walking a bit easier, although the snow was deeper here than in the woods. Fifty feet or so farther along, Jesse stopped again.

"Look! Look up there, see that big mound? That's where I fell!"

Gussie stopped to blow her nose. She was soaked through and aching in every joint.

" Maybe you'd better let me do this, kid. Is this about the right spot, I mean the right spot?"

Glad of the chance for a rest, she knelt down and started brushing the snow from the top of a pile of branches. Underneath the branches were leaves and under the leaves were a couple of rocks and what looked like a chunk of wood. She needed both hands to lift the rocks out of the way. Something was making a peculiar clicking sound. Gussie stopped to listen and realized it was Jesse's teeth, which had started chattering. Before she could say anything, he turned his face away and pretended to be looking for something high up in one of the trees.

"Boy, I should have brought a shovel or a hayfork or something, this is tough going kid, I mean tough going. Are you sure this is the right place?" Gussie said, swiping at the sweat dripping off the end of her nose with the back of one glove. She took a closer look at what she had uncovered.

"There's something here all right! Oh boy, Jesse. Maybe you shouldn't be seeing this," and she started digging harder than ever. But Jesse couldn't stand the suspense any longer and came to look over her shoulder. The shape of an arm in a light-coloured sleeve began to emerge and then the outline of a jacket pocket.

"That can't be Pop, he doesn't have a jacket like that," Jesse said in a loud voice, making Gussie jump.

"I don't think you should see this, Jesse," she said, again. She was beginning to regret bringing the boy with her. He seemed calm enough, almost too calm, after the outburst of the previous night. Maybe she should have brought one of the Auxiliaries instead. Or even Mac. Oh heck, what was she thinking? Without the boy, they wouldn't have had the vaguest idea where to look.

"No, it's okay," he said, and bent down to help her. Gradually the body of a man came into view. With her policeman's eye, Gussie took careful note of its position. The left leg was slightly bent at the knee. The other leg rested on top of it. Both feet were clad in stout brown leather work boots. The boot that Jesse had tripped over the afternoon before was sticking straight up, propped up by the leg underneath. She could well imagine that in the fading light it could indeed have looked like a stump. The arms were folded across the chest and the hands were bare. An expensive gold watch hung from one wrist. When she cleared the last of the snow away from the man's head, she noticed some raw patches on the face. Other than that, his skin was as white as wax. He looked like he had just fallen asleep.

Digging the snow out from around the back, Gussie drew in a sharp breath.

"What in heck is this? Looks like a stick or something." Using a gloved finger, she carefully traced the edges of the object that protruded from under the body. "Oh my God, it's an arrow!"

7

COMPANY FOR CEECEE

When she'd hung up the phone, CeeCee stayed where she was on the living room sofa. The cat came bounding down the stairs and jumped into her lap, stretching out a paw and placing it lightly on her chest. CeeCee gathered him in and held him close.

"I wonder how cats always seem to know when we need comforting," said Francy, sitting down beside her. Ferd was still standing by the front window, wondering what to do next. He swung around and came over to stand squarely in front of the two women.

"Look here", he said after a moment, "would you like us to stay here tonight? I mean, I probably won't get any sleep in a strange bed, but ..."

Francy cut him off with a disgusted look. "Maybe there's someone else you'd rather have here with you," she said to CeeCee, nervously running her plump little hands in circles over her knees. Her round face with its rosy cheeks, large blue eyes and wispy reddish bangs made Francy look for all the world like a Raggedy Ann doll.

"Well", said CeeCee after a silence, "kind of you to offer. But no. Wouldn't want to put you out. Only other person might be Dottie. You know, Dottie Kibbidge? Over in East Thorne? Hate to ask her to come out on a night like this, though."

"Is she by any chance related to the funny little guy who owns the grocery near us?" asked Ferd, relieved to hear that he might get to enjoy his own bed after all. "Where they sell the dried fish?"

"His sister. Never been married. Got stuck looking after their mother. Too late for Dottie by the time the old lady died. Keeps house for Rab. Doesn't seem to mind. Likes to feel useful. Cheerful kind of person. Maybe I'll give her a call, she can only say no," CeeCee said, reaching for the phone again.

Dottie said, "Oh dear me no, lovey, t'will be no problem a-tall a-tall, I'd be some happy to help ya out ya poor poor thing and Rab'll bring me over in his pickup. It's got good snow tires on it. He'll be goin' back to open the store anyways case someone might be needin' somethin' case we get snowed in, which we might be from the looka things and I've a fair big shepherd's pie here so don't bother makin' supper lovey.We can have that when I get there. Just put on the kettle won't you, lovey?"

CeeCee, who'd grown fond of Dottie in the short time they'd known each other, always felt short of breath after talking to her. The woman barely paused for breath. The Kibbidges came from Back East somewhere, CeeCee wasn't sure where exactly. She smiled and nodded at Francy.

"That's great. We'll stay 'til she gets here, won't we, Ferd? You sure you'll be all right?"

"Yes, yes. No need for you to stay. I can manage now. Thanks for coming. Couldn't think straight by myself. Not like Hink to do something like this," and CeeCee started crying again, hugging the cat so tightly that he struggled to escape and she had to put him down.

Francy put her arms around CeeCee and said there, there now, but Ferd went back to the window and parted the drapes. The snow was coming down so heavily, he couldn't see a thing, but he'd rather look at nothing than watch CeeCee cry. They'd better get a move on or they'd be stuck here anyway. How did the

Dentons stand to live so far from town? Figured Hink Denton to have more sense.

Ferd Otterley was a tall man, angular and thin, with sparse grey hair and a full beard of the colour they call salt-and-pepper. Short and dumpy Francy barely came to his shoulder. Seeing the two of them as they said their goodbyes, standing there side by side, under the shadow cast by the hall chandelier, CeeCee couldn't help thinking what an odd sort of couple they made. Outwardly they acted devoted to each other, although every once in a while she could feel a strange sort of tension hanging in the air between them.

8

BLACKOUT!

Dottie and CeeCee sat in the Dentons' kitchen, eating apples and Cheddar cheese.

"Boy, that meat pie sure was delicious. Hink never makes anything like that," CeeCee said, gathering the apple peelings together to give herself something to do. She hadn't really tasted the pie. Her senses were so paralyzed with fear of what might have happened to Hink. But, she'd eaten the generous helping of pie automatically when it was put in front of her. She felt she had to say something to show Dottie her gratitude.

"Does he do *all* the cookin'?" asked Dottie, looking shocked. "I never knew a man as could cook. They don't even like makin' tea, least not the ones I ever knew. How'd ya manage that?" She got up and brought the teapot and two large mugs over to the table.

CeeCee shrugged her shoulders.

"Didn't have any choice. That's what he wanted after we came down here. Anyway, Hink's a pretty good cook except he never makes the dishes *I* like. Like anything in a casserole. You know. Macaroni and cheese, baked beans, corn pudding. You know the kind of stuff our mothers used to give us when we were kids," said CeeCee, adding some honey and milk to her tea. Her hand was shaking so much, some of the milk spilled onto the table.

"Rab wouldn't be caught dead doin' anythin' in the kitchen. When he was a kid, he wanted to help with the picklin' one time and our dad give him a good rap on the head and called him sissy. Anyways, our mam ruled the kitchen in our house, even us girls had a fight to learn how to make anythin'. I was always pesterin' her to let me do stuff, but she said I got in the way and made her nervous. Our gram was good, though, she taught me everythin' I know, pastry, dumplins, bread, even knittin'. Mam never had time nor patience for things like that. Oh, Gram and I, we had some grand old times, we did. I still miss her," said Dottie, wistfully. Dottie's black and white 'pokeydot' blouse gaped at the neck and her pink handknit cardigan hung limply about her shoulders, but she always had such a kindly expression on her face, CeeCee felt you could forgive her anything.

"Did ya get started on that knittin' pattern I give ya?" asked Dottie, wanting to keep CeeCee's mind off her missing husband. CeeCee shook her head and blew her nose into a linen handkerchief she took out of her sleeve.

Finishing off her apple, Dottie stood up, smoothing her skirt down over her ample hips. When she'd met CeeCee's husband, the first person Dottie had thought of was an old teacher she'd had back in The Valley. Mister Know-It-All the kids called him behind his back. But she liked CeeCee's unpretentious manner, even though the Dentons were probably worth more than most of the people around Bickerton. Just looking at CeeCee's clothes told Dottie there must be money there. The different shoes she'd seen CeeCee wearing must have cost a bundle.

The two women had met at the Bickerton library one day when Dottie was picking up some books for her neighbour, Mrs. Crumb, who'd taken a fair good tumble as Dottie put it, and broken her leg. CeeCee made some suggestions when she overheard Dottie asking for books about real people, Mrs. Crumb's favourites. They'd gotten into a conversation that led to Dottie suggesting they go for tea and a bite at the Cosy Corner, the restaurant down the street from the library. CeeCee accepted eagerly. It was the first chance she'd had to get to know someone who'd lived here for a while. Everyone else she'd met so far had been another newcomer like herself.

Funny thing about women, CeeCee thought, when she remembered that day. You meet them as total strangers and inside the first five minutes they're telling you their life story. That time in Toronto when she'd kept Hink waiting. They were supposed to meet downtown right after Hink finished work, but she'd gotten into a really interesting conversation with a woman she met while shopping for a slip. Hink was furious, couldn't understand how she could waste so much time with someone she'd probably never see again. Hink was fussy about who he spent time with, but then he made friends so easily that if one didn't live up to his high standards, he could always find another. CeeCee didn't consider herself that lucky. Usually shy, she considered the occasion in the lingerie department to be a rare one. It took a while before she was sure of her ground with someone new. Anyway, she sometimes thought Hink's friendships were superficial, a means to an end, someone to go places and do things with. They didn't seem to her to be the kind of friendships you'd call lasting, with people he really cared about.

CeeCee was what you would call a loner and she was well aware that her attitude towards people was a lot different from Hink's. She was inclined to look past the exterior and get to know the real person. She was delighted with Dottie, who maintained a cheerful outlook in spite of having had a tough life. Dottie told her she was the second youngest of nine children, whose father had fished all his life. When the fishing declined, he'd had to give up his boat. That was the finish of him, Dottie'd confided, on one of their many visits over tea and generous slices of the almond sponge cake that was a Cosy Corner specialty. The older Kibbidge boys had left home as soon as they could and were scattered right across the country. She wasn't even sure where some of them ended up. Her sisters were married and still lived with their families back in The Valley.

Rab, the baby of the family, like his brothers, couldn't wait to leave home, and had come through here on his way West, got off the bus at that rest stop up on the highway to stretch his legs, liked what he saw and let the bus go on without him. He found his way down to East Thorne, sweet talked the owner of the little grocery into letting him do odd jobs around the place. Combined with other odd jobs, he managed to save enough to buy a small cottage down at the far end of the Canal. He was a hard worker, reliable and honest. Eventually, he went into partnership with the grocer and when the old man died, took over the business, rented out his cottage and moved his few belongings into the living quarters behind the back of the store. He was so friendly and helpful to his customers that word got around and soon he was making a comfortable living, so comfortable that when their mother died, he was able to send for Dottie to come and live with him.

"Where'd he get the name Rab?" CeeCee asked one day, her natural curiosity getting the better of her. "Short for Robert?"

"Oh dear me no," Dottie laughed, "he was always out huntin' rabbits. Sometimes caught a few of 'em and kept 'em in cages behind the house. He found people who'd buy 'em, people who were always comin' by and askin' for the 'rabbit man'. After a while, they took to callin' him Rab and it stuck. His real name's Dougal." She paused for a moment and then said, "All Ds in our family. David, Donald, Doreen, Dennis, Daniel, Daisy, Delia, Dougal. My real name's Dorothy." She laughed and added, "but please, don't never call me that, would ya? Sounds too lah-dee-dah."

CeeCee promised, smiling inwardly at her new friend, who was the last person she could imagine putting on airs.

After Dottie cleared away the dishes, insisting that CeeCee just rest easy, they moved into the living room, taking their mugs of tea with them. This was her first visit to CeeCee's home and Dottie was gratified to see that her instincts about the Dentons being well off had been right. A velvet sofa in a rich shade of forest green dominated the room, soft and sleek, with colourful silk cushions heaped at one end. In front of the sofa was a coffee table that looked as if it were made of polished ebony.

Oil paintings in elaborate frames were tastefully arranged on walls the colour of fresh cream. A pair of those double-globed lamps her mother used to call Gone with the Wind stood at either end of the sofa on matching ebony tables. A lavishly decorated Christmas tree occupied the space between the tall windows, which were draped in a creamy taffeta. Figurines of ladies in long dresses, and crystal vases crowded the mantelpiece of the dark green marble fireplace, which took up one end wall.

The muted shades of deep red, green and gold in the Oriental carpets spread over the honey-coloured pine floors added to the grandeur of the room, which appeared to be well used in spite of its expensive furnishings. Books and magazines were piled haphazardly at the base of a rosewood bookcase lining the other end wall and a heap of newspapers lay on the floor half under the sofa. Dottie thought someone must have a sweet tooth: a crystal bowl filled with gold wrapped toffees sat on the coffee table, which was littered with empty candy papers.

"My, what a grand room." Dottie said. "Never seen anythin' like it."

CeeCee lowered herself into one of the two green-and-cream velvet armchairs that flanked the fireplace and looked around as though she'd never seen the room before.

"It's all Hink. Picked out everything. Except for my figurine collection. And some of the books. I'd have settled for something plainer, maple or cherry wood maybe. Not ebony and rosewood. He let me keep my grandparents' old pine table as long as it stays in the kitchen. Never use the dining room. Close it off in the winter. Shall I make us a fire, do you think?" she asked, without enthusiasm.

"Oh dear, lovey, it's gettin' on to bedtime. I'm an early riser, have to be, got to get Rab goin' don't ya know," Dottie said from the depths of other chair. "Let's just let our supper settle. Where's your bathroom, is there one down here?"

"Sorry," said CeeCee. "Not a very good hostess tonight."

"Never mind, lovey, I just didn't want to go pokin' about in your house, is all. No no, stay where y' are," Dottie said, quickly, as CeeCee made a move to get up.

"Upstairs second right, light switch's outside, I put a towel on the washstand for you," CeeCee said, gratefully. She made no effort to move, but continued to sit staring into space while Dottie was gone.

Through a kind of haze, she heard the wind hurling snow against the front windows. The lights in the room began to flicker. *Blast. That's all I need right now, a power failure,* she thought dully, unable to rouse herself to action. By the time Dottie came back downstairs, the lamps had dimmed down to about half their normal brightness.

"Got some candles somewheres, lovey?" asked Dottie, in the gloom.

CeeCee indicated two fat red candles on one of the end tables.

"Ya never know, do ya, out here in the country, when the power's goin' to go on ya," Dottie said, striking a match from the little enameled matchbox she'd found between the candle-holders. Just as she was lighting the second candle, the lights went out. They sat there silently for a moment until their eyes had adjusted, watching the play of shadows cast by the waver-ing candlelight.

Then CeeCee said wearily, "May as well go to bed. Power could be out all night. Happens here a lot. We're at the end of the line on this road. Could be morning before they find out what's wrong."

Dottie agreed, handing her one of the candles and picking up the other. The two women made their way carefully up the narrow staircase, CeeCee, imagining that this must have been what it was like to live in this house a hundred years ago, going up to bed by candlelight and Dottie, trying not to drip candle grease on the dark green stair carpeting. After showing Dottie to the spare room at the end of the hall, CeeCee got ready for bed in the large front room she shared with Hink.

She was glad the wind was making so much noise it drowned out the sound of her crying.

9

STRANGERS IN TOWN

Retracing their tracks to the snow-clogged Old Barge Canal Road, Gussie made a mental note to put the boots to the Roads Superintendent to get the heck over and clear the road before she brought in the coroner. *Why did I bring Jesse,* she wondered. *That was a fool thing to do, for sure.* If she'd really believed him, she should've brought out someone else and just gone by Jesse's description, however vague, of where he'd fallen down.

Mac was right. She was too impulsive. Was she really just wishing for something drastic to happen, something more exciting than handing out parking tickets to tourists who'd overstayed their time on Main Street? What on earth was she thinking? Now she had what looked like a suspicious death on her hands. *Who in heck would be running around with a bow and arrow over here? And why was the guy with the boots in the woods in the first place?*

On the way back to town, she was so preoccupied with the questions that were milling around in her head, she'd almost forgotten about the boy in the seat beside her. He hadn't uttered a sound since they'd left the woods. But Jesse, sensing her distraction, was quick to remind her that his house was down on Maple. As she pulled in the driveway of the little cottage, Gussie made Jesse promise not to say anything to anyone about what they'd found. Except his mother, of course. She explained she needed to get some people to help. Until they were one hundred per cent sure who it was, she didn't want to upset anyone. Jesse mumbled okay, he promised, but did she think he could stay home for the rest of the day? He couldn't face school just yet. Gussie said that was up to his mom.

"Maybe there'll be no school today if the snow's so bad," Jesse said, as he slid off the seat. Gussie couldn't help smiling to herself. Wasn't that just like a kid, ever hopeful the school might have to close or burn down or something awful like that?

When Kitty heard their story, she was appalled. "Dear God in Heaven, Jesse really did find a body." She put a protective arm around her son and drew him close to her. "By all means, if he doesn't feel like going, he can stay home," she said. "But, oh dear God! I can't believe this. Jesse found a dead man."

Gussie went on to say what a really big help Jesse had been. That she couldn't have managed without him. From what he told her, she was sure the man they'd found wasn't Albie Woodcock, but she would definitely call later to see how things were going with Jesse. She made an attempt to apologize for having exposed him to such a shock, but Kitty waved her away.

"That's life," she said to Gussie, who at this point didn't know what more she could say. Kitty pulled Jesse into the house with her and shut the door. He stayed snuggled up close to her, hugging her tightly around the waist.

"Oh Mom, I thought it might be Pop, I thought it might be Pop. It wasn't, but I thought it might be. Oh Mom, oh Mom, oh Mom."

Kitty could barely understand him with his face buried in her sweater. They stood there together quietly for a few moments. Darn Albie, leaving us like this. What a scare the kid's had. "Poor Jess, my poor little boy, it'll be okay, Mom's here, Mom's here."

In the town of Bickerton, the side streets were usually the last to be cleared after a heavy snowfall, but a narrow strip down the middle of most of them had already been plowed, making them barely passable. People were out in droves struggling to clear their driveways. *There'll be a lot of people late for work today, that's for sure,* Gussie mused as she waved to the busy shovellers on the way back to her office. She hated to leave the body in the woods, but she had to remove Jesse from the scene as quickly as possible and get help. She hoped that no animals, two- or four-legged, would disturb it before she could get back over there. Odd though. The man hadn't been carrying papers or a wallet or anything that would have identified him.

Swinging into the police station lot, which was already plowed out, she spotted the truck belonging to the Auxiliary Police parked at the far end. So, they were still around, thank goodness. You never know with volunteers, they could've just as easily gotten fed up and left before she got back. Unlocking the back entrance to the building, she went along the short hall to her office. The pungent odour of cigar smoke mingled with wet wool met her as she opened the door. Mac stood up from where he'd been sitting at her desk.

"What the dickens are you doing here, Dad? How'd you get out so fast? The snow's real deep, I mean real deep," Gussie asked, startled to see him. These days, Mac usually slept late and didn't get around to showing up in town until noon. She knew he had a lot of late night meetings and had a hard time getting out of bed most mornings.

"Uh, just thought I'd drop in and see how you were making out. No problem getting out with that little plow I got off Joe last year. You know, the guy owns the Quick Bite down by The Landing? Jim-dandy little machine. Don't know why he wanted to get rid of it."

Mac reached across to knock the ash off the end of his cigar into the ashtray Gussie kept for visitors.

"Pretty wild night, wasn't it?" he continued, moving around to the front of the desk. "Thought at one stage that wackety old chimney over the back kitchen was going to come down, the wind was so awful." Mac still lived in the same house where he was born, down by the Lake about half a mile from town. The place was falling apart, but he refused to give it up.

Mac's heavy white brows drew together as he scrutinized her.

"My God, Gus, you look like death warmed over." He gave her a quick hug, then took her cold narrow hands between his warm solid ones.

"You're freezing, girl. Weren't you wearing gloves?"

Gussie withdrew her hands and began rubbing them together. She hadn't realized how cold she was until she felt the warmth of Mac's presence. Even though she was easily as tall as he, Mac always seemed to loom over her. He had on his favourite black turtleneck under a red and black checked bush shirt and the jeans with the black leather patches he'd talked her into sewing on the knees. For some reason, he favoured black cowboy boots, which he wore year round. His thick white hair looked damp and he was unshaven.

"Oh, Dad, you know how I hate the smell of cigars. Now you've gone and stunk up the office, I mean stunk up the office," Gussie said, ignoring his question while draping her jacket over the back of her chair and plumping herself down at the desk. "I've got a million things to do, Dad. Couldn't we talk later, meet for lunch or something?"

Mac came closer and peered down at her with pale brown eyes through the horn-rimmed glasses he'd worn for years. Perched halfway down his nose, they added to the concerned expression on his ruddy face and made him look like a kindly physician, the type you might see in an ad for some kind of pills. He would have hated it if he knew she thought he looked like a doctor, considering his contempt for the medical profession in general.

"Hey, you look like you didn't get any sleep last night," he admonished. "Where were you this morning anyway? The guys from up at Cooley's said you blew in and out again without telling them where you were going. They were kind of ticked off. Said they'd been out and around all night."

"Where'd they get to? I saw their truck outside," Gussie said, trying to distract him. She didn't want him around when she got busy on the phone, but never knew how to get him out without offending him. Mac had a reputation as a bit of a snoop. He liked to think he knew everybody in town and wanted to know every single little thing that went on. She couldn't afford to let slip that she might have a serious problem on her hands. It would be all over town in no time. *That woman doesn't know her job. Have to get rid of her. Need a man here. What was Mac thinking?* She could just hear the talk. Up until now, she hadn't given Bickerton too much to talk about except the thing with the Watson twins. And her split with Syd, of course.

Besides having a reputation for gossip, Bickerton is like most small towns: if you drive right straight through it, as most people do on their way to their summer lodge vacation or a cottage farther north, you'll think nothing ever happens here. And if you chance to stop for a cold can of pop or a newspaper, you'll be treated politely but distantly. Doing the shopping for your two-week camping vacation down by the Lake in the summer is one thing, but if you stay on much past Labour Day, you'll be met with undisguised resentful looks: *oh no, these ones must be here to stay.*

CeeCee remarked on this chilly reception from the towns-people when she and Hink had first come down.

"Don't let it get you, they'll settle down after a while, just keep on being polite, they'll soon get used to you," he said.

But CeeCee wasn't mollified. "They take our money quick enough, you'd think they'd be a bit friendlier," she complained. Hink just laughed and said she was expecting too much. "Some of them have never been out of here their whole lives, they're afraid of strangers, especially those from the City," he said.

"Oh Hinky! You've got to be kidding! What on earth have they got to be afraid of," she asked."Probably it's because we've been places, done things, seen things they can only read about. That makes them nervous," he said.

"But nobody else has noticed this, I already asked Maggie and Francy," she persisted.

"Now CeeCee, you're forgetting, Pete's Dad lived here for years so they know the name. And Francy, well, Francy wouldn't notice if they used foul language or turned their backs on her, she's so dumb," Hink said, scathingly.

CeeCee promptly dropped the subject. She thought he was being decidedly unfair to poor little Francy.

On the surface, life in Bickerton seems sedate enough, far removed from the noisy chaos of the City. Solemn looking buildings from another century, watched over by big old trees, line the main street, with the handful of businesses essential to the life of any town clustered near the centre close to the Town Hall: bank, post office, food market, variety store, library, restaurant, ladies'wear, flower shop, pharmacy, hairdresser, hardware.

The police station is up one side street handy to the main highway, the funeral home with its dark green awnings and huge parking lot up another, three churches with their manses huddle at one end of town, the Senior School, along with the arena, the swimming pool and the ballpark sprawl at the other. On the outskirts up beyond the police station are two used car dealers, a gas station, and a Co-op for the farmers in the region. Ordinary enough. But beneath the ordinariness lies something else, some indefinable atmosphere, which is seldom penetrated by outsiders, no matter how long they live here. Looks are exchanged between people in the shops or at the library, or when they meet each other in the street. Things left unsaid are somehow understood, as if the inhabitants are in some kind of symbiotic contact, like a school of fish or a flock of birds. For a newcomer trying to fit in, this could be unsettling.

If CeeCee had been acquainted with Kitty Woodcock, she would have learned she was not alone in feeling the way she did. Kitty had never been accepted either. Bad enough that she came from some obscure settlement in the Far North, when it got around that her husband wasn't home much and that her son was different from the other kids, most people looked the other way when they met her on the street or in the shops. But Kitty wasn't at all bothered by things like that. People could think what they liked. Kitty had learned long ago to ignore the nasty looks and went her own carefree way.

Most Bickerton residents work at one of the two factories on the fringes of town. One factory makes candy. Not just any old candy. This stuff is special. Some time back, a descendant of one of the original settlers had the brilliant idea of starting up a business based on a recipe for a kind of toffee, which had been a cherished family secret for over two hundred years. Since the area around Bickerton is known for its rich cream and butter, prime ingredients for toffee, this was a good location for Spilsbury's Sweets. The business had started small, but word of how good it was quickly got around. Now the candy is being sold right across the country.

The other company manufactures an exclusive line of health equipment like crutches, braces and canes. A few years ago, when new signs were needed at the entrances to town, the Town Council held a contest for a slogan that was supposed to tell everyone what the town was known for. Someone entered the phrase *Bickerton: the Candy Cane Town* . The judges however, lacking any sense of humour, chose *Welcome to Bickerton: Yours to Visit, Ours to Enjoy* .

The winning slogan neatly reflected MacPherson Noble's attitude towards his hometown. Although he'd gone away to school in his twenties and learned long ago that people are people wherever you go, he still felt he had to protect his town, try to keep it the way it had always been, a network of families bound by blood and marriage, descended from the first settlers, safe from the outside world that was creeping closer every year. He'd been afraid Gussie would meet someone in the City and stay there, so he was overjoyed when she'd come back and married Syd Spilsbury. He'd never given up hope that the two would get back together and still regarded Syd as his son-in-law.

As soon as he realized she wasn't going to drop any hints about her whereabouts that morning, Mac kissed his daughter good-bye, leaving her free to get back to work. Part way through Gussie's conversation with the acting coroner, Mac suddenly popped back into her office to retrieve his cap, which he'd left hanging on the back of the door. Gussie stopped abruptly in midsentence and gave him a stern look. He winked at her and shut the door. She went back to explaining to Dr. Blair what she wanted. Then she called Len over at Perry's Funeral Parlour to see if his hearse was available. Finally, she went to find the two Auxiliaries down at the Cosy Corner where Mac had said they'd gone for breakfast. By the front desk she stopped to tell Myrna, the receptionist, who was on the phone, where she was going. Myrna waved a sheaf of pink telephone messages at her, but Gussie indicated that she'd be right back. Probably gabbing with her sister again, Gussie said to herself. Good thing Mac had some extra lines put in.

Making her way carefully along the sidewalk, which the deep snow had made all but impassable, Gussie arrived at the Cosy Corner just as two burly fellows in their distinctive orange-red vests marked **AUXILIARY POLICE** were paying their bill. Inside, the air was seductive with the smell of bacon and coffee. Jennie Brant came out from the kitchen with a tray of steaming cinnamon buns and plopped them on the counter right under Gussie's nose. Her stomach rumbled in response and she found herself paying for a large bag of buns and a coffee. The two men were waiting outside for her.

"Hi Perce, how'd you make out?" Gussie asked, trying to balance the coffee on top of the buns. "And who've you got here?" she added, realizing that she didn't recognize the other man, who was nodding and smiling at her through the black forest of his beard.

"This here's Butch. He's new last month," Perce said, who was built like a wrestler, but was as nervous as a deer. "Say, we can go home now, eh? We've been at it all night."

He looked down at his boots and stammered, "That is, if it's okay with you. We know you've been up just as long as us. Myrna told us when we got back from taking the detour down. We thought you'd gone home, you left so fast."

"Sorry about that," Gussie wondered if she could trust these two. "I've got a bit of a problem, I mean a bit of a problem. Can you come back to the office so we can talk in private? This is real serious business, I mean real serious business. I'm going to need two strong men for a special job right off. You'll have to leave those vests behind, though."

Perce said sure thing, he'd be glad to come, but Butch hesitated. He told his wife he'd be back late, but not this late. She got real upset when he didn't come when she thought he should. Torn between his natural curiosity, which had led him to volunteer for the job in the first place and his desire to keep his wife happy, he lumbered along behind Perce and Gussie, trying to follow Perce's reporting on the night's events.

Back at the station, Dr. Bill Blair had already arrived. Dressed for the weather in a parka and boots, he was scanning the **WANTED!** posters on the wall by the door and greeted them with a smile on his darkly handsome face. He'd been interested in Gussie ever since he came to Bickerton, but she was all business. Twice he'd asked her out for dinner, but she firmly refused, without so much as a hint of a reason. Probably just as well, with all the old ladies he had as patients watching his every move. But he wasn't ready to give up on her yet.

"Boy, that was real quick, I mean real quick," Gussie said, setting the coffee and buns on Myrna's desk and trying not to make too much of the doctor's quick arrival. Picking up the pile of messages, she glanced through them. Most of them were from Mrs. Denton marked **Urgent** . Flinching inwardly, she put them on top of the coffee, picked up the whole works and headed to her office, the others trailing in her wake.

Ten minutes later, a small convoy led by Gussie in her four-wheeler, followed at a safe distance by the doctor in his pickup and the Auxiliaries' truck, was making its way over to the Old Barge Canal Road. The hearse was expected to meet them in about an hour. The Roads Superintendent had responded to Gussie's request. The plow had already gone through. She could just make out its flashing blue roof lights up ahead. A pale lemon-coloured sun was struggling to break through the clouds, just faintly illuminating the tops of the evergreen trees, which were bent over from the weight of their fluffy white coats, while the sides of the narrow road were banked so high it was difficult to see over them. Gussie was glad she had some idea of where they had to stop.

Emerging from their vehicles, the three men realized this was going to be a tough job indeed. Butch had decided he didn't want to miss out on the excitement, while Perce was sweating with anticipation. Busy with hauling out their gear, they didn't notice a small grey car pull up at some distance behind them.

10

MISS SNELGROVE TAKES CHARGE

Jesse lay flat on his back on his bed with his hands under his head, staring at the ceiling. No amount of coaxing by Kitty could get out of him what had happened with Gussie in the woods. All he would say was, it wasn't Pop, it wasn't Pop, it wasn't Pop, in a kind of litany. Kitty didn't know what to do with him. She phoned the school to see if it was open. It was, even though the buses that brought the kids in from the surrounding country-side had been cancelled. She tried to persuade Jesse that maybe it would be a good idea to get up and go to school after all, but he just lay without moving, not looking at her.

After a while, Kitty gave up and went back downstairs to her desk. *Maybe he'll get up when it's lunchtime. I shouldn't have let him go alone with the cop, I should've gone with them. Why do I always think of these things too late? Oh well, Jesse's a tough kid, he's like me, he'll get over it.* No doubt she'd find out soon enough who the poor soul was that they found in the woods. *Thank God it wasn't Albie .* Gussie had called like she said she would and said it wasn't. Kitty wished he would call, but she knew wishing for that was useless. It wasn't the first time he'd taken off on her. She turned her attention to her work and was soon so lost in it that she was startled when Jesse came in and said it was noon and could he have something to eat, please?

THE TROUBLE WITH SOME PEOPLE   **63**

Not long after Kitty had left him in his room, Jesse decided that his mom was right. Staying home had been a mistake. He got up and tried working on his bird charts, but all he could see was the boot with the orange sock. After a while, he gave up and picked up one of the new adventure books Kitty had bought him the last time they were up in Cooley's Mills. But still there were those images in the snow — the heap of branches, the bare hands, the pale face, the boot, the sock — shimmering on the page, engraved on his brain. He put the book down and lay back on the bed. *The poor guy. Who'd do that to him? Who was he anyway? How'd he get in there?* Jesse doubted he'd ever go back in the woods by himself again. He'd always be expecting to see another body. Just thinking about it made him feel sick. He longed to tell someone, but he'd promised the lady cop he wouldn't, and anyway Pop was always telling him, over and over, it was very important to always keep your promises.

Stumbling into the half empty classroom while the bell was still ringing, Jesse hung his jacket on its hook and fell into his seat just as Miss Snelgrove swept into the room, her navy crêpe skirt swinging importantly from side to side. She wore a sleeveless plum-coloured vest over an old- fashioned white blouse with lace at the collar and cuffs and sensible shoes. Her faded hair was scraped back into a bun at the nape of her neck and her black-rimmed glasses made her look years older than her age. With only a short time until retirement, which she'd decided to take much earlier than she had to, she was determined to make a lasting impression on her pupils. She didn't particularly care whether they had fond memories of their days in her classroom, she just wanted to make sure they never forgot her.

Lettice Snelgrove was not a happy person. She knew it was her fault, she took life too seriously; everyone was always telling her lighten up, relax, smile more. There had been a time when she thought she'd have to leave Bickerton, after the stories about her mother started circulating. The shame she felt back then kept her indoors for a good month until she got seriously ill. That had been way back in old Doc Winter's time. He'd been sympathetic and had given her a prescription for a strong tonic, but told her to hold her head up, she wasn't her mother and anyway times have changed. Not that they had, nor probably ever would, in a place like Bickerton, but he felt he had to get her out of her house. She was already well on her way to turning into a recluse.

After a while, she forced herself to go back to work, but over time she'd become the stereotypical small town schoolteacher, never married, kept two cats, went to church every Sunday, dressed severely and would never admit to watching Front Page Challenge. She was so terrified she'd turn out like her mother, she stayed away from mixed social gatherings. Other than church. She avoided encountering men, even crossing over to the other side of the street if she saw a man coming towards her. Once or twice she'd been forced to walk in the road when there were men coming on both sides at once. In fact, the only man she had anything to do with was her half brother who was much younger and whom she had practically brought up after their mother died. And the school principal of course. Then there was that other one. But any thoughts of him she kept locked away.

"Good afternoon class, I trust you had a substantial lunch, especially on a cold day like today. I see a certain young man has decided to honour us with his presence. Jesse Woodcock, stand up. Where is your excuse?" Lettice put her hands on her hips and looked sternly down the narrow aisle at him.

"Here, please, miss. Right here." Jesse replied, fumbling in his pocket for the note Kitty had written.

"Well? Don't just stand there. Bring it up here to me," Lettice ordered.

Jesse started up the aisle and promptly tripped over his trailing shoelaces. There was a snicker from somewhere behind him, which broke off abruptly as Lettice glowered at the offender. Unfolding the note, she held it at arm's length.

"Another headache, I see," she sniffed, crumpling up the note and tossing it in her wastebasket. "Has your mother taken you to the doctor lately? Perhaps it's because you're using your binoculars too much." There was another snort.

"I'm warning you," Lettie said to the unidentified snickerer, "I'll have no nonsense in this class. Young man," she continued to Jesse, "when you get home, tell your mother I want to have a talk with her. Have her call me tonight.

"Class, we were at page 14 in the Blue Reader. Shall we go on?"

When recess came, Jesse looked around the schoolyard for Adam, but couldn't see him anywhere. He didn't feel like joining in with some of his classmates who were building snow forts or rolling up snow into giant balls for snowmen. As he stood by himself in the middle of the schoolyard wishing he'd stayed home after all, he saw a small group of boys coming towards him led by Tommy Bartlett, the biggest kid in the class.

Tommy strutted up to him, his face a sneering mask of insolence. "So, Mister Birdman," Tommy said. "Decided to goof off this morning, eh? Was there too much snow for the poor wittle baby, was it too deep for his wittle booties to get through, eh? Bet your mommie let you sleep in, you poor wittle fing. Bet your old man's gone for good this time, bet he's glad he doesn't have to look at *your* ugly mug every morning." Tommy moved a step closer. The other boys laughed and scuffed their feet in the snow, but stayed where they were.

"How about it, kid? Whatcha got to say for yourself? Speak up, I can't hear you." Tommy came even closer until he was squarely in front of Jesse. Tommy was a full head taller than anyone else in the class and had big thick hands, which he had balled into fists. Jesse stood his ground, trying hard not to show how scared he was. Adam had warned him about Tommy. If he doesn't like you, you're in for it, he'd said. In for what? Jesse asked. In for a pasting, that's what. Keep out of his way and if he ever comes after you, don't let him see you're afraid, or you'll really get it, Adam said. He tried it on me once, but I punched him in the nose and he left me alone. Jesse thought frantically of what he might have done to attract the bully's attention. Up until now, Tommy had ignored him.

Glancing around at his companions to make sure he had an audience, Tommy suddenly lunged forward and butted Jesse in the chest. The unexpected move made Jesse lose his balance and he fell over backwards. Tommy threw himself down on top of Jesse and started punching him in the ribs. The two rolled around in the snow, the other boys shouting, "Fight! Fight!" attracting the attention of the other kids who came running over to watch.

"That's it, Tommy, give it to him good, the big sissy," yelled one of Tommy's followers. "We don't want his kind around here!" shouted another.

One of the girls started to cry. Another girl, who looked like she could be a sister to Adam, tried to break through the ring of excited kids, but her friends held her back. Jesse was helpless to defend himself, but he had the advantage of being thin and wiry. He wriggled around and suddenly slipped out of Tommy's grasp. In his struggle to escape his tormentor, one of Jesse's boots caught the bully in the head. Tommy sat up, holding his ear. "Did you see that, you guys?" he roared. "The little stiff kicked me in the head. I'm gonna kill him!"

At that point, Miss Snelgrove came hurrying across the schoolyard, slipping and sliding through the deep snow, red-faced and coatless.

"What is the meaning of this?" she shrieked, gasping for breath. Little tendrils of her hair had escaped from the imprisoning bun and were whipping around in the wind. "Both of you. GET UP THIS INSTANT! You know fighting is forbidden on school grounds. I'm marching you straight into Mr.

Roxton's office. We'll see what *he* has to say about this *disgrace-ful* behaviour!"

She grasped each boy firmly by the collar and yanked him to his feet, turning him in the direction of the school building. She'd really wanted to take hold of them by the ears, but she could be in trouble for doing that. Tommy's father was an important person in the community and she didn't want any unpleasant phone calls. Jesse strained to hold back the tears, while Tommy looked defiant. The other children drew back. Although they were afraid of Tommy, they were even more afraid of the teacher. When the trio had almost reached the school steps, a volley of snowballs landed behind them, but Miss Snelgrove was too angry to stop and find out where they came from. She dragged the two cul-prits up the steps and into the school. The bell marking the end of recess started ringing just as Adam Brant, his hands full of snowballs, came out from behind one of the trees.

11

BREAKFAST AT CEECEE'S

A persistent tickle in her throat set CeeCee to coughing, waking her up. Raising herself on her elbows, she could see it was still pitch dark out. That was strange. She could hear music. *Sounds like it's coming from downstairs,* she thought groggily. She strained to listen. Yep. Someone was singing in a thin reedy voice...

"or when the va-a-a-lley's hushed and whi-i-i-te with sno-o-o-w"...

Could she have left the radio on? At that thought, the events of the previous night came flooding back. She peered through the gloom, trying to make out if Hink was in the bed. His side was smooth, untouched. A memory popped into her head, the memory of being afraid to go to sleep alone when she was a little girl. Every night she'd turn her other pillow sideways and pretend it was a friend come to keep her company. Then she'd fill the space between them with dolls and stuffed animals until her mother, coming in to kiss her good night, would laugh and say, soon there'll be no room for CeeCee.

Ignoring her housecoat and slippers, she went out into the hall and crept cautiously down the stairs towards the sound. The voice went on...

"oh Danny boy, oh Danny boy, I miss you so-o-o"

A sliver of light was coming from under the door to the kitchen. Her first reaction was Good. That means the power's back on. Opening the door wide, she discovered Dottie, fully dressed, with one of Hink's aprons tied around her waist, seated at the old pine table singing and making toast.

"Mornin', lovey, I hope I didn't wake ya, I tried to sing quietly," Dottie said, breaking off in the middle of the next verse. "I just couldn't stay in the bed another minute. Not that it wasn't right comfortable, mind. It sure is some lovely room. Did ya have a good night, love, not that I 'spect ya did, seein' as how your hubby's still out somewheres. Oh dear, I shouldn't've said that, I forgot. In our house the men were always comin' and goin', half the time we didn't know where they were at. Come and sit down and have a nice hot cuppa tea. I hope ya don't mind me gettin' into your kitchen on me own." Dottie finished buttering the toast and reached for some strawberry jam. Still half asleep, CeeCee mumbled a g'morning, shook her head and said, no, she didn't mind at all, it wasn't her kitchen it was Hink's.

When she'd first woken up and found herself alone, CeeCee thought maybe Hink'd come in late and, not wanting to disturb her, had spent the night on the sofa. Now, crossing over into the living room, her heart sank. Everything was just as she and Dottie had left it. Checking the thermostat, she could see the furnace was running all right, but the house still felt chilly. She knelt down by the fireplace and started to build a fire the way Hink had shown her. She thought vaguely about the pipes. Had it gotten cold enough for them to burst? *Better make a fire first and then check the basement.* Hink always worried about the pipes in the winter. Once before, in the City, they'd had a flood from a burst water pipe after the temperature dropped suddenly overnight.

As she fumbled with the fireplace things, the cat who had hidden himself away somewhere, probably on Dottie's bed, came thumping down the stairs. Mewing and stretching, he padded over to wind his sleek body coaxingly around her, his green eyes glowing in the half light.

"Breakfast for you first, my boy," she said, picking him up and forgetting about the fireplace, "otherwise I'll never have any peace." She carried the cat into the kitchen, set him down by the stove and got out his bowl. Rummaging around in the refrigerator, she located the tin of cat food near the back.

Dottie, who had been sipping her tea in spoonfuls, watched as the cat settled down contentedly with his food. Seeing CeeCee shivering in her nightgown, she got up and went into the living room to get the dark red afghan she'd noticed heaped at the end of the sofa the night before.

"Do have a little something, lovey," Dottie urged, draping the warm wrap over CeeCee's shoulders and tucking it down behind her back, "or would ya drather go back up to bed til it's a wee bit warmer? I heard the furnace come back on a while ago. Probably a good thing we shut off the lights and all last night. Might've had a power surge, although probably not a little house like this with just a tv, radio, fridge and a few lamps. Rab always worries about it when the power goes because it knocks out his fridge cases and all when it comes back on."

CeeCee sat down heavily at the table. She was finding it hard to think how only yesterday afternoon she'd been sitting here in this same chair with no idea that something might have happened to Hink. Seemed like years ago now. She wondered if that lady cop had taken her seriously, that Hink really was missing. All at once, the anxiety that had been weighing on her for so long overcame her and she started to cry.

"There, there, lovey, let yourself go, it'll help," Dottie said, fetching a box of tissues from the counter. "I'm sure we'll hear from Miz Spilsbury real soon. Let me make ya a proper breakfast. Ya'll feel better if ya gets somethin' inside of ya."

"Oh, Dottie, I feel so helpless," CeeCee was sobbing in earnest now, the tears streaming down her face. "I don't know what to do. After I'd been in bed for a while, I couldn't get to sleep. Called the police station several times, but that lady cop was still out.

All the woman at the other end could say was there was a lot of trouble on the roads with the snowstorm. Said they'd call me in the morning. I was so worried I had to take one of Hink's sleeping pills. Didn't help much. Had horrible dreams all night."

"Would ya like me to cook ya up a mess a eggs? There's lots in the fridge. I could do them any which way ya likes," offered Dottie, passing the plate of toast to CeeCee who took a slice, but put it down in front of her untouched.

"Is it still snowing?" CeeCee looked about in a daze "Forgot to look. Oh, darn! Forgot to plug in the block heater on the car. Hink'll be mad if it doesn't start right away. What am I saying? Hink's not even here." And CeeCee gave in to tears yet again, wiping her damp cheeks with a wad of tissue. "This is so embarrassing," she whispered, blowing her nose loudly to hide her discomfiture.

"Don't ya worry none, lovey. Ya got a right to be upset. Look here, I'm goin' to make us a mess a scrambled eggs. I found some odds and ends a cheese what'll go real good on top. Nothin' like a good hot breakfast, that's what my Gram always said. Snow's still comin' down but not so bad as before. Eat your toast while it's hot. Ya got someone to do your plowin' out?"

"Neighbour up the road usually does it. Hink has to call him first. Won't take orders from a woman," CeeCee bit off a corner of her toast.

"So he says. Isn't that just like the country! We'll see what he has to say when *I* gets him on the phone. It'll be light soon. What's his number?"

CeeCee looked gratefully across at Dottie who'd left the table and was hunting through the cupboards for a frying pan. After a couple of false starts, she emerged triumphant, brandishing a cast iron pan.

"Guess I could try some eggs, please, Dottie. You're a darling. What on earth would I've done here by myself?"

"Oh, ya'd have managed. Ya'd be right surprised what ya can do if ya have to. Like cheese on your eggs? And ketchup? Don't much like it meself, but lots do."

Dottie was in full swing now, breaking the eggs into a bowl and whisking them together with some milk. CeeCee envied her. She'd never felt comfortable in the kitchen, even her own, and here was Dottie right at home in a strange one.

"What about the girls? Are ya goin' to give 'em a call?" Dottie asked over her shoulder.

CeeCee gasped. "Oh my God, the girls! I never even thought. They'll be terribly upset! Dote on their father. Didn't like it when we moved out here. Thought it was a crazy idea. Said they'd never see us. Said why didn't we take a nice apartment in the City and go some place warm for the winter. Wouldn't come out here to visit for months after we moved. Then they only came because their husbands were looking for some place to camp. The two guys like fishing and hiking. Coralee, she was okay, but Janette hardly said a word all day. Wasn't sorry to see them go. Hink was disappointed none of them liked it here."

Dottie set a steaming plate in front of CeeCee and popped more bread in the toaster. Taking off her apron, she settled in to tackle her own breakfast. It was growing steadily lighter outside now and the house was starting to feel warmer. As she worked her way through the softly scrambled eggs and melted cheese, CeeCee began to feel much better. Surely as soon as it was properly morning she would hear from the police.

When they'd finished eating, she gave the plowing neighbour's number to Dottie who went in to the front hall to use the phone. Dottie had never been in a house where there wasn't a phone in the kitchen, but CeeCee explained it was all Hink's doing. No stupid telephone was going to interrupt him when he was busy working on a complicated dish or trying a new recipe. Or in the middle of a meal. To CeeCee he was being overly fussy since they rarely got many phone calls at any time of the day.

Now she thought she'd almost welcome an interruption if it was about Hink.

While Dottie was busy on the phone, CeeCee felt the need for something stronger to drink. Tea was all very well in the afternoon as a pick-me-up, but right now what she wanted was something stronger. Why not? Hink wasn't here to stop her. Drawing the afghan around her, she got a stool and went into the pantry. Then she looked in the freezer. In no time at all, the tantalizing smell of fresh perked coffee began wafting through the kitchen. She smiled to herself; she'd managed to hide the tin of coffee from Hink after all.

"Neighbour woman said her man was out doin' the chores," announced Dottie coming back into the kitchen, "so I told her as ya had to be out this mornin', could she please tell him to come over as soon as he gets in. I didn't tell her anythin' else but I could tell she was real curious to know where ya were goin' and why it was me callin' and not your hubby. She said she'd tell him first thing. I must call Rab," she went on, "he'll be wonderin' what's happenin'. I'll just be a minute. I don't want to tie up the line ... in case ..."

"That's okay, Dottie, you go right ahead. If I don't hear from that lady cop by eight, I'm going to call again."

CeeCee leaned back in her chair. That coffee sure hit the spot, she mused. She wondered how she'd ever given it up. She tried to remember where she'd stashed those marvelous French cigarettes when she and Hink had quit smoking. She jumped when the phone rang, her heart beginning to pound.

"I'll get it, love," Dottie called from the hall. CeeCee could hear her chattering away to someone and then she was back.

"That was Miz Otterley from over to East Thorne. She wondered if Mister Denton was back and could she talk to ya, but I told her ya was still in bed and I'd give ya the message and could ya call her back a bit later. Was that all right, love? I never said a word 'bout Mister Denton bein' gone, but I could tell she was real curious. She can wait. I'm callin' Rab now." And she was gone again.

CeeCee poured herself another cup of coffee, then looked down at herself, suddenly aware she was still in her nightgown. Better get dressed, she thought. As she started up the stairs, she heard the rumble of a plow working its way up the lane.

"Rab says I can stay as long as ya needs me, he's got a heap of snow to clear before he can open," Dottie called up to CeeCee who had reached the upper level. As CeeCee was about to reply, the telephone rang again.

12

PETE AND MAGGIE

By morning, the outside temperature had risen to a more comfortable level, but in the Wychwood household, the atmosphere was decidedly chilly. Maggie slept late and when she finally came downstairs, she got herself some coffee and disappeared into the tiny room off the kitchen where Pete's Mom used to do her sewing. Pete, who'd been up for hours and feeling guilty from the night before, knew it was no use trying to talk to her when she went in there.

When Maggie wanted privacy, she went to extremes. The day they moved to Bickerton, Maggie insisted she and Pete have separate bedrooms. Pete didn't like sleeping apart from her, but learned to relish his peaceful nights alone, without her constant tossing and turning. When Maggie began spending hours on end in the bathtub, he was happy they had separate bathrooms as well. Weekdays, he went down to his office, evenings he had his men's service clubs, weekends his golf and tennis, while she played endless games of cards and went out shopping in Dunhampton and to lunch with her girlfriends. There were days when they scarcely saw one another.

Those friends who knew about his situation wondered why Pete had stuck with this unconventional arrangement. But Pete knew why. He was still crazy about his wife. He'd fallen for Maggie the first day she walked into the office where he was working as a junior accountant. After pursuing her for months and nearly going broke in the process, Pete finally persuaded her to marry him. That had been nearly thirty-seven years ago. But he sometimes wondered how *she* felt. In some strange way, she seemed to need him. Every once in a while, this need would show itself and then he knew that the other things about her that were hard to take — the meals eaten alone, the solitary evenings, the lonely nights — didn't matter. Those times made up for it all.

Right from the start, Maggie controlled their relationship. She was obsessively ambitious, and determined to have the best of everything. Designer clothes, the latest in home furnishings, the most luxurious car. Especially the biggest house. In the town where they'd started out, that had been easy. But in Bickerton, where Pete set up his accounting business, she had to settle for second best. Pete didn't agree with her on this subject. Bewyching Wood, which his father had left him, was situated on the highest point of land overlooking the town, was certainly spacious enough. But it was neither the largest nor, more important to Maggie, at the very top of the hill. That house belonged to old Mrs. Roxton. Maggie had lusted for Hill House ever since they moved to town. She was impatient for the old lady to die, but Pete told her not to count on the house being available even then. Eliza Roxton had several heirs still living, he was continually reminding her.

But Maggie wasn't to be deterred from her goal. I've simply got to have it, this house isn't good enough, she'd say over and over. Pete couldn't see it. Privately he thought Bewyching Wood was a much finer property, nestled as it was in the shelter of maple and pine trees and surrounded by gently sloping lawns and shrubs that bloomed gloriously in season. It had a wide front porch that was cooled in summer by breezes off the Lake, a rose garden at the back and a widow's walk on the roof with a stupendous view.

By the time you got all the way up to Hill House, the ground was barren treeless rock. The massive structure of dark grey stone, built by some long dead Roxton, had tiny windows and no landscaping to speak of. Pete had always thought it looked like a funeral home with its imposing white pillars and severe aspect. His Dad's house, now his and Maggie's, was built of a warm Western red cedar, a house that looked like home from the time it went up. His father had considered himself lucky to be able to buy the lot and had demolished the dilapidated cottage that had stood there, vacant, for years. Pete had often been sorry he'd given in to Maggie and agreed not to have children. He hated the idea of strangers taking over the house in which his parents had spent so many happy years after his Dad retired.

Well into middle age now, Maggie was still stunningly beautiful, with hair she kept a glossy black and a translucent skin that she never allowed to be exposed to the sun. Her eyes were a piercing blue; she had a way of looking at you sideways from under her eyelashes that was irresistible. She worked hard at keeping her figure and wore close-fitting things like black velvet leggings and angora sweaters. Pete was sure she'd never been unfaithful. She didn't like men, she'd told him often enough, just enjoyed teasing them. She'd made Hink Denton look ridiculous more than once. *And* Ferd Otterley. Even George Roxton, the principal over at the Junior School, had been left standing with a silly grin on his face, that time the three men stopped by to pick up Pete for their annual hunting trip and Maggie had gone up and whispered something in his ear.

She was still furious with Pete from the day before. Weeks ago, they had arranged to go in to the City to take in a show and then stay for dinner with some old friends. After lunch, she had been putting the finishing touches to her makeup when she heard a car pull up in the drive. At that instant, Pete called up the stairs that he had to go out and to bring his car down to the Quick Bite sharp at five. She ran to the bedroom window, but whoever it was stayed behind the wheel and she didn't recognize the car. Pete was out and gone without a word about where he was going. Maggie was livid; her own car had been up in Cooley's Mills for repairs since last week when she'd run it off the road into a fence and damaged the front end. Something in the tone of his voice told her she'd better do what he asked. Anyway, five o'clock was too late to start driving to the City. She was left having to make some excuse to their friends.

Later, when she picked Pete up from outside the Quick Bite, he was silent and withdrawn and made no response to her barrage of questions. After they had said hello to CeeCee outside the restaurant, Maggie drove them home, a niggling feeling inside her that something serious was up. Pete had never done anything like this before and the thought was disturbing. She'd always been able to have things her own way with him. Not this time. Maggie prepared a cold plate and took it off to her private room. The rest of the evening passed the same way.

The next morning, Pete wasn't feeling well. He'd lain in his bed like a stone all night, unable to unwind. The few times he had drifted off, a jumble of nightmares brought him awake again. Around four-thirty, he'd given up and come downstairs to his Dad's old study, where the early morning light found him still sitting in his Dad's worn and shabby Morris chair, smoking cigarette after cigarette, staring out the glass doors that led to the garden. The snow had blanketed everything, burying the mounds of hilled-over roses and leaving the garden looking vast and alien. The only thing plainly visible was the top of a piece of garden statuary mounted on a pedestal that his Mom had brought from their other house. It had been given to her when his sister died and was in the form of a young girl with her arms full of roses. Only the head was showing now, with its tiara of snow crystals.

Just after eight, when he'd decided it was time he was getting some breakfast, the telephone on the table beside him rang. It was Francy Otterley. In her high little-girl voice, she told him Hink Denton was missing, she'd just spoken to some woman at the Dentons, CeeCee was too upset to come to the phone and shouldn't they be doing something. Pete thanked her and said he'd call back when he'd talked to Maggie. The sick feeling began to well up inside him again.

The door down the hall banged and Maggie came into the study. She was looking paler than usual, her uncombed hair hanging loosely about her shoulders. She leaned against the back of his chair and followed his gaze outside.

"Looks real pretty, doesn't she?" Maggie said slowly. "A real little angel. Your Mom never got over her, did she?"

Pete stood up suddenly. "Let's not get into that again," he said shortly. He picked up the overflowing ashtray and carried it out to the hall.

"Interested in some breakfast?" he called back over his shoulder, hoping she'd say yes.

"Maybe some more coffee. And a couple of those sweet rolls I got yesterday at the Cosy Corner. And some cheese," she responded, surprising him. It was weeks since they'd eaten together in the morning.

Pete's spirits rose. This was Maggie's way of softening towards him after being angry. He didn't know what he was going to tell her about yesterday. It was better she didn't know what was going on. But he knew he'd have to think fast and make up something to satisfy her. As she was putting things on the table in the breakfast room, he could see she was about to start in on him again. To distract her, he said, "We just had a phone call from Francy Otterley. Hink Denton's missing and she thinks we ought to do something."

"You mean he's still missing from last night? What's CeeCee doing about it? Has she called Gussie? And all that snow!" Pete was astonished. For once, Maggie was interested in someone outside herself.

13

A FLICKERING FLAME

Lettice slumped in her easy chair by a cold fireplace, resting her poor swollen feet on the worn leather hassock she loved to play on when she was a child. She felt done in. Her legs had been aching like crazy the last few weeks. Days like today didn't help them at all. What a comfort it was to have cats, they're such good company and make so few demands. As if he had been reading her mind, Foozle jumped up on her lap and stretched out to his full length. She ran one hand over his back and scratched his neck with the other. The bigger of the two cats she had left from the original five kittens she found abandoned in her back shed, Foo was a plump grey fuzzy ball of a creature who could never get enough love and affection. Woozle, thin and as black as tar and more independent than his brother, had assumed his customary perch on the back of her chair and was purring contentedly in her ear. Every once in a while, he would bunt at her neck with his nose or nibble at her hair which had been released from its bun.

"Stop it now, Woo, that tickles," she said tapping him lightly on the head. "Just wanting your share of attention, I know, I know." She wished she could relax as easily as her cats. She thought vaguely of getting herself a drink, a nice glass of sherry maybe, but couldn't summon up the energy. Today had been one of those days when she wondered if maybe her mother had been right after all. Momma had wanted her to get a job at the candy factory. Just think, Letty, she'd said in her bubbly way, you could start on the line, work real hard and maybe in a few years, you could make it to supervisor, I hear the pay's decent. But Lettice had stubbornly refused to waste a single thought on the possibility of spending her life surrounded by candy. She wanted something better for herself.

Teaching, now. Yes, teaching. Even though that had been her Auntie Plum's suggestion. Auntie Plum, who took great delight in introducing her as 'Meet my niece, Lettice' which Lettice hated, and who looked more like she should be called Auntie Prune when her skin went all wrinkly in old age. Anyway, Auntie Plum said now Lettice that's a job which'll give you some status, lift you miles above those girls you're always hanging around with who just want to work until they can hook a man.

Auntie Plum had been right. Lettice's two best friends thought working at Spilsbury's was 'a great idea, but just 'til we get married, eh?' Julie was doing okay until one of the packers got her pregnant and dumped her as soon as he found out. She'd had to leave town, the disgrace was too much for her family. No one, not even her family, had any idea where she was now. Or even seemed to care. Margie stayed with it until she'd lost most of a hand in one of the mixing machines. She'd had an awful time getting any compensation out of the company. They said it was her fault, if she'd been having dizzy spells, she should have stayed home and seen a doctor. She couldn't tell them she was getting next to no sleep from her sick mother's ranting and raving all night. The company had to be threatened with bad publicity by Margie's tough-guy cousin, Albert, before they came across with a decent sum of money. Poor Margie couldn't find another job and no one would date her until a much older man convinced her he'd look after her if she married him. Turned out all he really wanted was someone to swear at and knock about on the nights when he came home drunk. Which was almost every night, Lettice recalled hearing. Margie was a widow now and looked ten years older than her age. No, it may have been much harder work, but teaching had been the better choice. Anyway, she would never have done what Momma wanted her to do. Who was she to give advice anyway. Look at the mess she'd made of her own life.

Still, more and more often, there were days when Lettice wondered if a straight factory job might have been easier. Take today, for example. Nothing had gone right. When her car refused to start, she'd been forced to struggle on foot through heavy snow to get to the school on time (she had to set an example to the pupils, didn't she). Then there was the dreary history lesson and the equally dreary reader (who on earth had set this curriculum anyway). And, when the kids were so distracted by all that lovely snow just waiting to be played in, they were next to impossible to get settled down and she hadn't been able to get through the work she'd planned for that day (no need to worry about the absentees catching up). Then there was that fight in the schoolyard (that Tommy Bartlett was definitely getting worse and Jesse Woodcock--well, what could you expect with such a lackadaisical creature for a mother). And to top it all off, the confrontation in George Roxton's office (she'd been so angry and out of breath she could hardly speak). Thinking about it all, she knew she'd made the correct decision to retire early. She was getting too old for it, no question. The thrill of seeing some of her pupils grow up and go on to greater things outside the stuffy confines of Bickerton had evaporated ages ago and she longed for some peace.

She was still reeling from the events of the afternoon. She'd been dumbfounded when George Roxton hadn't backed her up and had behaved as though the fight between Tommy and Jesse was somehow her fault. Boys will be boys, he'd said stiffly. As if that excused everything. She couldn't understand what had gotten into him. He hated fighting on school property and usually came down like a ton of bricks on troublemakers. Give 'em a few lines, that ought to do it, he'd said, I'm sure they'd rather be out building snow forts or something. Then he'd winked at the boys, who were standing there grinning. Lines they'll get, she'd retorted, but I'm contacting their folks anyway.

Setting the boys to writing I MUST NOT FIGHT ON SCHOOL PROPERTY a hundred times on the blackboard after the others had left, she composed a note to Jesse's mother and Tommy's father, with a postscript to telephone her at home that night. Keeping the boys in after school meant she'd had to stay late as well, and although she could sit down at her desk, her legs kept reminding her they didn't like that any better than standing. She'd had to fight to keep herself from massaging them in front of the boys. Just as the two culprits were beginning to run out of space (she could have sworn they wrote bigger on purpose), the intercom buzzed and the sepulchral voice of the school secretary announced she was wanted on the phone. She asked the secretary to take a message and handed the boys their notes.

"Now remember, you two," she cautioned, "I expect an answer from your parents tonight. Without fail."

Both boys looked sullen as they left the classroom. She hoped they wouldn't pick up from where they'd left off that afternoon. Oh, well. Once they were off school property, they weren't her responsibility.

She was surprised to learn the phone call had been from Tom Bartlett Senior, Tommy's father. What an odd coincidence. And what could he possibly want. He can't know about the fight already, she thought. She was dying to get home and put her feet up, but decided to call him back before she left the school. The telephone rang, forever, it seemed, before a weary sounding Tom Senior answered.

"Sorry to take so long," he said, stifling a yawn. "Uh, I must have dozed off for a second."

"That's all right," Lettice said, briskly. "I understand you called earlier."

"Listen, I hate to bother you with this, Letty, but I'm at my wits' end. I really need to talk to you and I don't want to do it over the phone. Uh, is there some place we could meet?"

Letty. He called her Letty. How dare he! Lettice was furious with him, but steeled herself to respond as professionally as she could. After all, he was one of her pupil's parents.

"Of course we can, Tom. But not at my place. And not at yours either. You know how people are in this town, they'd try to make something of it."

"Uh, sorry," Tom said again. "I wasn't thinking there for a moment. Maybe I better come over to the school. How about tomorrow afternoon? Is four-thirty too late? I have a meeting at three, but it should be over by quarter after four."

Lettice thought for a minute. She had some paperwork she'd been meaning to catch up on. Maybe tomorrow afternoon was as good a time as any. After agreeing, she hung up feeling drained, remembering how it had been with Tom. Once. It seemed like light years ago she'd been crazy about him and thought he felt the same about her. They'd already started making plans for after graduation, plans for a future together. Until the fragile little creature that had been Ella moved into town. Ella with her pale hair like spun sugar, her delicate skin, her turned up nose, her rosebud mouth with its tiny little teeth, and her slender wraith-like body. Like a china doll she was. Ella, who had all the boys following her home after school, making fools of themselves, vying for her attention. But she just laughed at all of them. All of them except Tom. He was lost to Lettice right from the first day Ella appeared. Poor little Ella. Marriage and an early pregnancy had been too much for her. After her baby girl was stillborn, Ella's mind collapsed and she had been taken away to an institution Up North somewhere where she wasted away and was gone within the year. Tom was left a widower.

When she thought of those days, Lettice remembered how sick at heart she'd felt. People had said to her, right to her face, well, now's your chance, Lettice, what're you waiting for, at least he doesn't have any kids for you to take on, why don't you go after him? She'd been stunned. How could people be so unfeeling, so cruel. People she'd known all her life. She'd clamped her teeth together, smiled at her tormentors and went out of her way to avoid meeting Tom. Not long after that, he'd left town. Gone to the City, to a real good job, burying his sorrows, people said. Too bad for you, Lettice. But Lettice had gotten on with her life, such as it was, gotten into teaching, gotten through the tortured years when the gossip about her poor foolish mother spread all over town.

Then Tom came back to Bickerton with a new wife and a son. People said he hadn't managed too well in the City, had to come back to his roots, back to where he could make a fresh start. But his wife didn't fit in. Too citified, people said, thinks she's better than the rest of us. Very quickly Tom's wife got bored with small town life and with Tom and ran off with one of the seasonal pickers, leaving her son behind and Tom with a demanding child on his hands. Now young Tommy was growing up and becoming a nuisance to everyone.

Lettice didn't feel comfortable with Tom's son in her class and watched with growing alarm as Tommy grew daily more aggressive. She couldn't help feeling a certain amount of vindication. *Serves Tom right, the fool, choosing that weak and silly Ella over me,* she'd told herself over and over after Ella died. *Then having the bad luck to pick another fool for a wife.* She'd dreaded the annual 'Meet the Teachers' night. All for nothing. Tom Bartlett hadn't bothered to show up. Now he needed her help with the boy whose growing reputation as a bully was upsetting her class, something she couldn't tolerate no matter how close to retirement she was.

Funny about the candy factory, though. She never could stomach the stuff. Too sweet. Too cloying. Just the smell of it, as it wafted through the town on hot and humid summer days, made her want to gag. And that was where Tom was employed as a senior manager.

14

OUT AT THE RESERVE

Jesse and Adam sat slouching on the sagging sofa in the Brants' cabin. The cabin was a small place, much smaller than Jesse's little house. It had one room, which served as living room, and bedroom for Adam, and another small room for Adam's parents, with a tiny bathroom tucked into one corner. Between the boys, with his head on Jesse's lap, was Adam's dog Lickapaw. Every time Jesse moved, the dog wagged his tail, smacking Adam in the ribs. Adam didn't seem to mind, but continued stroking the dog's back and murmuring to him in low measured tones.

"Gee, you're so lucky," said Jesse, scooching around to get more comfortable. He loved coming out here. He was glad his mom fixed things so this time he could spend the whole weekend. The excuse she gave him was she had to get ready for Christmas and he'd just be in the way. But he knew the real reason. She wanted him to have a change of scene so he could get the body in the woods off his mind. Fine during the daytime. But Jesse knew deep inside it wouldn't work at night. As soon as he got into bed and tried to fall asleep, all he could see was the orange sock in the heavy boot. It looked so pitiful, as though its owner had dropped it on the way into the Hidden Swamp and forgotten to come back and get it.

He shut his eyes tight to squeeze out the memory and said again, "You're a lucky guy, having your own dog. My mom says we can't afford one. Says the food's too 'spensive. Does he do it very much?"

"It's *ex* pensive, dummy. Do what?" Adam said, absently.

"Lick his paws," Jesse responded, kicking his legs against the sofa, making the dog wag his tail harder than ever.

"Not much," Adam replied, "only when he gets left alone too long. Dad usually takes him in the truck, but sometimes he has to leave him here 'n that's when he does the licking. What do you want to know that for?"

" 'Cuz of his name, dummy. Lickapaw. Why'd you call him that then?"

"Oh, Dad thought it sounded like a good Indian name, that's all."

"Um, what kind of a dog is he?"

"Gee, you ask a lot of questions," Adam said, amiably. "Dad said his mother was a black Lab, but we don't know who his father is. Could be one of those strays that hang around the Rec Hall."

Both boys were exhausted. They had been playing in the snow since Jesse's arrival that morning. Forts had been built, besieged, destroyed. Piles of snowballs had been made, hurled and replenished. A giant snow thing now stood outside the front door. Snow thing, because it was hard to tell what it was exactly. The boys agreed it looked like a big, scary monster, whatever it was. The four gigantic snowballs that had gone into its creation had been rolled and stacked with a great deal of heaving and pushing. After that, the boys had had enough and dragged themselves in the back door. Their snow soaked clothes were hanging behind the old woodstove, which gave off a comforting heat from its corner of the room. Little tendrils of vapour spiraled above the clothes as they dried, making them look as though they were smouldering.

After rummaging around in an old chest in the other room, Adam had hauled out two well-worn flannel shirts that smelled strongly of wood smoke and stale tobacco. The shirts came down below their knees where they were met by thick grey work socks that Adam took out of a cardboard carton under the sofa. Adam's shirt fit him much better than Jesse's, who looked lost inside his. Like most boys his age, he didn't care how he looked, but sat happily dangling the too long sleeves as he chattered away to his friend. It was Saturday, their favourite day of the week.

The dog's black coat began to gleam as it was struck by the sunlight coming through the only window in the room. Jesse pushed one sleeve back and gently ran the palm of his hand over the dog's head. It felt like he imagined silk would feel. Smooth and slippery.

"Um, hey Adam," Jesse said solemnly, "can I ask you something?"

"Another question," Adam laughed. "Uh, sure," he said, scratching the dog behind his ears. "What?"

"Um, ah, you won't get mad or anything?"

Adam snorted. "Why should I get mad? We're friends, aren't we?"

"Yeah, I know but, um … well it's kind of, um … well …"

"Well, what? I'm not gonna hit you, dummy. Come on, what is it?"

"Well, um, uh, I just wondered. You're so much darker than me … well, um, well does it bother you when guys call you black?"

"Better black than red," Adam said, laughing. "You know how they like to call us Indians redskins. Must be from the days we used war paint. Me, I don't care what they say. Why do you ask?"

"Well, um, they're always calling me black and I'm not, I'm brown. See?" And the two rolled back their sleeves, put their bare arms side by side and looked at them critically.

"What the heck, black, brown, what's the difference? At least we don't have to worry about getting sunburned. *They're* the red-skins, not us," said Adam, rubbing his arm with the shirt sleeve.

"Yeah. Imagine if your skin was red," giggled Jesse. "You'd look like a lobster."

"Yeah. Red, like you fell in red paint. Or, or someone dipped you in blood."

Jesse stopped giggling and fell silent. Then he gave a slight shudder and slid off the sofa, startling the dog. The work socks slipped down around his ankles.

"Hey, what else are we going to do today? Where's your Dad anyway? Want to arm wrestle? Can I have a drink of water?" Jesse jigged up and down on one foot.

"Hey, what's got into you? Ants in your pants?" Adam laughed again.

He let out a whoop, dumped the dog off the sofa and joined Jesse in a spontaneous dance, both of them shrieking and laughing, setting the floor of the cabin bouncing up and down like a springboard. Dust motes rose in the air, the dog started barking while round and round they went, stamping their feet in a crazy wild rhythm until dizzy and spent, they fell together in a heap on the sofa. They lay there breathless as the dust they'd stirred up slowly settled. The dog came over and sat down in front of them, his long, pink tongue hanging out, looking at them as if to ask what's next. Then when nothing more seemed likely to be happening, he went over and lay down near the wood stove. There was a loud thud from inside the stove.

"Just a piece of wood," said Adam, yawning and rubbing his nose with the back of his hand. "Hey, it's my turn for a question. Has your Pop come home yet?" He knew how upset Jesse was that his father had left.

"No," Jesse said abruptly and shut his eyes. He really didn't want to talk about Pop to anyone. Not even to Adam.

"I got to tell you something. But you got to promise to keep it a secret, or you might get me in heck with my Dad."

"What? How could I do that?" Jesse sat upright, putting his feet down on the floor with a thump.

"Well, the other night Mom and Dad weren't home yet 'n I couldn't get to sleep so I got up 'n took Lickapaw out for a walk 'n I saw a light coming from over at the Rec. It was real late. No one, but no one's supposed to be in there that late. So, uh, I sneaked over to take a look." Adam paused and bit his lip.

"Go on, go on, what'd you see?" Jesse was getting impatient.

"Well, it was kinda gloomy in there. There's just one light bulb, you know. Hanging on a cord over the big table? There were these three guys, sitting at the table, all hunched up, like this you know?" And Adam bent over with his chin on his chest. "I'm not sure who they were, couldn't see their faces too good, but, but I swear one guy was your Pop. You know that old cap he has with 'Big A' on the side? Well, one of the guys had a cap on just like it."

Jesse drew in a rapid breath. Pop's cap, the one he got ages ago. At a gas station up past Cooley's Mills. Pop was so proud of it, said it was made just for him. Holding his breath, he waited for Adam to continue.

"Well, all of a sudden, one of the other guys, not your Pop, started pounding his fist on the table 'n I real got scared 'n ran back here. But, um, I heard a bit of what they were saying. When I got back in bed, I remembered." Adam rubbed his nose again. "It was something about some land. Over to Bickerton some- where. Just before he started hitting the table, the guy started shouting real loud, it's our land, they can't have it, it's ours!"

"Gee whiz!" Jesse exploded. "What's my Pop got to do with it? What's he doing over here anyway? Why doesn't he call us?" And he felt the tears starting. He turned away and flung a sleeve over his face.

Adam was beginning to feel uncomfortable. Maybe he shouldn't have told Jesse anything. But Jesse was his best friend. If it had been *his* Dad, he'd want to know. Trying to think of something to distract Jesse, he said, "Hey, let's go over to my Auntie Alma's place. She's always got cookies, remember? We went over there the last time you came, huh? You said they were the best cookies you'd ever eaten? Anyway, I'm starved 'n who knows when my mom'll be back from work. Auntie Alma'll look after us."

And that was the end of that. For now. For Adam. But not for Jesse. He knew he'd have to tell his mom as soon as she came out to get him. She'd want to know for sure. Or would she just worry more? Anyway, so far he'd managed to keep his discovery in the woods a secret. Even from his best friend.

His Pop would have been proud.

15

FRANCY FUSSES, MAGGIE IS ENVIOUS

Francy Otterley stared out her living room window at the snowy ribbons decorating the railings of the front porch, feeling sorry for herself. *I hate, loathe and detest winter. Out there's the reason why. Where is everyone? As soon as there's a few flakes of snow, everyone retreats into their houses and you don't see hide nor hair of 'em until spring. They could be dead for all I know. Gee whiz, what's the matter with me, I forgot about poor Hink and CeeCee.*

As she stood there, City memories began to superimpose themselves on the bleak landscape outside, conjuring up a vision of twilight in late December, of houses tightly packed together with their jumble of roofs and chimneys and their multitude of windows from which a warm and friendly light streamed out over the frozen lawns; a vision peopled with figures in furry coats and colourful headgear hurrying back and forth on the pavement, some with briefcases, others weighed down with shopping bags of gaily wrapped parcels, all intent on their destinations, all with purpose in their stride, with somewhere to go, something to do, and someone to do it with. Francy shook herself and the vision faded. *I shouldn't be thinking like this, it's so lovely and quiet here and isn't that what we wanted? Peace and quiet? Thank goodness the snow's stopped for now. I'd hate to be stuck in the house all day with Ferd the way he's been acting lately.* She shivered and turned up the collar of her woollen dressing gown. Just looking at all that white stuff was making her feel chilly.

In spite of the melancholy feeling the view gave her, she remained standing there, staring at nothing. Out beyond the end of their front lawn lay the Old Barge Canal, hidden deep beneath what Francy liked to think of as icy sheets and a snowy blanket. It was hard to make out where the lawn ended and the Canal began. If you didn't know any better, it looked like you could walk across to the other side, like it was a proper road. She'd heard stories of people who'd tried it and come to grief. The Canal could be treacherous in the places where the warmer water from the sewers flowed under the thick crust of ice. The spring before they'd moved out to East Thorne, the Otterleys had seen a story in one of the City newspapers about the bodies of two young girls having been found down near The Landing. According to the article, one afternoon late in January they decided to cut across the Canal on the ice instead of going the long way around by the bridge and had broken through that deceptively smooth surface. A passer-by saw it happen, but it was too late to rescue them. They disappeared under the ice.

Francy shuddered at the recollection. She'd always hated the cold and would have liked nothing better at that very moment than to be somewhere else, somewhere where there were wide sandy beaches and palm trees. And not one single solitary flake of snow in sight. But Ferd wouldn't hear of it. What's wrong with a little cold, makes a nice change, he said when she complained. And anyway, winter means no traffic on the Canal. No noisy boaters to keep us awake the way they do on hot summer nights. But Francy suspected he just didn't want to spend the money on another place. Maybe we should've bought that house we looked at over closer to Bickerton, she said, tentatively. No, Ferd said, this side of the Canal's far and away the better side. Besides, East Tee'ers aren't as stuck on themselves. You'd have hated it there. But Hink and CeeCee live on the other side and they're our closest friends, she wanted to say. But Francy had kept that last thought to herself. No use arguing with Ferd. He was always right, no matter what.

As she had a hundred times before, she wondered what was really bothering Ferd. For a week now, he'd been flailing about, talking in his sleep, nothing she could make any sense of, keeping her awake for hours. Last night she couldn't stand it any longer and escaped to the spare room. It meant warming up another bed, which kept her awake even longer, but at least she wasn't being jiggled and jounced around every few minutes. It set her nerves on edge. *He can't sleep at night, then he's miserable with me in the morning,* she'd thought, pulling her knees up under her nightgown to get them warm. *I wish he'd tell me what's wrong. Maybe he doesn't like being retired. Or maybe he wishes we could have stayed in the City. Maybe he's afraid to admit we made a mistake coming here. Oh I don't know, maybe it's my fault. That's enough, now I'm being really stupid. We couldn't stay in the City and we both know it.* Her last thought, just before slipping away into sleep, was that coming to East Thorne was Ferd's idea in the first place. *Maybe we will be safer here. He always insists he knows what's best for us. And he's right. It is friendlier here, on this side of the Canal. CeeCee even said so.*

While Francy was making herself miserable staring at the blankness outside, across the Canal and away over on the far side of Bickerton, Dottie had cleared away the last of the breakfast dishes and was just mopping the kitchen floor, which looked like it hadn't been done in a month of Sundays — her old Gram's favourite expression — when a large black car came lumbering up the lane.

"Now what," she grumbled under her breath. "Who's this now, comin' to pester poor CeeCee?"

She shoved the mop in the pantry, threw her apron over a kitchen chair and went to open the door. The two people emerging from the car were unknown to her. They came bounding confidently up the steps as if they had been expected.

"Hello there," the woman said breezily, when she saw Dottie. "We're the Wychwoods, old friends of the Dentons. We came to see if there's anything we can do to help."

As she spoke, the woman flung back her long dark hair. Her clothes were the first thing Dottie noticed. She was dressed like someone fresh off the pages of a fashion magazine. Tight black leather pants and a sleek black jacket of some kind of fur Dottie didn't know what, mink maybe? The bright blue scarf around her neck accentuated the blueness of her eyes, which seemed to look right through you. The tall man standing behind her smiled slightly and nodded. He seemed embarrassed to be there. Dottie couldn't help staring at his overcoat. It too was black with a deep fur collar that was an exact match of the woman's jacket. *Hmph, these two must be loaded, and will you look at their car for pity's sake, it's some big. Of all the nerve, traipsin' way out here without so much as a call first to see if it's okay.*

Aloud, she said abruptly, "I'm Dottie. Miz Denton's upstairs. I'll see if she feels up to comin' down." She stepped back to let them come in.

Without waiting to be asked, the Wychwoods took off their snowy boots and went into the living room. Everything seemed normal to Pete, although he realized he was hardly in a position to tell since he'd only been inside the place once before. And then it was only to pick Hink up for a meeting. Maggie walked slowly around the room, giving the furniture and the rest of the décor the once over. Poor thing, Pete was thinking, seeing the corners of her mouth turn down, she can never bear to think that someone might have a house nicer than hers. Or more richly furnished.

This room is gorgeous, Maggie thought enviously, running her hand along the back of the velvet sofa. *The furniture alone must have cost a mint.* She moved over to the mantelpiece where a ray of sunshine coming from the high windows fell across the collection of crystal, making it sparkle. Wow. There certainly were some exceptional pieces here. How did people like the Dentons afford stuff like this? She tried in vain to remember what she'd been told about the Dentons' life before they came to Bickerton and was just about to ask Pete when CeeCee appeared in the doorway, wearing a deep rose housecoat. Her face showed the strain she was under. She seemed surprised to see them.

"Nice of you to come," she said, with some effort. "Please. Sit down." She went over and lowered herself into one of the chairs beside the fireplace. "Excuse me," she said, leaning back and closing her eyes. "Feeling a bit lightheaded." Dottie disappeared into the kitchen so she would be out of earshot.

Maggie and Pete exchanged looks, then moved to take seats at opposite ends of the sofa.

"We don't want to intrude," Pete said hurriedly. "We just heard from Francy Otterley that Hink didn't come home last night. We didn't realize he was on the missing list when we bumped into you at the Quick Bite yesterday." He cleared his throat uncertainly.

Maggie sat erect, her hands in her lap, trying hard not to stare at the oil paintings on the wall across from her. She'd made a practice of studying the work of famous artists. Some of these looked familiar. Could they possibly be originals? But keeping such valuable pieces out here? In the back of beyond? What about security? *I don't see any kind of alarm system. The Dentons must be filthy rich. Or crazy. Or both.* She suddenly realized she'd been missing out on some of the conversation.

"... called the local police? Everyone says the gal who runs the place is pretty good," Pete was saying. Privately he thought women shouldn't be involved in police work, especially ones that looked like Gussie Spilsbury. Too dangerous. What could her father have been thinking?

"Already did. Still looking ... though ... don't know if she believed me," CeeCee replied slowly without opening her eyes. She knew she wasn't being very welcoming, but she didn't care. She felt as if she were caught in the middle of a bad dream, that it was happening to someone else.

"Who *is* that person who let us in?" Maggie asked. "I've never seen her around here before. Is she a relative?"

"That's Dottie. Dottie Kibbidge. Her brother has the grocery store. Over in East Thorne."

"Oh. East Thorne. We *never* go over there," Maggie said. "It's such a low class neighbourhood."

Pete shifted uncomfortably in his seat. Maggie didn't know it, but he'd been over there dozens of times. He knew who Rab Kibbidge was, in fact he kind of liked the guy. Rab had an original sense of humour and loved a good joke. This was the first time he'd seen the sister though; she was always busy with something somewhere else whenever he'd been there. Now that he'd seen her, he thought she looked like a capable sort of woman. A good person for CeeCee to have with her right now. He wondered about the Dentons' daughters, whether they'd been told their father was missing. Better not to mention them now. CeeCee appeared awfully upset. He might make things worse.

CeeCee sat up and opened her eyes. "Like some tea? Dottie makes lovely tea. Dottie?" she called.

"Oh no. Don't go to any bother," Pete said, quickly getting to his feet. There didn't seem to be anything he and Maggie could do. Over CeeCee's objections, they said goodbye and told CeeCee to let us know if you hear anything now won't you. CeeCee watched them out of sight.

On the way back to town, Maggie didn't say anything for the first couple of miles. Then she said in level tones, "At least we can go home with a clear conscience," and turned away to stare out at what she could see of the frozen fields over the high banks of snow.

Pete was startled. Conscience. He'd never heard her mention the word before. He'd always thought she didn't know what a conscience was. Typical of Maggie though, only thinking of herself.

After the Wychwoods' car had disappeared, CeeCee wondered aloud to Dottie, who'd come back into the living room as soon as they'd gone, why they'd bothered coming out in the first place.

"Humpf," Dottie said, and pursed her lips. "Nosey, that's what. Those kind of people give me the pip. I wouldn't give them another thought, lovey, they're not worth it. Say," she went on, "why don't I call Rab and have him come out and pick us up? Ya'd be much better off with us over to East Tee. That police lady can call ya over there just as easy."

"Well," said CeeCee slowly, "if you think he won't mind. Having me, I mean. Just for a short while, then. Awfully kind of you."

Anything, *anything* to take her mind off Hink.

16

LOOKING FOR ANSWERS

It was the third day after the grim discovery in the woods down by the Old Barge Canal Road and Gussie was feeling really awful. She didn't want to admit it, but she was sure she was coming down with a cold. *Too much running around in this weather and not enough rest, my girl.* She could hear Mac's voice as if he were right there in the room. Forcing herself to get out of bed, she'd dragged her aching body to the station and was glumly surveying the stack of papers in front of her, door closed, phone off the hook, this last a definite no-no. But Constable Spilsbury was in no mood to cope with any interruptions. Not for an hour or so anyway.

Bill Blair had done a thorough job. He determined the victim had been shot in the back with a hunting arrow fired at close range. The arrow had pierced his heart, killing him instantly. The force of the blow appeared to have knocked the victim off his feet; he had fallen and had landed face down. This could account for the abrasions on his nose and chin. Dr. Bill explained that the absence of blood at the scene was caused by the arrow blocking the wound to such an extent that the blood was unable to flow freely. Since the heart had stopped beating instantly, the blood had pooled in the body. But Denton had been found on his back. Gussie was sure this meant the body had been moved. But from where? And by whom?

Having the doctor on hand in the woods had been a tremendous boon to Gussie. He'd helped her stake out the area in spite of the deep snow, while the two Auxiliaries struggled to load the body onto the rescue sled they'd dragged into the woods with them. It had been such a strenuous trek back to the road and waiting vehicles that none of them had any breath left over to utter a word.

Perce and Butch had been sent on home to their families. Tired, hungry and badly shaken, it was their first experience with violent death up close. Gussie had been afraid Butch might pass out on them when they finally freed the body from its frozen grave, he'd turned such a peculiar shade of green. But she admired the way he forced himself to carry on. Perce was much more stoic. He simply took out a huge black and white striped handkerchief into which he loudly blew his nose.

The description of the clothing CeeCee Denton said she thought her husband was probably wearing when he disappeared was too general. Lots of people wear beige pants and jackets and hiking boots. Especially in the country. And, especially in the fall. But the socks! They really were a brilliant fluorescent orange. When Gussie saw those socks under the penetrating lights of Dr. Bill's surgery, her heart sank. From her experience with the Watson twins, she knew the most difficult job a cop has to do is to break the sad news to the next of kin. Unable to face CeeCee Denton alone, she asked the doctor to go with her, using the excuse that Mrs. Denton might need him. At least they didn't have to drive out as far as the Denton place. Dottie Kibbidge had left a message with Myrna that CeeCee was staying with her over in East Thorne for the time being.

When CeeCee was confronted with their solemn faces, she burst into tears. Dottie had taken over then, ushered them into her cosy kitchen, made them all sit down and busied herself with the tea things, apologizing for Rab's absence, on a little trip, she said, to look for something for the store she couldn't remember just exactly what. She really was a big help under the circum-stances, Gussie acknowledged, even though she was inclined to fuss.

"I'm sorry, I mean, I'm so terribly sorry," was all Gussie could muster, aware that her professional mask, which had never been all that secure to begin with, was slipping away. After all, here was this poor woman, no family close by, having to deal with the tragedy alone. How different it had been for the Watsons who had a whole network of relatives for support. CeeCee kept saying over and over, knew it, just knew it, all night I knew it, he never stayed out before, was it quick do you think, did he suffer much, oh Hinky, knew it, I just knew it. In an attempt to calm her down, the doctor offered to give her an injection of something just to take the edge off, he said. But CeeCee vehemently refused. She remained hunched over the table with her hands pressed tightly against her face, rocking herself back and forth, back and forth.

Sitting in the warmth of the kitchen with Dottie hovering in the background making sympathetic noises, Gussie asked gently if there wasn't someone else she could call to come and make the formal identification. "No, no one," CeeCee said in a voice barely above a whisper, "I'll come. Want to do it. Give me a few minutes. Be all right. I'll do it. Just give me a minute."

"Ya poor thing, ya poor, poor thing," Dottie soothed. This was a new experience for her. She'd been there when the bodies of fishermen who drowned at sea had been brought home. But that was different somehow. That happened often and was expected. They'd been glad to have a body to bury. But this? Violent death? Violent and mysterious ? This wasn't like that at all, as she told Gussie much later.

Dottie did the only thing she knew how to do in times of crisis, make tea, endless cups of strong, sweet tea, and make sure it was drunk by the person in pain. And by everyone else in the room. Eventually, she sat down at the table and began patting CeeCee gently on the arm. CeeCee ignored her and went on rocking, rocking, drinking the tea mechanically, not hearing, not seeing.

Gussie was grateful for Dottie's ministrations. Mentally she scolded herself for not being more in control of her own emotions. She'd given CeeCee only the barest details of how Hink's body had been found in the woods over by the Old Barge Canal. She dreaded to think what her reaction might be if CeeCee knew a young boy had been the one to find the body. After a second and then a third cup of Dottie's restorative brew, CeeCee pulled herself together and announced she was ready to go with them over to Bickerton.

Now Gussie was faced with the biggest challenge of her short career. There would have to be an inquest. Dr. Blair said, in his opinion, it looked like a hunting accident. But who in heck hunted with bow and arrows around here? And anyway, the hunting season had been over for almost ten days. *Must have been a stranger.* No. That would have been too easy. Most things that went wrong in Bickerton were too quickly blamed on outsiders. She'd driven back over to the scene, but found no clues. More snow had fallen in the meantime, making it impossible to look for much of anything. She left the area barricaded and hoped and prayed no one would go around the barricades until she'd had time to figure out what could have happened.

She'd gone home then for some long overdue sleep, ignoring the messages that had been piling up in her absence. She was beginning to think maybe a job like this was too much for one person. Forcing herself to eat a bowl of cold cereal, she'd climbed into bed, her body aching like she'd been run over with a truck. *I should have taken a shower. I must stink.* But sleep eluded her. The sight of Hink Denton's poor defenceless body lying on the examining table, the look on CeeCee Denton's face when she saw her dead husband, Butch's green face, Perce's striped hankie, all jiggetted around in her brain, making sleep impossible.

She tried to imagine what it would be like to be CeeCee Denton, losing her life partner in such a horrible way. Having to go home to an empty house, to the silence. Having to get through the days somehow. And then to bed, without the familiar presence beside her, without the warmth of the man with whom she'd shared countless nights over the years. Gussie's own marriage had been too brief to be able to relate to a situation like this. Listening to CeeCee on the phone in the doctor's office, telling her daughter that her beloved Dad was gone and could she please find out where her sister was and let her know, then breaking down completely when she hung up the phone. It was all too much. *Hink Denton's naked body. Butch's green face. CeeCee's stricken eyes. Perce's striped hankie …*

The sight of that hankie reminded her of a black and white bathing suit she had once, back when she and Syd started going together. Syd teased her about it, said it made her look like some kind of glamorous jailbird. But she thought it made her figure look fabulous. Back then, she still carried some baby fat and those stripes meeting in a V down the front made her look slimmer. Or so she thought. Syd used to take her to a secluded spot up on the Lonesome River, way north of town, so secluded you had to go through a farmer's property and then through a long stretch of woods to get to it. Gussie was always afraid they might get caught, or worse, be attacked by some farm dog. The fear heightened the excitement she felt when they finally reached the bank of the slow-moving river, kicked off their shoes, spread the old plaid blanket from Syd's truck under an enormous willow tree whose branches hung so low its fronds trailed in the water. Gussie always thought it was like lying under a giant grass skirt, the long thin leaves rasped together and shimmied and shook in the slightest breeze. Then they'd race each other to plunge into the river, shrieking at the sudden shock of cold, thrash around to get used to the chilly water. Then Syd would dive under, grasp her around the legs, pull her under with him and they'd come up kissing in spite of the water that streamed down their faces.

They never had time to stay long. Syd had to get back to work or his Dad would start yelling at him. Hauling themselves up on the riverbank, they'd eat whatever they'd managed to bring with them, maybe some of Syd's mom's gingerbread, then wash it down with cream soda, and sneak back the way they came to Syd's old truck. Gussie always insisted on changing before climbing into the high truck seat. She could never stand the clammy feeling of the wet suit against her skin. Syd was good and turned his back while she wriggled out of the sodden bathing suit and into her clothes that felt so good after the searing cold of the river. Then they'd tie her suit on his antenna where it fluttered and flapped like a little striped pennant. It would almost be dry by the time they got back to town. Those were the good times. So romantic. So innocent. Before they were married. Afterwards, everything changed.

Lying in bed that night, Gussie wondered how many people in town knew something unusual had happened. That terrible afternoon that seemed to go on forever, before she'd had a chance to get out of her office, Mac had burst in. He didn't want to sit down, but strode back and forth, demanding to know why her car had been spotted going over to the Old Barge Canal Road. More than once, he added accusingly. He came closer as she hesitated, trying to think of what to say to satisfy him. Close enough for her to catch a whiff of cigar smoke and an alcohol smell that was definitely not after shave lotion.

"Dad! You smell boozy. You've been drinking again, I mean drinking again. You know what you were told the last time. I thought you were finished with that. Hand me your keys, Dad. Now, you just walk yourself over to Jimmie's and get a coffee. Get two coffees. I'll talk to you tomorrow when you're sober, I mean sober," Gussie scolded, furious with him. Why couldn't he let her get on with her job?

"Aw, c'mon, Gus, let your ol' dad in on it. Somethin's up. What'er you doin' gallivantin' 'round the countryside with Billy Boy Blair?" Mac persisted, trying unsuccessfully to balance himself on the edge of her desk.

"Dad, for the last time, this is police business. You'll find out when everyone else does. Now, go straight over to Jimmie's and get some coffee into you. Do you want me to get someone to drive you home?" Was she being too hard on him? No, he should stay out of it.

Mac brushed away the offer of a ride and lurched out of her office. She could hear him stumbling down the hall. If she'd been out there, she'd have heard him muttering that he'd gotten her the blasted job, it was his idea for her to become a cop, was this all the thanks he was going to get?

As soon as he left, she gave Jimmie's a call and asked him to call her so she could stop by and take Mac home. Now, absently shuffling the papers on her desk and thinking about his visit, a tiny suspicion began gnawing at her that Mac might know something about the mystery of Hink Denton's death. Maybe that would account for his erratic behaviour. He hadn't touched a drop of alcohol in years, not since he found out about her split from Syd. He'd really tied one on that night, was sick in bed for four days, first with a hangover and then a nagging pain in his stomach. Old Doc Winter had done what he could, read him the riot act and told him his ulcer couldn't take much more. Lay off the booze, MacPherson, my friend, he'd warned, or you'll end up on the surgeon's table. Or worse.

What could Mac possibly have had to do with Hink Denton? Gussie wracked her brains trying to remember if he'd ever said anything that might give her a clue. Had they gone hunting together? No. Denton had been a birder. She had almost forgotten that fact. Not likely to be a killer of wildlife, although she'd heard some avid birders had been hunters once. Look at Audubon. She remembered reading somewhere that the famous authority on birds had gone from slaughtering them to trying to save them. Who were Denton's cronies? What did he do when he wasn't out birdwatching?

Rummaging around in her desk drawer on a vain hunt for aspirins and trying not to let the pressure get to her, Gussie knew she'd have to find some answers and soon.

17

GETTING NOWHERE FAST!

Since the discovery of Hink Denton's body, Syd's behaviour was becoming something of a puzzle to Gussie. She felt badly having to keep him in the dark. *Oh well, that's how police business has to be. Can't have interference at this stage. Especially from the press.* At the time, she thought Syd had been grateful for the sparse details she'd given him and had published a short piece in the *Bugler*:

Mysterious Death of Local Resident

The body of a man, identified as being that of Mr. Hinchcliffe Denton, 68, of Fifth Line, Rural Route 2, Bickerton, was discovered yesterday in the vicinity of the Old Barge Canal Road. He had been missing since Wednesday. Bickerton Police Constable Augusta Spilsbury said the matter is undergoing thorough investigation. She refused any further comment, but assured this newspaper that details will follow when they become available. Mr. Denton was a newcomer to the area. He leaves his wife, Cecilia and two daughters, Janette Williamson and Coralee Jeffords, both of Toronto. Funeral arrangements are incomplete.

But as to who had found the body and exactly where, well, she'd told him nothing. Not even so much as a hint. When he persisted, asked how she expected him to do his job properly with so little to go on, she replied crisply that he'd get the answers in due course. Somehow she didn't think the change in his behaviour was linked to her refusal to tell him more. There was obviously something else going on with him. Another puzzle with no quick answer.

It was getting worse: for the last few days, he'd been calling her more often than usual, at odd hours, which wasn't like him at all. He knew how busy she was. Once he even showed up unannounced in her office. Normally he'd call first to see if it was convenient. When she'd expressed surprise and asked him why he was there, his response had been vague. He stood just inside the doorway, looking distracted, nervously jingling the change in his pocket. She thought he might disappear at any moment, he seemed so distracted, jumpy even. His usually smooth dark hair, which she noticed with a pang was beginning to show streaks of grey, was every which way, and he looked like he'd slept in his clothes. The creases around his eyes had deepened and his face was blotchy.

"Um, uh, just wanted to see how you were. Uh, er, you know, Gus ... you know we haven't ... well, we haven't seen each other for, well for ages ..."

"Id case you've forgodden, I bean, forgodden—we're divorced. Remebber? You said you couldn't stad livink wid be eddy bore, I bean eddy bore. You said I god od your derves, rebebber? You said de sound of by voice bade you sick, remebber?"

Gussie's voice cracked and she blew her nose in the cotton handkerchief she kept handy in her sleeve. She hated tissues; they made her skin on her poor nose red and raw. Mac said they were made of wood pulp, so no wonder. When he'd said that, she'd laughed uproariously at the idea of blowing her nose into a tree. Her nerves were beyond frayed since her cold had worsened.

What in heck was eating Syd anyway? So okay, she'd be the first one to admit that, ever since the day they had separated, they'd started going out together for the odd drink, usually after he finished work on Tuesday nights. Maybe that hadn't been such a good idea. But he'd been so persistent. He seemed to need to talk to her then, more than at any other time. Talk. That is, he talked. She seldom got a word in. But then talking had been their trouble. Right from the beginning. Syd simply couldn't get used to her peculiar habit of repeating herself.

One Saturday morning over breakfast, after they'd been married for almost a year, he'd come out with it. Said when they first started dating, he thought everything she did was cute. Said he hadn't noticed it much at first. But living with it on a daily basis was just too much. Said he felt like screaming every time she opened her mouth. When he said that, Gussie dropped the blueberry muffin she'd been enjoying, ran upstairs and cried her eyes out. After that episode, she tried everything she knew to change how she talked. She went to an expensive speech therapist over in Dunhampton and practised what he taught her for hours on end. All in vain. As soon as she started talking to someone, it was back, that stupid repetition. It was all Mac's fault, she thought angrily. He'd been so fussy about how she expressed herself when she was growing up that, out of a desire to please him, she'd fallen into the habit, a silly little habit that had driven a wedge between two people who'd once been so much in love. Syd moved out the day before their first anniversary.

After a while, she'd gotten used to seeing him occasionally, painful though it still was. She told herself it was better than nothing. He still called her regularly every Monday morning to get the latest police news for his 'On the Bickerton Beat' column. But this. This calling her every day, day after day, and sometimes late at night was different. He wasn't involved with anyone else, so far as she knew. Sometimes she wished he were. He was always alone when she saw him in the Cosy Corner sitting at a small table down near the back, staring into a mug of coffee. Or driving slowly along the main street in his truck, the same old truck they'd happily roared around the countryside in for so many months. She wondered how well the paper was doing. Most of the time she'd been too busy to do more than glance at the headlines. Maybe he had money problems. *Why do I still care? I must be crazy after what happened.*

Thinking about why he might have come to her office, she wondered if maybe he'd been feeling sentimental. He was such a kid about Christmas, making a great mystery of his gift to her. The year they got engaged, an enormous box had appeared under her tree. He'd laughed and joked about 'the mink coat you've always wanted' and 'that new radio you've been admiring in the Sound Shop window'. She had to use a sharp knife to open the box, which was tightly packed with chunks of wood, a couple of bricks and old newspapers. Way down near the bottom she spotted a tiny heart-shaped box wrapped in gold foil. Inside was a delicately filigreed diamond ring. At her look of surprise, he'd turned serious and had gotten down on one knee and proposed. So romantic, after all the teasing. She sighed at the recollection. They'd always had such fun together. Deep down, she was full of regret things had turned out the way they had, but was determined not to let it show. What good would it do now?

That day in her office, Syd appeared a bit shocked at her outburst. They'd stood, looking at each other for a stunned moment, then he'd mumbled, yeah, you're right, and was gone. Gussie tried to settle down to her work, but couldn't concentrate. What on earth did he want? Was he ill? Or was he trying to tell her something? She'd never been good at picking up on subtleties. As a policewoman, she preferred to deal in facts. Detective work, especially that kind, was unfamiliar territory.

The inquest into the death of Hinchcliffe Denton returned a verdict of 'death by person or persons unknown'. Gussie was determined to uncover who those persons were, even if it meant working through the holidays. Reconsidering her situation, it really was a bit much to expect one person to do all the policing required, even in a town the size of Bickerton. When something happened up on the main highway — and lately it seemed accidents up there were becoming more and more frequent — she had to drop what she was doing, it didn't matter what, and head up there. The territory she was responsible for was extensive, covering far more than just Bickerton. It stretched north to just below Cooley's Mills. The Lake was the southern boundary. West it went half way to Dunhampton while the eastern boundary was erratic and included East Thorne and part of the Old Barge Canal Road. If Jesse Woodcock had found the body floating in the Canal, all this would have been someone else's problem. Gussie was set on finding out who the perpetrator was, even if she had to work alone. She couldn't help thinking of poor CeeCee Denton and how she must be feeling.

She was really under pressure now. She had only a few days before someone from Dunhampton would be calling to check on her progress, maybe even take over what she regarded as her case. Even if she often felt that, on top of everything else, this job was at times too much for her. And, after all, this *was* her town. And her big chance to prove to everyone that Mac had been right to give the job to a mere woman.

She'd interviewed quite a few people already. First the Otterleys. She'd made an early evening visit to them over in East Thorne. Francy Otterley just sat crying and clasping and unclasping her hands, looking utterly miserable. Ferd paced back and forth, swearing under his breath at every question she asked. No (dammit). They didn't know who Hink's friends were outside of Bickerton. No (dammit). They had ab-so-lute-ly no idea who might own a bow and arrow. No, no, and again no, they didn't know anything. They'd never even met the daughters. The time she'd spent there was next to useless. The Otterleys had been no help at all. Still, it was a start.

Then she'd tried the Wychwoods. She'd had an awful time getting a hold of them. Every time she called, they were either on their way out to a social engagement, as Maggie called it, or getting ready to host a party themselves. She'd finally had enough of their excuses and went straight to the house first thing one morning. Maggie had been decidedly hostile and stared at her as if she were some kind of annoying insect. Pete's face had been ashen. He looked like he'd been up all night and kept his eyes fixed on Maggie, answering Gussie's questions with yesses and noes. Mostly the latter. She'd gotten absolutely nowhere with them either.

While she was over in East Thorne, she'd dropped in on the Kibbidges to see how CeeCee Denton was managing. She found the two women in the kitchen surrounded by knitting books and balls of colourful yarn. There was a sweet syrupy smell coming from a platter of freshly baked butter tarts. After Dottie had offered her a sample or two and a cup of her strong tea, and CeeCee was listening patiently to her questions, both women remembered simultaneously that in the shock of hearing Hink's body had been found, they'd forgotten to tell her someone had driven into the Dentons' lane that afternoon after Rab had picked them up and they'd had to go back for something.

"More than once, I tell you. More than once. Someone's been out to the house," CeeCee said in a small scared voice, putting down the pale blue sweater sleeve she'd been working on. "First time was when I came back from looking for Hink the night he disappeared. Found the back window smashed. Figured it must have been a branch came down in the wind. But now I'm … I'm afraid to go back there. Rab had to go out and get Shadow and bring him over here." She gestured in the direction of the stove where a wicker basket held a sleeping cat.

"It doesn't seem to have bothered him any, the change I mean. You know how cats are, they hate change, I mean they hate change," Gussie said earnestly. "CeeCee, are you sure, I mean, are you sure it wasn't someone coming by to say they were sorry to hear your husband was, well, missing?" Gussie felt a twinge of alarm. What was going on here?

"Mmm. Could have been that ... the second time," Dottie said, slowly, "but then, who's got that big of a rig? Them tire tracks sure went deep. Like they was carrying a real heavy load of somethin'. " Dottie was looking quite outlandish in a brightly coloured vest covered in some sort of Indian design, with bunches of yellow ribbons dangling down the front. A wide headband made of braided red, yellow and green yarn held her hair back from her face.

CeeCee shivered in spite of the warm kitchen and thrust her arms through the sleeves of the dark red cardigan that was slung over her shoulders. Trying to behave calmly and rationally, she picked up her knitting again.

"Well," she said, taking a moment to reflect. "Don't think so. All the ones we know had already called." Her nerves were all on edge. She still couldn't take in the fact that Hink was gone. For good.

Gently, Gussie asked after the girls. CeeCee looked uncomfortable at the mention of her family. She was bitterly disappointed in the way her daughters had reacted to their father's death. And to her own situation. She felt they'd been no help to her at all. On the contrary, they'd been a pain in the neck.

Janette had come out for a day and spent the whole time trying to persuade her mother to come back to the City with her. How can you stand it out here, Mom? Especially now. You haven't been here long enough to know anyone. What are you going to do with yourself? Why on earth won't you come home with me? I'll look after you, I promise. Janette was impatient to get back to the City. That much was obvious when she turned down Dottie's invitation to stay over. She didn't like her mother staying with strangers, staying away from her own house, and bluntly said so. Right in front of Dottie.

You should be there to keep an eye on things, Mom, you know you should, she said more than once during her visit. CeeCee wondered what 'things' she had in mind. The paintings maybe. Janette had always made a fuss over them whenever she visited. At this point, CeeCee didn't give a hoot what happened to the house. The place could burn down for all she cared. She'd closed her mind to any thoughts of it since Hink's death. Her younger daughter Coralee was on an extended trip overseas and called to say she'd come down as soon as she got back. Coralee wasn't as acquisitive as Janette, but she still thought her mother should give up the experiment as she called it, of living out in the boonies.

CeeCee wanted a private funeral for Hink, just for the immediate family, she said, and had scheduled it for after Christmas. The girls were upset when she told them. Don't you think any of Dad's old friends from work would like to come? How about his cousins Out West? How can you do this, Mom? But CeeCee was adamant. Hink's former workmates hadn't bothered with him since he retired. Oh, one of them had called once on his way through town, but said he didn't have time to drop by. Hink didn't seem disappointed, just shrugged it off. That part of my life was over the day I retired, he'd said when he told her. As for the western cousins, they'd been out of touch with them for years. Anyway, I couldn't take the pitying looks, the sympathy, was CeeCee's response.

"It's all just too much. Guess people do it because they think it's expected of them. Make a big fuss, I mean. Rather be left alone. Anyway, how does anyone know how I feel? And do they even care?" she'd complained to Dottie after a particularly upsetting phone call from Janette. "I'm the one who's suffering the most, don't they care what I want? Always thought the girls preferred me to their Dad, he was home so seldom when they were growing up. They always came to me for everything. Why are they being so pig-headed and inconsiderate? Now, of all times."

In her calming way, Dottie'd said, "Now try not to mind 'em too much, lovey, everyone has their own way of grievin' when there's a death in the family. 'Specially when it's a parent."

CeeCee'd been grateful for the understanding. Dottie may have seemed a simple person, but she was wiser than most about the basic things in life. And she'd never felt like a stranger to CeeCee, no matter what the girls thought.

Now CeeCee didn't know what she would have done without the Kibbidges and said so to Gussie. Dottie turned pink when she said that.

"Hasn't helped much we've had another dump of snow. It's depressin' and all," she said gruffly. Dottie was one of those gifted knitters who could follow a complicated knitting pattern and talk at the same time without missing a stitch. Dozens of bobbins in various pastel shades of yarn hung from her needles as she worked on what looked to Gussie like an afghan. "And all that wind!" Dottie went on. "What awful weather! It was bad enough Back East, but never this early. Not before Christmas anyways."

"Are you sure it wasn't just someone dropping by, I mean dropping by for a visit?" Gussie asked again, trying not to think of how all the new snow was hampering her investigation. It was now impossible to even think of searching the area where the body had been found. She would have to wait until the snow was gone. And goodness knows when that would be. Winter had barely started.

"Doubt it. Not the kind that people drop in on. Usually call first. Hink doesn't like ... I mean didn't ..."

"We wondered if someone was snoopin'," offered Dottie. She shifted in her chair and looked worried. "None of my business, but maybe they was lookin' for somethin'." She glanced over at CeeCee, who bit her lip. "Shall I tell her? Or do ya want to?"

"No, no, I'll do it." CeeCee put her knitting down again and swallowed hard. "Um, well. Hink's been, well, I mean had been, how should I say, well, he'd been acting a bit, a bit weird lately. Gotten secretive. Thought maybe he was having trouble adjusting. To being retired, I mean."

"Huh!" Dottie scoffed. "Most men don't like givin' up their life's work. They don't know what to do with themselves. Look at my Dad, it near killed him. He just sat in the kitchen day after day, makin' Mam's life miserable. She couldn't go anywheres, not even into the next room without he wanted to know where she was goin'. Then he'd go off at night and get drunk and ..." She stopped abruptly. This was CeeCee's time to talk, not hers.

"Happens to some," CeeCee agreed. "Read about it. Before we came out here. But Hink, well, he had his life all organized. Or, or I *thought* he did. He retired me. Right out of the kitchen. Not that I really minded. He was a much better cook than I'll ever be. No. Didn't think too much about it. The retirement thing, I mean. But now ..."

"Who else did he know around here?" asked Gussie, trying another tack. "Besides Ferd Otterley. And Pete Wychwood."

"Well," CeeCee said, "there's that fellow from down at The Landing. Nick Fearnley. You know. The one who takes people out looking for birds? And, um, let's see. There's Tom Bartlett. Hink mentioned him a couple of times. And let me think. Well, there was one other one. Used to call when Hink was out. Never left his name. Or a message. But I don't know. They never came out to the house. Hink met them in town somewhere, I guess. Thought maybe they were just all birdwatchers together. And, um, oh yes. Your dad, Gussie. He called a couple of times. Didn't tell me what he wanted, though."

"That's interesting," said Gussie after a moment. Odd. Mac had been cagey when she'd asked him if he'd known Hink

Denton. She'd have to go after him on that. Nick Fearnley she could see, with Hink being so crazy about birding. Nick was the big expert in town. But Tom Bartlett? As far as she knew, no one had ever suggested Tom was interested in birds.

Was she missing something here?

18

SYD'S WOES

If Gussie had only known, the truth was things weren't going at all well for Syd. Not at all well. He'd only just come to realize how much he hated the newspaper. He'd never really liked working on it. But all the time he was growing up, his dad told him repeatedly, once you get a few whiffs of printing ink up your nostrils, my boy, you're hooked for life. Nothing like it, son, absolutely nothing like it. And just think of the power you'll have. In a small town like Bickerton? You'll have power here, believe me. All the power you'll ever want. Everybody in town, every man jack of 'em will be reading what you write. Waiting to see what you think. Of everything that goes on in this burg. And the best thing of all, you'll be your own boss.

His dad had been dead wrong. On all counts. Ever since Syd had taken over the *Bickerton Bugler*, he felt like there was a huge weight pressing down on his chest, trying to suffocate him. He thought he'd get used to it after a while. But that hadn't happened. The newspaper ruled his life. He had time for little else. The smell of the ink made him feel sick. And as for power, that was a laugh. His carefully researched articles on the new fire hall equipment, the recent outbreak of a rare disease on a local pig farm and the need for a night watchman on Main Street, aroused very little interest.

Most people read the paper to see if their names or their photographs were in this week's issue. Avid for gossip, they combed the articles for some juicy tidbit to talk about and then if he wrote anything that so much as hinted at any goings-on, they bombarded him with nasty phone calls. They rarely wrote 'Letters to the Editor' except to complain. If he made the slightest mistake in spelling, he was sure to get a call from one of the teachers telling him he ought to set a better example. If, God forbid, he left out someone's name under a group photograph, he'd get an irate phone call from the offended person. If he couldn't make it to every single Town Council meeting, or sports event, or school concert, or wedding, or even funeral, he was taken to task. Some people even had the nerve to phone him late at night. After one of these episodes, he wished with all his heart he could leave the annoying telephone off the hook. But that was a no-no in this business. He might miss something important. Like a major accident up on the highway. Or someone's farm being foreclosed.

Tuesdays were the worst. Tuesday nights were when he missed Gussie most of all. When they were still together, she'd have a hot meal waiting for him. If she couldn't be there, she'd leave a casserole in the oven with a note saying she'd be home as soon as she could, and not to wait for her. When she did get home, they'd sit down with toast and cocoa and he'd tell her about the problems he'd had with the latest edition. She was a good listener, just let him ramble on and on until he'd run out of steam and drag himself upstairs to try and sleep, dreading the next morning when it would start all over again. Whenever Gussie suggested he might think about doing something else, he said he couldn't let his dad down. He had to give Gussie credit for one thing though. She didn't point out, but your dad's gone, I mean, he's gone now. Isn't he. His dad had died of a massive heart attack the month after he and Gussie got married and suddenly the *Bickerton Bugler* was his. All his.

It always took longer than he figured to put the paper to bed, as they say in the trade. He had to be finished with the printing by nine or his secretary, who came back in after supper to do the labelling for the subscriptions, wouldn't get it done by eleven when she had to leave. Her husband was on the graveyard shift at Spilsbury's and she had to get home for her kids. If that happened, Syd would have to finish the labelling himself. Then the papers had to be sorted for the delivery boys who'd show up at the shop by seven Wednesday mornings to get the *Bugler* out to their customers before they went to school. Most of them were reliable enough, but they got sick, or overslept, as kids will and then he'd have to take over the route himself. Otherwise, more complaints. He wondered how his dad had stuck to the job for so long.

Trouble was, Syd didn't know how to do anything else. He'd always worked for his dad. After school, weekends, even the whole summer vacation. His dad took it for granted Syd would succeed him, told everyone how lucky he was to have a son to take over the business, told Syd how lucky he was not to have to start from scratch. Like some people.

He was stupid to have left Gussie, he knew that now. But his pride wouldn't let him admit it to her. He thought maybe his nerves would calm down when he was on his own. But they were worse. Definitely worse. Why had he picked on her way of talking? He must have been in worse shape than he thought. No other woman he knew would have put up with the hours he kept. Gus had her own career and understood deadlines and late nights. She'd always managed to find time for him in spite of her job. Even now, when she was obviously in the middle of something big, and when he couldn't stop himself from calling her.

He wished he could help her with her investigation. But he didn't have the time, having to be practically a one man band at the paper. So much for being your own boss. That was the biggest laugh of all. Why did people always think the boss had it easy. They ought to trade places with him, just for a day. They'd soon find out how easy it was. He wished he could afford to hire a part-time reporter, a student from the Senior School even, to cover some of the events in town. But he was barely able to keep going as it was.

Every year, he dreaded the approach of the Christmas season. School concerts, Santa parades, turkey dinners with long-winded speeches by the mayor and other worthies, all expecting to read about themselves (and be quoted one hundred per cent accurately) in the *Bugler*. In his wilder moments, Syd thought of renaming the paper the *Bickerton Baloney*. That's all it was. Pure baloney. In print.

What would happen if I just took off and left it all? he often asked himself. But the response was always the same. *I couldn't do that to Dad's memory, I wouldn't be able to live with myself. What the heck am I going to do?*

19

SURPRISE AND DISMAY

It was almost three o'clock in the morning and Lettice still lay, hopelessly wide awake. What an evening it had been. Not long after that day they'd met to discuss his son's unruly behaviour, Tom Bartlett had called her and said he'd liked to take her out to dinner, that is, if she'd consent to go with him. Lettice was taken aback at first, but found herself accepting, much to her surprise. In spite of the weatherman's threat of more snow, they'd driven up to an inn north of Cooley's Mills. The place was originally a stagecoach stop on the old pioneer route and had only recently been renovated by someone from the City. It boasted a comfortable dining room, extravagantly decorated for Christmas, where a cosy fireplace with real logs winked cheerfully at them. A satin-shiny dance floor beckoned, with music provided by an old-time local band 'Franklyn and Friends', none of them under sixty. Even if you didn't want to dance, which Lettice didn't, it was a decided pleasure just to sit and listen to Franklyn, who played a real mellow horn, as Tom termed it.

The meal had been outstanding, at least to Lettice, who seldom had the luxury of eating out. Cream of asparagus soup was followed by prime rib of beef with Duchesse potatoes, (these last were new to Lettice, but Tom said they were just mashed potatoes dolled up with egg yolks and cream), broccoli with a cheese sauce. The whole was topped off with profiteroles, their delicious chocolate filling oozing out on plates decorated with crème de menthe and chocolate sprinkles. At the end of it all, Lettice was glad she'd worn a loose fitting dress. A flattering shade of peacock blue, it was the only decent dress she owned. Everything else in her wardrobe was geared to her teaching — sensible and hardwearing. At least she'd remembered to put on some jewellery — her mother's double strand pearl choker with the matching earrings. The pearls lent a softening effect to her face, which was inclined to look weather-beaten in the winter. She'd never seen the need for using cosmetics. After all, who would look at her now. At her age.

They lingered a long time over their coffee, listening to the band and watching the dancers swirl past. Franklyn's version of the old standard, "Stardust," put Lettice in a nostalgic mood.

' ... *though I dream in vain ... in my heart ... it will remain* '

She refused the snifter of brandy Tom proposed. She was anxious to keep a clear head and anyway, she wasn't all that fond of liqueurs. Tom seemed nervous and edgy. He kept fiddling with his tie as though he'd never worn one before, kept clearing his throat before every sentence. Lettice was hoping they'd talk about the old days when they were a couple. Or, she thought they had been. But Tom kept bringing the conversation back to himself and all his various problems. She had to bite her tongue to keep from asking him why her? What did he expect her to do about his life? And why had he come back into hers after so long? All the time he was talking, she tried to keep from staring at him, he was still so handsome. Older of course, but his dark brown eyes were as warm as ever. *When he smiles at me, it's as if no one else exists. But I know better.*

Tom brought her home just after midnight. They'd considered staying longer, the band had been so good, but when their waiter came over to their table and said, folks, just thought you'd like to know it's snowin' and blowin' out there, they decided they'd better leave before the weather got any worse and the roads turned hazardous. Tom hadn't said much on the drive down. When they got to her place, he helped her out of the car and accompanied her to the door. Before she'd had a chance to experience that awkward moment at the end of a date, he'd thrown his arms round her, kissed her on the cheek and called her a good sport. He was off down the path before she could respond.

Now she lay in despair, squeezing her eyelids shut as if that would hold back the tears that lurked there. Tom had kept coming back to his problems with Tommy Junior until she was ready to scream. She'd wanted to tell him the best thing he could do was send his difficult son to a private school for boys, one that had a military way of doing things. She'd wanted to ask him why he'd dumped her so many years before. At times during the evening, she felt like hitting him over the head with something, anything. Her handbag. Maybe the napkin. Anything to make him notice it was her sitting there. Good old Letty. His captive audience for the evening. He was so full of himself: his job at the candy factory, which he found tedious; his distaste for everything Bickertonian as he put it, and the narrow view of the world that still prevailed; his former wife whom he termed pushy (he never mentioned poor little Ella); his unhappy son; his house, which he called a money pit.

When he'd brought his little family back to Bickerton, Tom bought the old Blair homestead because, as he readily admitted to Lettice, his second wife, who'd come from a poor family, had grandiose ideas of fixing up the joint and lording it over the locals. Lettice had a vague memory of being inside the house once, why exactly she couldn't recall. It was a big barn of a place, with fifteen foot ceilings on the main floor and enormous gables that towered over the other houses on the street. Nowhere near as palatial as the old Roxton place up on the hill, of course, but nonetheless, one of the grander homes in town.

The Blairs had made their money in the lumber business and had used a lot of their own product in its construction, especially in the ornate mouldings that decorated the place inside and out. Dr. Bill Blair, the last of his family, had chosen, wisely Lettice thought, to live in a newer, smaller house, and the old house had stood vacant until, Tom told her, he'd bought it for a song. Lettice resisted the urge to giggle when he said that. She knew from past experience Tom couldn't carry a tune. Evidently, he hadn't been able to get it done up fast enough to suit his wife. That was why she left him, Tom said. Lettice had heard otherwise, but she let him go on. And on he went.

"The furnace conked out last winter, sure cost me a bundle. The floor squeaks like a hundred mice, so you can't walk around at night. The chimney flue needs re-lining, there goes another pile of dough. The front steps need replacing, and I can't decide whether they should be wood or concrete, what do *you* think, Letty? And every spring? The darned basement floods. I've got that mess to look forward to," he'd moaned.

"But that's the way of it with old houses," Lettice reminded him. "Especially one that's sat for ages with no one to look after it properly. Why don't you sell it then, if it's such a burden?"

"Can't do that. Young Tommy needs stability. He hates moving. The last time we were getting ready to move, he disappeared before breakfast one morning. I found him under the stairs in the basement, sitting all hunched up with one of his old baby blankets over his head. He refused to go to school that day. And the next. We had an awful time with him. He wouldn't eat. He wouldn't sleep. We finally took him to the doctor who said we'd been too soft on him. My wife cried and stormed out of the office. I saw the look on Young Tom's face when she did that." Tom picked up his glass, then set it down again. "After that, he started to become harder to handle. He has no real friends, just a gang of kids that hang around with him, trying to see who can be the toughest in the bunch. I'm at my wits' end. I don't know what to do with him. What do you think, Letty?" With that, he downed the contents of his glass in one gulp. And that was how the evening had gone. The glow Lettice had felt after the lovely meal faded quickly when they resumed their conversation. Every other sentence Tom uttered ended with 'What do *you* think, Letty?'

But he really didn't want to know what I thought, he just used me for a sounding board echoed and re-echoed in her head since he'd brought her home. *Why did I let it happen? Why wasn't I strong enough to stand up to him and say to his face, that's enough, Tom. What do you want me for? What do you expect me to do? About your job, your old house, your miserable son?* But as she lay there, watching the hands of her little bedside clock inching towards four, she knew why she hadn't.

You're still in love with him, you old fool.

20

GOSSIP, GOSSIP

It was the same every year. The Christmas season, so long anticipated, had come and gone through town like an express train. No longer the centre of attention in their starring roles as Christmas trees, Scotch pines and spruces had been stripped of their finery and cast out. They had to be satisfied to decorate the curb in front of each house, forgotten bits of tinsel glittering in their naked branches. Their final burst of glory would come soon, when they would be hauled down to the Lake, tossed onto a huge pile and set on fire, to the delight of the children. People smiled and joined in their oohs and aahs as the flames, shimmering like Northern Lights against a sooty sky, would rise up with a swoosh and a roar, sending millions of tiny sparks sailing out over the dark water.

As usual, Gussie spent Christmas Eve at her place with her father, a good-sized turkey and all the trimmings. Mac was in better spirits than she'd seen him in a while. They poked fun at each other as they pulled their bright Christmas crackers apart with a loud snap and donned the silly paper hats inside. Later, when they were enjoying some hot apple cider, enhanced with butter and a splash of rum, Gussie had taken advantage of his good mood and brought up the subject of Hink Denton. Mac leaned back in his chair and cleared his throat before replying in the offhand way he used when he really didn't want to talk about something. Yeah, he'd met the guy, once or twice. Somewhere around town. At some event or other. He couldn't remember exactly where. When Gussie asked what they'd talked about, he scratched the bald spot on the top of his head and mumbled something about the guy just wanting the dope on The Landing, don't know what in heck for, though.

"Dope! What do you mean by dope?" she asked, adding another dash of rum to her cider when she thought Mac wasn't looking.

"Dope. You know. How long people've been living there. Who owns that big hunk of vacant land down by the Lake. Was there always a public beach. You know. Stuff like that. If you ask me he was being awful nosey for a newcomer. Reach me over some of those cashews, would you, girl?"

He didn't dare ask her for more rum, he knew what she'd say.

"Maybe he was just curious, I mean, curious about the place, don't you think, Dad? Isn't that normal, I mean normal for someone who's just come to town? You have to admit, it is kind of an odd place. The Landing, I mean. Did you figure out what vacant land he was asking about?"

When Mac didn't answer her right away, she went on casually as if he had. "Don't you think that's all it was, Dad, just plain old curiosity?" and handed him a small, carved wooden platter loaded with chocolate truffles and assorted nuts. But not another word could she get out of him about Hink Denton. End of story as far as he was concerned.

It was also well after the New Year's Eve celebrations, which Gussie noted thankfully had been quieter than usual. Other than a broken window over at the Junior School, and a scuffle outside the arena between two members of rival hockey teams which Gussie was able to put a stop to before it got out of hand, nothing newsworthy had happened. Oh yes, there was that complaint from someone up on the hill. Too much noise coming from Bewyching Wood. When Gussie went up to check, she found Pete Wychwood sitting in a snowbank with a large bottle of bubbly singing at the top of his voice, off-key. He went like a lamb when she guided him back inside the house. The glamorous Maggie Wychwood was nowhere to be seen.

Most Bickertonians seemed to have preferred the comfort of their own homes to partying somewhere and then having to worry about getting home in one piece. Especially this winter, which looked like it was trying to set a record for snowfall. Nearly three feet more of the white stuff had accumulated over the holidays and the weather had stayed cold. Some back roads were still too treacherous for the school buses to navigate safely, so classes had been intermittent for some time following the Christmas break. Jesse hadn't seen Adam for ages, not since the weekend he stayed over at the Reserve. He was dying to show Adam what his Pop had sent him for Christmas. His mom said it was from Santa, but Jesse knew better. It had arrived wrapped in brown paper. That was a sure sign.

It was also well after the funeral service for Hink Denton, which was held on a bleak and snowy afternoon in late December. Service only and a perfunctory one at best. The Dentons were so new to the area, they hadn't gotten around to choosing a cemetery plot and anyway, as CeeCee told Dottie later, Hink changed the subject every time she brought it up. Now that decision would have to be put off until the snow was gone and the frost released the ground, which might not happen until May.

The service had been mercifully brief, during which CeeCee, to her embarrassment, was unable to keep from crying. This set the girls off and in spite of her best intentions Dottie found herself joining in. Following the service, CeeCee and her family, along with the faithful Dottie, fled to the Cosy Corner for an early supper. The girls and their husbands left as soon as the dismal meal was over. They'd given up trying to persuade CeeCee to come back with them and shook their heads in resignation at each other over her shoulder as they kissed her goodbye. Mother was being stupid and stubborn, but we did our best, they assured each other on the way back to the City.

Concentrating all her efforts on the Denton case, Gussie was finding herself frustrated at every turn. To handle the few minor problems that had come along, she'd been able to get Perce and Butch down from Cooley's. Since their experience over on the Old Barge Canal Road, they showed more enthusiasm for the job than before. They'd been guarded about asking her how things were going, but she knew their curiosity must have been tormenting them. But she didn't feel she could discuss the case with anyone at this stage. Far too many loose ends.

This detective work wasn't easy, that was for certain. She was still trying to set up an interview with the elusive Nick Fearnley. There was no answer at his home, although she'd called there countless times. None of the birding community had seen him since the day Hink Denton disappeared. Which was suspicious in itself. Nor could any of Nick's neighbours in the few homes still left down at The Landing tell her where he'd gone. Gussie never liked going down there, it was too depressing. Rusted out cars, roofless ice huts, ramshackle fishing boats that would never see the water again lay abandoned around the small frame cottages, which had withstood rough weather and blowing sand since the early part of the century. Piles of bald truck tires served as gate-posts to the entrance to the area. A dilapidated sign, which read **WEL OM TO TH L ND NG** dangled from one hook.

Landing people were different from the people in town. Descended from the earliest settlers, they were clannish, inbred, and staunchly proud of their background. Gussie wondered why, when most of their ancestors had been smugglers, pirates and others outside the law. Nothing to boast about. Not in her book, anyway.

Reviewing her notes, she remembered CeeCee mentioned encountering Nick with a young couple at the Quick Bite during her fruitless search for her husband the night he disappeared.

Gussie made a detour to the tiny restaurant one morning on her way over to check on Mac's place. He had gone Up North for a few days to visit an old buddy whose state of health was such he wasn't expected to last the winter.

That day it had been perishingly cold, putting Gussie in the mood for a hot drink and maybe a muffin. But after she pushed her way in through the heavy wooden door, a sickening smell of burnt coffee and stale cigarette smoke mixed in with rancid grease enveloped her, making her stomach heave. And there was another odour, indefinable at first, but after a moment she realized it was mouse. *Probably mice nests in the ceiling. Or blocking the ventilator shaft.* The place was deserted, the battered tables and chairs had a forlorn look about them. An ancient juke box was belting out some old-time Country and Western tune.

In one corner of the dimly lit room stood a large aquarium that might have held fish, but what was in it was anybody's guess. The glass sides were so coated in algae, it could have held a school of piranhas. Gussie made a mental note to find out when was the last time the Quick Bite had been given a good going over by the Health Inspector.

"Hello," she called, "anybody to home?"

She waited a few minutes. No one. The jukebox wailed on. She realized she'd have to shout over the din to bring any response. Finally, Joe Gaffield, the heavyset proprietor, stuck his head out of the kitchen. He seemed to be running the place alone, at least there was no sign of any help. When she inquired, Joe said he sometimes hired a girl to wait tables over the summer. He was obviously reluctant to talk to her, said he paid no never mind to anyone coming in with Nick. His heavily pockmarked face took on an expression of defiance. As if Gussie had been asking him to betray a friend. Evidently the bird man, as Joe called him, was a regular customer. Quite a few people came in during the tourist season saying Nick Fearnley had sent them, which Joe appreciated.

"Alls I ever do's fix what they order, quick like, 'n' make sure they pay up", he said after further prodding, wiping his thick fingers on a stained and greasy apron. "Don't much care as to who they be. Like, business is business." She'd interrupted him in the middle of cooking up a mess of chili, he told her. Joe didn't make a move to offer her anything, as most people in his position would have done. *Just as well,* she thought. *I certainly don't want to be beholden to the likes of him, even though everyone thinks the cops get their coffee and doughnuts on the house.* When she saw that Joe couldn't, or wouldn't, recall the day in question and was anxious to get back to his smelly kitchen, Gussie left. She was glad to fill her lungs with good fresh winter air even if it was freezing cold.

Rare for her, since she didn't believe in what she thought of as silly traditions, Gussie had made one New Year's resolution: to pay more attention to her looks. Normally, she was too busy to do more than shove her hair, which she wore pulled back in a ponytail, under her cap and slap on a bit of lipstick. It was about time she had a proper haircut. She couldn't remember when she'd last paid a visit to the Bo-Tay Hair Salon over by the library. There was always so much to do, she could never be sure she could keep an appointment. Or, if she did get around to making one, some emergency would crop up and she'd forget all about what she'd planned to do for herself.

Early one Saturday morning, Gussie found herself lying flat on her back, her pleasantly tingling body covered in a soft flannel sheet, her face swathed in hot towels, after enduring a scolding. Your skin is in turrible shape, how in the world could you let it go like that, tsk, tsk, you young gals are all the same, you think a little soap and water is all you need. Gussie smiled to herself in spite of the suffocating heat of the towels, which the operator, a bright brisk middle-aged lady, who was a distant cousin of Syd's, told her was necessary to let your poor little pores breathe, dear. After Maybelle unearthed it from the towels, Gussie's face glowed like a child's. Wow. She should do this more often. Since things were under control at the station with Perce and Butch down for the day again, she'd decided to go whole hog and have a massage while she was at it. Now she sat limp and relaxed in front of the mirror, while Maybelle ran a comb lightly through her freshly shampooed hair.

"My, you don't know how lucky you are to have hair like this," Maybelle enthused, as she draped Gussie's long mane this way and that. "And the colour! I know a couple of my reg'lers who'd kill to have such a gorgeous shade".

Gussie smiled again, figuring Maybelle was probably her own best client. Her hair, which she wore in a spiky fringe around her face, was a garish shade of henna. Her hazel eyes were high-lighted with more than ample eye shadow in a sort of bronze colour. Her brows had been plucked into thin crescents, giving her a perpetually startled look.

"You take that Miz Otterley now, from over to East Thorne? She's allus after me to make her into a redhead. But I keep tellin' her, the colour won't take on her kinda hair. Liable to go green or somethin'. Then she'd be suin' me for makin' her look a fright. Go off and tell all her friends that there Maybelle don't know what she's doin'. Then where would I be? How much do you want off this, Gus?"

"Isn't she a friend of CeeCee Denton? You know, the one whose husband—"

"That's her all right. Miz Denton brought her in here. Miz Denton's bin comin' here since she come to town. Nice lady, always so nice to talk to. Not like some. That Wychwood woman, now. She come in here once. For a trim that was. She asked an awful lot of questions. She wanted to know about old Miz Eliza, you know, Eliza Roxton. Wanted to know if I knew her. Wanted to know how old she was. Wanted to know how long she'd bin sick over to the Home. On and on and on. I told her I didn't know nothin' about any of it."

"Eliza Roxton, she's a great aunt to Sherry who works at the library, isn't she?" Gussie leaned forward and stared solemnly at herself in the mirror, trying to decide how much hair to part with.

"Only relative round these parts, beside old George over to the school, that is. S'posed to be some others Out West or some such. Nobody knows for sure. Them older Roxtons were an odd lot. Kept to themselves, probably thought everyone was after their money. Sherry, now she's a real nice lady. Smart too. How much shall I take off, now Gus? You don't want it real short, do you? Too cold out still."

After Gussie had settled for shoulder length, Maybelle got to work, prattling on and on about the Roxtons and about that awful time when Old Man Roxton ...

Gussie's mind drifted away, she was so relaxed. She came to with a start when something Maybelle said broke through her drowsiness.

"Sorry, Maybelle. You made me so comfy, I fell asleep there for a minute, I mean fell asleep. What was that you just said about Mrs. Wychwood's husband? Something about him and Syd?" Gussie was wide awake now.

Since when had Syd been a friend of Pete Wychwood?

21

FRANCY'S SECRET

Francy was folding up the last of the week's laundry in the spare room when she heard Ferd calling her from the downstairs hall. She thought he'd been closed in his study when she dragged the big mesh laundry bag down the stairs, but he materialized at her elbow, startling her as she was filling the washer in the back kitchen, saying he had some telephone calls to make and she wasn't to disturb him. If she interrupted him, he said, he'd lose his train of thought and it would be her fault if it all went wrong. What on earth was he talking about? What went wrong? And since when had she ever bothered him when he was on the phone? *Who's he to talk about interruptions,* she said to herself as she dumped another load into the machine.

The other night when she'd been trying to reach Marlene, he came in and started flipping the wall light switch off and on. I've told you before, Francy, he said, when she hung up. Long distance calls cost a fortune. Who were you calling anyway, not Marlene again. *The good old double standard,* she thought bitterly. *I never question any of his calls. He's definitely getting more impossible to live with. Thank God I'm at least able to sleep at night.*

Stacking the clean sheets and pillowcases on the shelves in the new linen closet, she was glad that job was over and done with for another week. She guessed she should be thankful she didn't have to iron all this stuff like her mother used to do. She remembered her mother slaving for hours, ironing everything, even underwear and socks. Imagine. The shiny new clothes dryer, wedged in next to the old washer they'd brought out with them, was a welcome addition to her army of housework helpers. At least Ferd had been good about getting her what she needed. Even if he was awfully fussy about how clean she kept the place. Old houses aren't well supplied with closets, so when she'd asked for a place to store the sheets and towels, he got some fellow from down at The Landing to build one in the upstairs hall, handy to the bedrooms. And since Ferd couldn't stand to see clothes hanging out on a line, said it looked like they were low class, he'd bought her the dryer.

For the hundredth time, she wished there was someone she could let her hair down and talk to about Ferd. Trying to get a hold of Marlene in the City was futile. Francy left numerous messages with the sleepy voice that finally answered the phone after dozens of rings at the number where her daughter was supposedly living. She was still waiting for a response. Why didn't Marlene get her own telephone, for goodness sakes? Francy had long ago given up any hope that her only child would grow up and take some responsibility for her life. Like CeeCee's girls for instance. Both had husbands and good jobs, both said they'd be happy to look after CeeCee if she'd just go back to the City. But take Marlene now, she rarely called her parents and when she did, it was only to ask for money. The last time she'd gone into the City, Francy bumped into an acquaintance who told her Marlene had taken on another part time job, this one at a drop-in centre for runaway teenagers. Maybe that's where all her money went. Marlene always did have a soft spot for lost lambs.

Francy often regretted they knew so little about Marlene's life. And worried that the girl didn't seem to be able to settle down into a normal lifestyle. Where had they gone wrong? They. That was a good one. Ferd was never around when any crisis involving Marlene arose. He'd always left difficult decisions to

Francy, using the excuse he was too busy with his students and after all, he never failed to remind her, Marlene was *her* daughter. You're too soft on the kid, Francy, he'd say, far too soft. Maybe he was right. Maybe she hadn't been tough enough. She'd always given in to everything Marlene wanted to do. She guessed it was probably because of the way she herself had been brought up.

The only child of older parents who had been so strict with her Francy often thought it was a wonder she'd ever been allowed out to meet anyone, let alone get married and leave home. Probably it was because they had so much in common, Ferd and her father, that her parents had encouraged the relationship. Both men had started out in the newspaper business and had quit to go into teaching. When she and Ferd first started dating, he used to come over really early to pick her up on Saturday nights. While she was hurrying to change from her cleaning job at the Five-and-Dime, Ferd and her father would disappear into her father's study and get into long and complicated discussions, discussions Francy couldn't make heads nor tails of. A couple of times, this had made them miss the beginning of the movie she'd been looking forward to all week. With the last show starting promptly at nine o'clock, it was sometimes too late to even bother going. She'd never figured out how to handle it. Certainly it was no use getting mad. The one time she lost her temper, both men looked at her in disgust and then shrugged their shoulders. *Isn't that just like a woman!* she could almost hear them thinking. After a while, she learned to live with her disappointment. When she told her parents Ferd wanted to marry her, with one voice they'd said Ferd was perfect and she should be grateful for the chance, as she wouldn't likely have another. She'd never understood why her parents had such a poor opinion of her.

"Francy! Oh Francy! Where the devil are you?" *Ferd again.* Francy made a face. *Where did he think I'd gone, to the moon?*

"Up here," she called, coming to the top of the stairs.

"Oh *there* you are," Ferd said, as he struggled into his parka. "I've got to go out, don't you know. I won't be back in time for lunch. You'll have to enjoy that feast alone, I'm afraid."

Feast. That was another good one. A can of soup. Some crackers. Peanut butter and cheese. That's all he ever wanted for lunch. Some feast. Alone? Francy didn't think so. As soon as Ferd's car turned the corner, she decided today was the day she was going to call CeeCee. Maybe they could meet for lunch, even do some shopping. That is, if CeeCee felt like going out. They hadn't seen each other since before the funeral. That is, if CeeCee had her car. Francy was sorry she'd never gotten up the nerve to learn to drive. Her father had discouraged her, said women were terrible drivers. So, if Ferd didn't take her where she wanted to go, she didn't get there. East Thorne was too small a community to support a taxi service, although recently there had been some talk of one starting up, maybe next summer.

Dottie answered the phone on the first ring and said in her breezy way, why Miz Otterley, good to hear from ya, how's things, how've ya been, sure an' I'll get Miz Denton for ya, won't be a minute. CeeCee had taken up Francy's suggestion with enthusiasm. It looked like it was shaping up to be another dull late winter day. It was still surreal to her, Hink being gone. Her whole life had been turned upside down. She'd tried to carry on, keep up a good front, but lately she'd been feeling restless and irritable. Goodness knows it wasn't Dottie's fault; she was unfailingly cheerful. But CeeCee felt she needed a break even if she knew she'd be trading Dottie's endless chatter for Francy's limited conversation. Just thinking about it that way made her feel guilty. Maybe Dottie needed a break from her. And Francy was okay. In her own way.

CeeCee hurried to change into something other than the old pants and sweater she'd put on to help Dottie clean out the kitchen cupboards. It was still cold enough for her to wear her heavy winter coat, which was stylishly cut and in her favourite shade of deep rose. When she heard why Francy had called, Dottie said good idea, lovey, do ya good to get out for a change, them cupboards can wait for another day, I've got lots more other things to do.

"Could we go as far as Dunhampton, do you think?" Francy asked when she was comfortably established in the front seat of the Dentons' sedan, and CeeCee said why not, let's do it, maybe there'll be some nice spring clothes in the shops, getting tired of my winter stuff, happens every year about now. Francy said, me too, although she was looking quite smart in her blue and red plaid coat. The morning traffic on the main highway was light and the hour or so it took to drive to the larger town went quickly with Francy and CeeCee talking in fits and starts with long gaps in between.

"Don't know why we haven't done this before," CeeCee said, turning off at the Dunhampton exit.

"I do," Francy replied, "between the snowstorms we've had this year and Ferd insisting that I'm home all the time."

"Highway was in good shape today," CeeCee said, ignoring the last remark. "Only a little sand left from the last batch of freezing rain."

"Or left there for the next."

"Don't even mention it. Sick of winter. Seems it's going to last forever this year. Can't wait for spring and some decent sunshine. Where shall we go first?"

After exploring what Dunhampton had to offer in the way of dress shops, which they agreed wasn't an awful lot better than either Bickerton (where the only way you could get decent clothes was to make them yourself) or Cooley's Mills (where a cramped and dingy department store specialized in work clothes, heavy boots and raincoats), they were beginning to get tired and hungry. Francy said her feet were getting sore, while CeeCee said it was because they were out of practice with shopping.

"I never get a chance to practise with Ferd. He hates shopping the way we just did it. You know, just looking around? He figures out what we need, then he goes out and buys it without looking at anything else," Francy complained, massaging her aching feet when they were back in the car and she could take off her high-heeled boots. "What was Hink...I mean -" Francy stopped in confusion then tried again. "What I mean is, does it bother you? I mean, to talk about him?"

CeeCee shook her head. "Sounds like Ferd shops the way most men do. I was lucky I guess. Hink liked to browse. And window shop. Took his time. Always gave me all the time I wanted. Liked to check around and see what there was, figure out where the best bargains were. Hated to pay full price for anything if he could get a bargain. Can't do that if you don't take lots of time to look around."

Dunhampton was about five times the size of Bickerton and, although it was lacking in suitable dress shops, it made up for it with a good selection of eating places. A pleasant drive around and down through the residential section took them past an attractive restaurant painted a cheerful blue and white and perched on the edge of the Lake.

"That place must be new since the last time we were here. I don't remember seeing it before," Francy said, twisting around in her seat trying to catch another glimpse. "What do you think, CeeCee? Should we maybe see what it's like?"

"Sure. Why not? Ready for something different. Getting a bit bored with the likes of the good old Cosy Corner," CeeCee said, and pulled into the empty parking lot in front of the marina next door to the restaurant.

The Topsail looked — and smelled — clean and inviting as they passed through the double front doors, each of which had a large porthole for a window. Inside, the spacious dining room was done up like the deck of a ship, with nautical charts on the walls and blue tablecloths with a pattern of white anchors spread on wooden tables. Floor to ceiling windows on the lake side made it seem like you were actually floating on the water. It was well past the usual lunch hour, but there were still a few patrons quietly enjoying a leisurely meal. The hostess, dressed in a perky navy and white sailor suit, showed them to a table by the wall of windows. The two women looked around with satisfaction. This place had been a good choice, they agreed. The view of the water and the islands beyond gave the promise of being much prettier in better weather.

Out across the leaden water, they could see that the ice was finally beginning to break up. Driven by a strong wind from the east, it lay in long irregular bands of pearl grey, the contrasting deeper grey water in between creating a pleasing stippled effect. Off to the west stood the weather-beaten docks of the marina, deserted now, but CeeCee could easily imagine that soon the scene in front of them would be a hive of activity, with weekend sailors eagerly getting their boats ready for another season. Bobbing up and down on the waves directly below them were a few ducks, the first of thousands that would soon be arriving on their way north. The sight of them reminded CeeCee of Hink and his bird list. Forcing herself not to think about that, she ordered two glasses of imported white wine and instructed the waitress to put both on her bill. No, no, my treat, she told Francy when she tried to object.

"But you did the driving and it was my idea in the first place," Francy noted.

"A great idea. Anyway, I like driving. How about those clothes we just waded through?" CeeCee said, changing the subject. "Weren't the colours awful?"

"Yeah, who was it decided we'd all look good in citrus shades anyway? That hot orange. Heatwave, I think it was called. And that yellow called Lemony Joy? Sounded like some kind of laundry soap to me. Ugh," Francy made a face.

"Looked like ancient egg yolk to me," responded CeeCee, making them both laugh. "Not to mention the green. Ivy. No. What was it again? Envy. That was it. Never did like the colour green. Never wore it either," she continued. "My mother thought wearing green brought bad luck. Where did she get that notion, I wonder? What ever happened to good old pinks and blues anyway? Or that pinkish purplish colour they used to call mauve?"

By the time their waitress came back, they'd both decided on the bouillabaisse and the fresh fruit salad plate with cottage cheese and whole wheat rolls, BAKED FRESH DAILY ON OUR PREMISES it said on the menu, Francy telling CeeCee after they'd ordered how much more appetising it all sounded than plain old tomato soup and soda crackers and CeeCee telling Francy how the Kibbidges ate mostly meat and potatoes with a thick starchy gravy over everything. Or kippers when they could get them. With potatoes. Never ate rice. Only potatoes.

"They don't like vegetables much. Or fruit either. Only apples. They said they didn't have those other things when they were growing up. Too expensive."

"That's odd, that they don't eat them. Now, I mean. Doesn't Rab sell them in his store?"

"Yes, but they don't know how to prepare them. Rab thought you ate a grapefruit like an apple, cut into quarters. Should have seen his face when he bit into it. Dottie got a real laugh."

"Are you sure you want to go on staying there?" Francy asked, spreading a liberal amount of butter on her warm roll which, after one tiny bite, proved to be living up to the menu's declaration of freshness. "I'm sure Ferd wouldn't mind if you came to us for a while." She hesitated to add she was dying for some company.

"Kind of you to offer. But no. Like it there. Rab's put me to work. Stocktaking. And a few other things. Keeps my mind off what happened," CeeCee said, heaping cottage cheese on her fork. "Getting to see what it's like to have a business. Always wondered about it. Can't bring myself to go back out to the house. Maybe in the spring." They stopped talking then and applied themselves to the steaming bowls of rich fish stew.

The dessert menu certainly looked tempting, but they felt they'd eaten enough, the servings of fruit were so generous. After their plates were removed, they sat quietly with their wine, enjoying the view. Then Francy broke the silence.

"CeeCee, I know it's been an awful time for you, but I just *have* to talk to someone and, um, well, you're the only one I feel comfortable talking to," Francy began, running her finger slowly around the base of her wineglass.

CeeCee tried to put an interested expression on her face. She didn't see what kind of problem Francy could possibly have that would come anywhere close to losing a husband. And in such a horrible way. Mentally she scolded herself. Something must be troubling Francy. She certainly wasn't her usual cheerful self today.

"Go on, go on. All ears," she said, wondering if she dared order them another glass of wine.

Francy hesitated. "Well, you see, it's Ferd. He's ... well, he's been worse. Worse than usual, I mean."

"Worse? What do you mean, worse?"

"Well, he's crosser with me than he's ever been, scolding me like I was a kid, I don't know why, well, most of the time I don't, and at night, well ..." Francy paused in her rush, "at night you see ... well, he's been ..." she stopped again and looked down at her hands.

"Sure you want me to hear this?" CeeCee said, nervously wondering what was going to come next. The thought of listening to the details of someone's intimate life made her cringe.

"Oh dear," Francy said, "it's not *that* ! What I meant to say was, at night he's been so restless I've had to move into the spare room." She picked up the salt shaker and put it down again.

"And he mutters. Talks, I mean. In his sleep, I mean. He's never done that before." She moved the salt shaker closer to its pepper mate. CeeCee wished she'd leave the condiments alone. She forced herself to look at Francy, instead of out the window at the ducks, whose numbers had increased since the last time she'd looked. "He's always been a real sound sleeper," Francy continued, straightening the tablecloth that didn't need it. "He's so lucky. He falls asleep as soon as his head hits the pillow. Not like me. I usually lie awake. For hours and hours sometimes. I hear every little sound. Our house creaks," she smiled. Apologetically, CeeCee thought.

"Old houses usually do. When did all this restlessness start?"

"Funny you should ask," Francy said, fiddling with her napkin. "I think it was right about ... about the time Hink ... disappeared."

"Odd." CeeCee's face looked grave. "Odd," she said again. "Are you sure, Francy? Think again. Can you remember exactly when it was?"

"I've already thought about it and I'm almost positive it was the same night when we came over to your place. After we heard. You know. About Hink. I remember thinking maybe he had a touch of indigestion. I mean, because we ate so late. We stopped for some fried chicken at the Cosy Corner and it did seem kind of greasy. And then we had some, ah, French fries to go with it and they were all out of vinegar to put on them. So there was nothing to cut all that grease. Ketchup never seems to do it. But he was just the same the next night. And it's ... well, it's been like that ever since. The only other thing I thought it ... might be ..." Francy stopped and looked away. Her face had flushed a bright scarlet.

"Excuse me," she said in a choked voice and left the table. CeeCee sat there stunned. What was going on here? She really could use another glass of wine, but thought better of it. There was still that long drive back to East Thorne. And there might be more snow.

When Francy came back to the table a few minutes later, her face was pale and her eyes were red. CeeCee hoped she hadn't been ill.

"I'm so sorry, CeeCee. I feel so stupid." Francy cleared her throat. "What I was going to say ... well ... I guess it's something I probably shouldn't be talking about." She seized her glass and quickly swallowed the last of her wine. "No, no, I'm okay," she said, seeing the look of surprise on CeeCee's face.

"Are you sure?" CeeCee asked, really concerned now. Maybe wine in the middle of the day hadn't been such a good idea after all.

"Oh CeeCee, I've gone this far, you might as well know the rest. You know, uh, well, we had to leave the City. It wasn't a case of 'oh let's move to the country'. Or a small town. Or something." Francy cleared her throat again. The pathetic way she was looking at CeeCee with those large blue eyes through a straggly fringe of pale hair reminded CeeCee of a little lost child.

"Never questioned why you came," CeeCee said a bit gruffly. She hated shows of emotion. "Go on," she said trying to inject some encouragement into her voice. "Why *did* you come then?"

"Well, it's Ferd's fault really. You see, there was some trouble. At the school, I mean. With one of his students. You see, she accused him of -" Francy's voice broke. She grasped the edge of the table, leaned forward suddenly and whispered, "of improper conduct I think they called it. He was hauled up on the carpet. It was awful. They didn't really listen to him. Only to her. They sure didn't waste any time. They said right off he was guilty. He was let go." She sighed. "He was lucky, I guess. It could have been a lot worse. Anyway, the story got out, I don't know how, and the scandal. Well, we couldn't stay there any more. Our friends dropped us. At least, I thought they were our friends. At least they let him collect his pension. If they hadn't, well ..." Her voice trailed off.

"Oh dear, I had no idea, no idea at all, how terrible for you," was all CeeCee could think to say. She was almost shocked speechless. That sad little confession helped explain the tension she'd detected between Francy and Ferd. She couldn't help wondering if the story were true. It certainly would have put a premature end to Ferd's career. Poor little Francy. Aloud she said, "Ever talked to him about it?"

"Oh no, no. No, the subject has never come up. After it happened, I thought for sure he'd deny everything, tell me it was just a stupid story made up by some lovesick student. There'd been others, you know." Francy's face flushed a deep pink. "Quite a few. Girls with crushes, I mean. They used to send him letters. One even called him on the phone one day. At our home! She sounded really embarrassed when I answered. Maybe she didn't know he was married."

She'd picked up her empty glass and was looking at it as if to make sure it really was empty. "She still had the nerve to ask if he was in. Girls at that age do some crazy things. I don't know, maybe this one thought he was seriously interested in her. He'd been helping her after school on some project or other. But then, he did that sort of thing all the time, it was part of the job. But since it happened, well, he's never said a single word. After they let him go, he just clammed up. And I was too scared to ask him about it. Maybe I was afraid of it being ... anyway, now you know our nasty little secret." She put her wineglass back down on the table. "You see, when Ferd started getting restless at night, I thought maybe something had happened to bring it all back. Maybe he ... but now—"

"Now you're wondering if he knows something about Hink's death," CeeCee made herself say it. She felt like screaming, but choked back the impulse.

"Yes. Yes I am. And I have to admit it. I'm scared, CeeCee," Francy said. The two women simultaneously reached across the table and took each other's hands.

"Don't be. Might be a perfectly simple explanation," CeeCee said gently, glad she'd regained some control. Whatever had happened with Ferd, it wasn't poor little Francy's fault.

"Do you think I should say anything to Gussie Spilsbury? I mean, I really don't have anything to go on, just a funny feeling about it."

"No, no," CeeCee said. "Don't. Don't say anything. Not to anyone. Not just yet. Let's wait a while and see what happens. Sure Gussie will find out what happened. Know she's working on it. Calls me every few days. In the meantime, see if you can listen in on Ferd's conversations. On the phone, I mean. Do you think you could do that? For me? You might overhear something that would clear things up."

Francy took a deep breath. "Anything, *anything*. I'll do anything you think might work. I sure can't go on living like this much longer," she said, weariness creeping into her voice.

"Should be getting back, I guess. Sky out there looks like more snow's coming," CeeCee said, after a moment, "but first, how about some coffee before we go?"

"Great idea," Francy replied, "and I better tell you that, well, Otterley isn't our real name."

"Better not tell me any more, Francy. Don't want you to be sorry afterwards."

"Oh no, I won't be sorry. In fact, I feel better already. For telling you, I mean. I never was much good at keeping secrets, you know, and it's been so hard having to keep quiet about my problem. Thanks for being so understanding. I'm not sure I would be. If I were in your place."

CeeCee was inclined to agree with her. Thank goodness she'd followed her instincts about not staying with the Otterleys. She was under enough of a strain without having to deal with other people's problems. She didn't think she could stand the tension. It was so different with the Kibbidges. Sometimes she wished she wasn't so sensitive. Or so, what was the word, empathetic.

Tucking Francy's revelation in the back of her mind, CeeCee got set to enjoy a good strong cup of the beverage she denied herself for far too long. As she was stirring cream and sugar into her coffee, with Francy chattering away inconsequentially about how much laundry she'd done that morning, CeeCee had a disturbing thought. Something in Francy's tale didn't ring true. If Ferd was Francy's first and only husband but not the father of her daughter, then who was? And since she was in such a confiding mood, why had Francy failed to mention this important detail? Or was it important? Not likely it had anything to do with Ferd's downfall. And yet ...

CeeCee was beginning to realize there was more to little Francy than she'd thought.

22

GUSSIE DOES A JUGGLING ACT

As January dragged itself into February and February slogged on into March, Gussie found herself getting more and more apprehensive. It was depressing; she should have been looking forward to spring like everyone else in Bickerton. More especially so this year, when Old Man Winter seemed to be considering taking up permanent residence. Starting with that awful night when Hink Denton disappeared, a continuing, and at times seemingly never-ending sequence of snowstorms, followed by periods of intense cold, meant the ground had been covered with several feet of the white stuff since well before Christmas. The proverbial January thaw never happened. Meaning that it had been out of the question to make a trip into the woods over by the Old Barge Canal Road.

But the normally intrepid Gussie found herself dreading the day when the snow would finally be gone. Or at least melted down enough for her to carry out a proper search. Every morning while she was getting ready for work, Gussie carried on a discussion with herself, trying to understand why she was feeling so uneasy and hoping it didn't show on the job. It was true, she reasoned, once the masses of snow were gone, she'd be able to get into the section of woods beside the Old Barge Canal Road where Jesse Woodcock, bless his little heart, had stumbled over Hink Denton's body, and could search for clues — bits of paper, scraps of cloth, even footprints if she was lucky although that was unlikely after all this time — anything that might lead her to his killer. For she felt in her bones, in spite of the coroner's verdict, that he had been murdered.

She was dismayed she hadn't managed to get any further ahead on what was turning out to be her first really important case, than she had been back before Christmas. Her superiors over in Dunhampton ordered her to keep on working on it. Gussie thanked her lucky stars they were astute enough to realize because of the exceptionally long and snowbound winter nothing could be done at the actual crime scene. They requested copies of her reports on all the interviews she'd conducted so far. Thank goodness that boring task was done. So much for the professional side. But Gussie couldn't help feeling badly for CeeCee Denton's sake. The poor woman maintained an absolute faith in her detecting abilities and had told her so any number of times. CeeCee didn't believe her husband's death was any accident. Gussie just hoped and prayed that CeeCee's faith in her wasn't misplaced.

There were still a few people she needed to question, including the elusive Nick Fearnley. Gussie made another trip back down to The Landing and checked his place again. Even to the most casual observer it was obvious from the untracked driveway, the pristine piles of snow around the front and back that no one had been there since the day she'd come by on her way to the Quick Bite to see Joe Gaffield. Nick's immediate neighbour stuck her head out her front door to see what the constable was doing. She was a bit more forthcoming than the rest had been and said in answer to Gussie's question that no, ma'am, not a soul had been near to Nick's place. Not since he took off afore Christmas. The mailman stopped bringin' up his mail after the first big snow-storm last fall. He could easily be gone for months, she said. Often was. This news was a relief to Gussie. She'd been worried Nick might have come back, gotten wind she wanted to talk to him and left town again. There were lots of ways to do that if you lived down at The Landing. Without any prompting, the woman volunteered to let Gussie know the minute he showed up. Or if anything happened at the house. Meaning some stranger poking around. Gussie found her spontaneous offer of cooperation surprising. Maybe the folks down at The Landing weren't as bad as they'd been painted.

Gussie knew it was crucial to her investigation that she get back into the woods. But after some of the things she'd heard over the past couple of weeks, she was half afraid of what she might find. There were those hints dropped by Maybelle who'd convinced her to come back to see her at the Bo-Tay regularly for some badly needed skin care. She simply had to find time to follow up on the hints and see where they led. And then there was the curious behaviour of Pete Wychwood who'd gotten roaring drunk several times since the New Year (at the Snake Pit of all places) and had to be taken home (by Tom Bartlett of all people) when he refused to leave. This last she'd heard from the doctor, Bill Blair, who called to ask her to dinner but because of her work commitments, they'd been unable to settle on a date. At least, Gussie thought, that was the best excuse she could think of for not going out with him.

Thinking back to New Year's Eve, Gussie figured Pete's noisy celebrating had been because of the season. She'd never known him to get drunk. Or belligerent. Not in public anyway. Bill said Tom had called him, wondering if Pete were sick or on some new kind of pills that might cause a reaction if he took a drink. Bill told him Pete hadn't been near his office for over a year. Unless he'd gone somewhere else for a prescription. Out of town maybe. Or into the City.

Then there was CeeCee Denton's mention of Mac's phone calls to her husband. Gussie didn't know what to make of that information. She wondered what on earth she'd do if she found any evidence in the woods connecting Mac to Hink Denton's death. Mac had been making himself scarce lately which was strange in itself. She didn't want to think it meant anything serious. Knowing him as she did, she figured sooner or later his curiosity was bound to get the better of him and he'd be sniffing around her desk again.

Another development she didn't know quite how to deal with was the reappearance of Syd in her life. She still hadn't found out what had been bothering him that day he showed up at the office. What she did know was that he was being hounded by *The Weekly* up in Cooley's Mills. Even the *Daily Dispatch* Dunhampton's pride and joy, which barely acknowledged Bickerton's existence in its regular news coverage, hadn't let up on him since he'd run the short piece on Hink Denton's unexplained death in the *Bugler* .

"They're still on my tail, Gus. Every week someone calls me. 'Hey, c'mon, Syd, old buddy, what're you guys down there in Bickerton up to, what's going on, was the guy murdered or what, what's wrong with your lady cop?' They're driving me crazy," he complained, his voice heavy with fatigue. "They swear they're going to come down and sit on my doorstep, even threatened to come down and follow you around. I guess nothing this exciting's happened in ages. The whole thing's becoming a real nuisance. We need a world war. Or an epidemic, God forbid. Something big to take their attention away from little old Bickerton. Isn't there anything more you can give me, anything to shut them up, make them lay off? For a while at least? Before I go nuts?"

It was late on a Tuesday night and Gussie had come back to the office to catch up on some overdue paperwork. She was exhausted after a long day, which started off on the wrong foot and stayed that way. The area had been hit with an unpredicted sleet storm that left the roads dangerously slick and caught many drivers unawares. Several ended up in the ditch. They'd had to wait for ages until the town's only tow truck could haul them all out. Luckily no one was hurt, but she'd had to quell a couple of confrontations between angry drivers that could have turned ugly. She was dying for some sleep, but since Cooley's had been hit with the same storm, neither Perce nor Butch had been able to get down to relieve her. Then Mac called. He wasn't feeling too terrific, he said, and could she come over and fix him some soup or an egg or something.

Alarmed at her usually independent father's request and the quaver in his voice, she'd skipped dinner and rushed down to the old house by the Lake. She found Mac running a fever and after settling him with some chicken broth and toast, left a call in for the doctor to drop by. That is, if he could manage to get down with the roads in such terrible shape. The sander had been dispatched and gone around once, but late in the day, the sleet had turned to freezing rain that was still falling. Wow. More trouble on the highway tonight, for sure, she thought wearily. Again she wondered if the job was getting to be too much for her.

"Kind of funny, isn't it, the lack of interest in the case. Around here, I mean," Syd said, trying unsuccessfully to stifle a yawn. "Is it because Denton was a newcomer do you think? I mean, he could have been murdered. Don't they even care?"

"Oh I think they care all right. But I think they're scared, I mean really scared. Terrified even," Gussie replied. "They want to believe it's someone from outside. They can't bear to think it might be one of us."

"Yeah, that's what I can't understand. It *could* be one of us. What's the odds that it was?"

"It's hard for me to even think about it, I mean even think about it," Gussie said, painfully aware that she'd slipped into her old habit and the chance it was going to irritate Syd. But he seemed oblivious and kept on talking.

"Remember the last time we had a mysterious death around here? Back when we were still kids? Some guy, I think it was one of the Bartletts from up by Cooley's, I can't remember which one, anyway, the guy was out hiking with his dog up along the

Lonesome. Dog sniffed out some bones, the guy thought they looked funny, brought 'em down here to old Doc Winter's. He sent 'em off to some lab in the City. Turned out they were human bones all right."

"How could I forget?" Gussie sighed. "Us kids scared each other for weeks afterwards. We made a game of it. Leaving weird notes in the mailboxes. Popping out of the bushes at each other on the way home from school. Tom Bartlett frightened me half to death, I mean half to death, one night when Dad was late picking me up from basketball practice. Did I ever tell you about that? No? Well, Tom had his old bomber jacket pulled up over his head. Just as I came out the door, he stepped out from behind that big signboard that used to be at the front of the school. He thought it was funny. I could have killed him, I was so mad, I mean so mad!"

Syd laughed. "Would have served him right if you had, the jerk. Look what kind of a guy he turned out to be, anyway. He's totally full of himself. I heard he's been seen with Lettice Snelgrove over in Dunhampton, getting cosy with her in some fancy new eatery over there. He gave her the bum's rush years ago. Poor old Lettice! You'd think at her age she'd know better."

There was a pause. When Gussie didn't react to this remark, he continued, shifting on the seat so he could look at her.

"Yeah well," he went on, still trying to capture Gussie's full attention. "I remember Dad having to write up the bone story. He had an awful time with it. Said he didn't want to hurt anyone's feelings and wanted to be sure he had all his facts right. It took a long time before we found out whose bones they were. You remember? When the Roxtons were having all that trouble and one of the girls who worked for them, the skinny one, what was her name?"

"Skinny Minnie we called her. I think it was Jean," supplied Gussie. "Yeah, she disappeared. Ran away or something. Because of Jeff Roxton, at least that's what the gossip said. He was always after her, just wouldn't leave her alone, they said. Probably she just couldn't take it any more."

"Well? What was I just saying? Wasn't that one of our own? Drove her to suicide, I mean. Might as well have killed her. You just never know, could have been something funny going on with Denton and somebody else around here we don't know about."

Gussie was reluctant to get into a long conversation with anyone, let alone Syd, at this hour. In a weak moment, she'd let him persuade her to climb into his truck and sit with him for a few minutes. It felt unsettling being back in the old truck again. Almost the same as she'd felt when she'd come back to Bickerton from the City after graduation. There'd been times she'd felt like she didn't belong here any more.

While she and Syd had been talking, she'd been running her fingers over the splits in the covering on the truck seat. They were the same old rips and tears that had been there when she and Syd were courting. The broken handle on the passenger door that she'd always found such a nuisance was still broken; the deodorizer Syd insisted on hanging on the rear view mirror was still the same old familiar woodsy scent of pine. Nothing had changed.

She felt a pang of concern for him. Even in the dimness of the old truck's roof light she could see the circles under his eyes. Darn him anyway, she thought, I don't need this now, I've got enough of my own worries. Remembering the trick with the broken handle, she unlatched the door and slid quickly off the seat. Back to the safety of the sidewalk, away from the renewed attraction of his presence, the sight of his hands, always so gentle, with their squared off nails that he could never keep clean from the printing ink, the leathery smell of his old cowhide jacket. *It's got to be the spring coming that's making me feel like this, nothing else,* she told herself. Closing the truck door firmly, she said good night to him through the open window, promising that he would be the first to hear if she turned up anything new.

She hurried into the building before he could see the expression on her face.

Syd sat for a moment, watching the rain trickling down the windshield, wishing he could have said something to keep her there longer. *What kind of an idiot am I, anyway. I should have told her how much I miss her instead of saddling her with my problems. Or bringing up ancient history.* Because of his stupidity, he never had a chance to tell her what he had really come for. He wasn't sure how to broach the subject. But she'd have to know soon. Mac had called him that morning. He drove home, feeling worse than ever.

Inside her office again, Gussie tried to settle down to work. Before she could tackle the pile of paperwork, she had another pile to sort through. Telephone messages. Everything seemed to be happening at once. One call was from George Roxton at the Junior School — could she come over next week and talk to the children about safety? With spring coming, there would be new hazards — bicycles, roller skates, pick-up baseball — all kinds of street games played in the middle of the road. This was a task she usually enjoyed, talking to the kids. She remembered when the old policeman she'd replaced, Constable Gerry they'd called him, had come to the school to talk on the same subject when she was a kid. He always brought some kind of treats with him, a bag of toffees or a box of cookies. She'd have to dream up some goodies to take. Another message was from Kitty Woodcock. Could Gussie please call her. No, it wasn't urgent, but she really needed to talk to Constable Spilsbury. As soon as possible was underlined. Gussie wondered vaguely how young Jesse was getting along. Or was Kitty just looking for news of her missing husband? CeeCee Denton had called twice. Probably wondering if there's anything new. And — that neighbour of Nick Fearnley's had called! No message, just the name and number. Shoving the rest of the messages under the edge of her desk pad, she looked at the last one again. It was too late to return any of

the calls. But she was determined to phone the woman down at
The Landing.

First thing in the morning.

23

LETTY SPEAKS HER MIND

Meanwhile, Lettice Snelgrove was having her own problems. Tom Bartlett was demanding more and more of her time. Telephoning her late at night when she was too tired to do more than listen. Complaining about his son and his house repairs and his on-going dispute with another senior manager at the plant. Wanting, well, it was more like urging her to go out with him again. Each time she told herself she was going to say no the next time he asked her, the nerve of him anyway after all this time, then found herself agreeing to go and afterwards being furious with herself for being so weak.

When she thought about it, though, she had to admit going out with him was doing a lot for her self-confidence. She was secretly thrilled to be able to get out of her house instead of staying home night after night with only the cats for company. She found to her amazement she had no trouble holding her own in a conversation, that is, when she got the chance. Once or twice she'd managed to get Tom to talk about something other than himself, so maybe things were getting better in that respect. They discovered that in spite of Lettice never having lived anywhere but Bickerton, she and Tom had a lot in common. They talked about books they'd read and about the possibility of travelling to Europe. Or maybe even the Orient. And they loved good food. He was teaching her about the pleasures of the table and encouraged her to try new cheeses and pastries from one of those quaint little places called a deli that you had to know where to find in the City. She found herself getting seriously interested in wines and how to tell the good from the not so good. Her waistline, which never had been something to boast about, was beginning to suffer from these culinary delights and she had to make periodic checks when she got out of bed every morning to see if she could still see her feet.

She guessed this is what people meant by having fun. Doing things with someone whose company you really enjoyed. All this was an entirely new experience for her. She was secretly over-joyed that it was bringing her closer to the only person she'd ever cared for. But, in spite of that closeness, she still hadn't worked up the courage to tell Tom that the best thing he could do about Young Tommy at this stage would be to send the little hell-raiser away to that military style boarding school.

She was dismayed how quickly word spread through town that she and Tom were going together. They'd driven as far away as the other side of Dunhampton, but it soon became obvious the local gossip mill was in its usual efficient working order. She'd had to endure some looks of contempt at the supermarket and in the post office. Once she'd even noticed a couple of her pupils whispering in the corner and giving her sidelong looks. But something deep inside her, some new-found strength left her able to ignore the stares and the whispers. *That Lettice Snelgrove, isn't it disgusting. And at her age too. The trouble with some people is they never learn. Guess it's true you can't teach an old dog new tricks. And him having gone through two wives already.* She ignored it all. As long as she had Tom interested in her again, even if he did dump all his problems on her. She was going to enjoy their eve-nings out and see how things between them developed. She felt a sudden urge to make some drastic changes in her life. Maybe all this gallivanting, this wining and dining, required a brand new wardrobe. And, maybe, just maybe it would even be worth her fixing herself up a bit more.

Following up on this last thought, Lettice made an appointment with Maybelle one Friday afternoon after school to have her hair cut. It had been another horrible week. She was feeling really dragged out. A new hairstyle might just give her a lift. Besides, she had a dinner date with Tom that evening. He'd found yet another restaurant way over past Dunhampton he wanted them to try.

"Dearie me, here's another one who's not taking care of her skin," said Maybelle after a cursory glance at Lettice, who felt her face grow hot. Thinking at first she'd made a mistake coming here instead of going out of town as she usually did to some place where she wasn't known, again she was aware of some inner strength emerging and the blush quickly faded. She felt a stirring of hope. Was she at last overcoming her old fear of rejection?

"Never mind, dearie, you're not alone," Maybelle hastened to reassure her when she saw Lettice's reaction. "Most ladies in this here town don't take proper care of theirselves. And don't you worry none, what goes on inside these walls is safe with me," she continued in her chirpy way, forgetting that she wasn't always that discreet. "Looks like you've been outdoors a lot. Oh yes, I forget. It's that school yard duty that does it to you, eh?"

When Lettice admitted what she really wanted was a makeover, Maybelle handed her a robe and directed her to the change room. "Let me set you up with some steam, dearie, and then we'll try some nice refreshers 'n creams 'n things. You'll be surprised what a difference they'll make. Then we'll get to the hair. Did I tell you about my Spring Special? Everything half off, this week only."

"I hope you're not referring to my hair," said Lettice, being to feel excited at the idea of a change. She was relieved to hear the whole process wasn't going to cost as much as she'd figured. Maybe she'd splurge and get her nails done while she was at it.

Two hours later, she left the Bo-Tay feeling like a new woman. Like Gussie before her, she wondered why she hadn't done this more often. Taking a close look at herself in the hall mirror when she got home, she was delighted with what she saw. Maybelle had given her a different look, the look of a much younger woman. No longer confined to a severe bun, her hair, which Maybelle had cut in layers, looked like soft feathers framing her face which, after liberal administrations of steam, toners and lotions, was now a pearly shade of pinkish ivory. Before letting her go, Maybelle had applied some of her newest cosmetics, 'just to see how they look, dearie, you can always wipe it off when you get home if it doesn't suit', quite of few of which Lettice promptly bought, since she had saved so much on the Special. The haircut, along with the makeup, accentuated her high cheekbones and made her eyes look enormous. On the way home she picked up her best skirt and vest outfit from the cleaners. It was a fine wool tweed in a lovely shade of violet.

As she was contemplating which of her new silk blouses to wear, the winter white or the pale grey, the telephone rang. It was Tom. In a grave voice that sounded very far away, he told her Young Tommy was in big trouble.

"It took me ages to find out what happened, Letty," he said wearily. "Seems he went skating at the rink down by the Senior School, you know the one? One of the parents who was there said he saw Tommy crash into one of the smaller boys from behind, pushing him into another boy. He said the second boy fell backwards and the first boy's skate blade went right into his eye. The doctors in emergency over in Dunhampton aren't sure they can save the kid's eye, it was so badly injured. Someone called the police station and Gussie Spilsbury is down there now talking to the other kids. I managed to hang around long enough to overhear some of it before hauling Tommy home. The kids were all saying the same thing. No chasing, no fighting, nothing. Tommy wasn't provoked, he just skated full tilt into the first kid, deliberately they said, and gave him a real good push. I'm afraid our date's off, Letty. I'm sorry, but I've got to stay here until things have been straightened out with Gussie. She's coming by our place in a few minutes. Oh, Letty, I just can't believe Young Tommy would do something like that on purpose. I mean I know he's been -"

Lettice took a deep breath and said to herself, *well, old girl, it's now or never.*

"Tom. Tom, hold on a minute and listen to me. There's something you should know. Young Tommy's been caught several times over the past few weeks threatening the other kids in my class. He punched one of them pretty hard on the arm the day before yesterday, for no good reason I could see, and he got lippy with me when I reprimanded him. The kids are all scared to death of him. He's even making *me* nervous. I'm never sure what he might do next. He's very strong, you know. And big for his age."

"Why didn't you tell me this sooner?" Tom said, after a long pause.

"Oh, Tom! I've tried any number of times to tell you," Lettice replied in level tones. "I tried to tell you there's a serious problem with your son, but you didn't want to hear it. I was going to bring it up again tonight, even though you're always so busy talking about yourself you hardly let me get a word in edgeways."

There. She'd said it at last. While she'd been talking to him, she realized this must have been what his wives had to put up with, his constant preoccupation with himself. He'd talked so much about the problems with his old house but refused to even consider giving it up, she'd decided he was the one who'd wanted it in the first place, not his second wife. And as for poor little Ella...

There was another long pause. She thought maybe he'd hung up, but she could still hear him breathing into the receiver.

"Am I really *that* bad, Letty?" he said in a low voice. "Is this really all my fault, the trouble with Young Tommy, I mean? I thought it was because his mother took off and left him and he blames me. Come to think of it, maybe that was all my fault, too." He stopped for another long minute and then said, plaintively she thought, "What am I going to do now? About Tommy? What do you think, Letty? I really want to know this time."

So she told him.

24
GOOD NEWS/BAD NEWS

Down at the Woodcocks' little house, everything was in an upheaval. Earlier in the evening, they'd had a call from Albie. A short one, but long enough for him to let Kitty know he was okay and not to worry about him. He said he couldn't come home just yet, but to expect him sometime in the next couple of weeks. As soon as he got there, he said, he promised to tell them what had been going on, but he couldn't talk about it now, especially on the telephone.

Kitty had been the one to take the call and when she'd hung up, sat there with the phone in her hand for the longest time, just staring at it as if it were something she'd never seen before. Jesse was in the kitchen working on a crossword puzzle in his newest birding magazine. When he heard his mother's brief conversation, 'hello, yes … yes, oh yes … no … no … no, I understand … okay … okay I will … love you too, bye', he sat transfixed for a moment, then threw down his pencil and dashed into the living room.

"Mom, Mom, was that Pop, was it him, was it really *really* him, tell me, Mom, was it, *was it?*"

Kitty came to herself, put the phone back on its cradle and said slowly, "Yes … yes. It was your Pop all right."

"Well? Is he coming home? Is he? When's he coming? Mom? M-o-m!" He drew her name out in a long singsong sound.

"I guess so," Kitty said in a whisper. "He said he was. But not right away. Stop it, Jess, you're hurting me!" Jesse had pulled her to her feet and was hugging her so tightly she could hardly speak. Gently detaching his arms from around her waist, she drew him over to sit with her on the sofa to tell him what his Pop had said. At least she tried to, but Jesse was wildly excited and broke away from her. Dancing back and forth in front of her, he was laughing and crying at the same time.

"What'd he say, Mom, what'd he say? Where's he been all this time? Why didn't he come home for Christmas? What was he doing over at the Reserve?"

"At the Reserve?" Kitty looked up in surprise, "I didn't know he was over there."

"Oh yeah, um, I guess I forgot to tell you."

"Forgot to tell me! Jesse Woodcock, stop your hopping about and come over here this instant! What do you mean, forgot to tell me?"

"Well, you remember that time I was over at Adam's? That time after ... after, um, well, Adam told me he saw Pop, well, he thought it was Pop, anyway, he saw Pop with some guys in the old Rec Hall and well, um, Adam got scared and ran home, he said, um, he said they started shouting and he got scared."

"Why didn't you tell me this before?"

"Well I didn't want ... I thought ... well I thought you'd start crying again and—"

"You mean you didn't want to upset me, is that it? Well, I sure am upset now. What in the world he's been doing over there, I can't think. All this time I thought—"

"I know. You thought he was dead. Well he isn't. I knew he wasn't and he isn't, isn't *isn't* dead. And he's coming home!"

Jesse was off again, "He's coming home, Pop's coming home, coming home. Home, home, home!"

Kitty's mind was in a whirl. She leaned back on the sofa, watching her son in his excitement, his eyes shining, his dusky little face aglow, a big smile on it, the kind of smile she hadn't seen since before the episode in the woods. And even though now they knew he was okay, she couldn't help her feelings of resentment towards Albie for having caused them so much anxiety. On top of that, she hadn't gotten around to confronting Jesse with something else.

That morning she'd had a call from Miss Snelgrove, the teacher he was always complaining about. Without any greeting like, 'how are you today, Mrs Woodcock, terrible weather we've been having', Miss Snelgrove said she had been having a lot of trouble with Jesse the past couple of weeks. He was unresponsive in class and was surly and, dare she say it, rude to her when she tried to find out what was bothering him.

"What really concerns me", she went on crisply, "and you should know about this, your son Jesse has not been finishing his classroom assignments on time and three times he has been late handing in his homework."

While Kitty was frantically trying to think of how to respond, Miss Snelgrove said in a still sharper tone, "Mrs. Woodcock, I had better tell you straight out. Your young lad had better pull up his socks soon or I am afraid he will not be passing on to the next grade in June."

By now thoroughly intimidated, all Kitty could manage to do was squeak out a 'thank you' and promise to look into it.

When Jesse came home that afternoon, he'd looked so withdrawn and sad, she didn't have the heart to question him about what was going on at school. He mumbled 'hi, Mom', ignoring the snack she'd set out for him, went slowly up the stairs to his room and closed the door. She nearly went up after him, but thought better of it. Later, at suppertime, he'd sat as silent as a little shadow, pushing the food around on his plate, saying he wasn't hungry when she commented on his lack of appetite. She wondered if he was coming down with something. There was a lot of 'flu around. Maybe that was it. But then again ...

Ever since it happened, he hadn't uttered a word about his discovery in the woods, but changed the subject every time she tried to bring it up. She thought it would be much better for him if she could get him to talk about it. She knew it still preyed on his mind, she could hear him muttering in his sleep at night. And he'd lost the happy little boy look she loved so much. He was growing up so fast, it was scary.

Seeing the transformation that came over him when he heard his Pop was coming home, her pride took a blow. *I wonder how he'd act if I'd been the one who left and was coming back, would he have been as excited to see me?* And then she scolded herself. *What a silly fool you're being, Kathryn Woodcock! Get away from me, you green-eyed monster, this is no time to be thinking like this. You know he idolizes his Pop and that's as it should be with a young boy.*

Was he having trouble at school because of his uncertainty over Albie's whereabouts? Or was it because the discovery of the body had upset him so much that he couldn't think about anything else? For someone his age, not being able to tell anyone about it had put him under still more of a strain. All of this went milling around in her head as she listened to her son singing happily to himself in the kitchen.

By the time Jesse enjoyed a nightcap mug of cocoa with her and had been sent off to bed, still up in the clouds about his Pop coming home, she was almost too tired to think over the events of the day. She knew she'd have to question Jesse about his schoolwork. Maybe tomorrow, when things had calmed down a bit. As for the other problem, maybe a call to the lady cop wouldn't hurt. She made up her mind to get a hold of Gussie first thing in the morning and see if she had any ideas on how to handle the situation with the body. After all, she'd been the one to take Jess into the woods, something Kitty regretted having allowed. She should have insisted on going with them. But then, what if it had been Albie he found? There was no easy answer to that one and anyway it was done now. In her heart of hearts,

Kitty knew this time she was beyond her depth. She realized she should have done something about the situation with Jess before now, but somehow she'd just let things drift. *She* was the one who'd have to pull up her socks or she'd fail her son. She needed help and she needed it right now. She couldn't wait for Albie to put in an appearance. It might be too late.

And there was no use pretending she could handle this situation on her own.

25
MORE SURPRISES

"I hear Miz Crumb's taken another tumble," announced Dottie one evening early in March, while she and CeeCee were clearing away the supper dishes. Rab had gone back out to the shop to straighten up the shelves for the next day. The two women usually used the brief time he was away to exchange the latest gossip gleaned from the day's customers.

"My, that woman does fall down some," Dottie continued, putting the milk and the butter in the refrigerator. "Her nephew Hughie, ya know, that nice looking redhead comes in for a loaf of brown bread and a quart of buttermilk every other day? He told me all about it this afternoon when ya were out back. Looks like she'll be housebound for another long spell. Thought I'd drop in and see if she'd be wantin' a few books to pass the time with. Maybe I'll get Rab to take me up to Bickerton tomorrow. There's a few other things I'm after over there."

CeeCee dried her hands carefully on an old towel and took off her apron. "That poor soul! What bad luck. How many times has it been now?"

"Three, I make it. Must be somethin' not right with her ballast," replied Dottie, who was stacking the clean plates in the cupboard.

CeeCee smiled to herself. Dottie must have meant balance. Unless that was another language peculiarity from Back East.

Sitting herself back down at the kitchen table after giving it a good swipe with the dishrag, CeeCee leaned forward on her elbows, heedless of the damp oilcloth.

"You know, Dottie," she began, "Been thinking—"

"Don't think too hard, ya might strain somethin'." Dottie's laugh was muffled, as she stored the last of the pots in the tiny pantry off the kitchen. "Just teasin', don't ya know?" she said, reappearing in the doorway. "That's what my old Gram used to say to us kids. Go on. Ya were sayin'?"

"Well," began CeeCee again, rubbing at the damp spots on her sleeves, "about time I went back over to the house and, well, started clearing out. Put it off long enough. Got to face it some-time. Don't think I can bear to live there any more," she added as an afterthought.

"I bin waitin' to hear ya say that, lovey. The clearin' out I mean. I knew ya'd come round to it in your own good time," said Dottie, foreseeing a minefield ahead if she referred to the last part. Draping her favourite cardigan with the frayed cuffs over her shoulders, she sat down on the opposite side of the table. "Want me to come with ya? I'd be glad to give ya a hand."

"Awfully good of you, but no. Ought to do this myself."

"Are ya sure 'bout that? Goin' over there all on your lonesome?"

"Well, what we could do is, I could drop you off at the library and—"

"Oh, 'twon't take all that long," Dottie said, airily. "If Miz Crumb wants books, young Sherry has a list of what I already took her. I got fed up with tryin' to figure what to pick out for her the last time. Anyways, I don't think much of the idea of ya goin' way out there alone. To the house, I mean. We don't know what all might have been goin' on. It's been awhile since Rab could get over and check."

"You're right as usual," CeeCee sighed. "Let's go tomorrow morning then, right after breakfast. Before I change my mind."

Inside the Bickerton library, Sherry Roxton looked up from the stack of books she'd been sorting and greeted them with a smile. "I haven't seen you two here for quite a spell. What've you been up to? Terribly long winter, isn't it. Spring's forgotten all about us. What can I do for you? Something in particular you're looking for?"

"It's Miz Crumb. You see—" Dottie began, but Sherry interrupted her. "I already heard. Yesterday, on my way home. Too bad, eh? More of those real people books, is it? Let me have a looksee."

While the librarian and Dottie were putting their heads together over the 'Crumb List', CeeCee wandered over to check out the NEW ARRIVALS shelf. She hadn't felt much like reading lately. Since Hink's death, everything she'd picked up to read seemed so trite, especially the murder mysteries she used to devour with such eagerness. *I'm living in the middle of a murder mystery right now,* she thought, as she absentmindedly leafed through a shiny new paperback with an enormous eye dripping blood on its cover.

As soon as CeeCee was out of earshot, Sherry moved closer to Dottie and said in a low voice, "Something I think you should know, Miss Kibbidge, seeing as how Mrs. Denton seems to be staying at your place. You probably know how she's feeling about — you know — better than anyone."

And she went on to tell Dottie about Jesse Woodcock.

"He comes in here several times a week, mostly to look at bird books, he's crazy about them you know. Birds, I mean," Sherry confided. "But the other day he asked me if we had any books on bows and arrows. Of course I thought he meant Robin Hood or something like that, but he said, no he'd already read that one. No, not books of stories about long long ago, he said, but something that really happened. Like now, he said. 'What exactly do you mean, bows and arrows?' I asked him and he said, looking down at the floor, 'I mean about guys using them to kill other guys, do you have any books like that?' I didn't know what to think. I mean, his mother is a little odd, never goes out much, they say. Do you suppose she was talking to him about what happened to Mr Denton? Surely it's not a fit subject for a kid. The other thing," she said as she opened the books they had chosen for the unfortunate Miz Crumb and started checking them out, "the other thing I forgot all about until that moment. The day before Mr Denton was found? I told the kid about the Great Blue Heron someone spotted over in the Hidden Swamp. Do you suppose—"

Dottie who had been listening attentively, gasped suddenly and whispered back, "It could be, yes, could be *he's* the one what found the body. We were never told exactly what happened and I know it's bothered CeeCee ever since. I wonder ..." And they moved off to continue their conversation between the D to F and G to J aisles.

Out at the Dentons' place, it appeared no one had been there recently. Except for Rab. Dottie pointed out his sunken tire tracks close to the house to CeeCee, who thought she probably wouldn't have noticed them otherwise. She had to admit to Dottie she had never been all that observant. Once inside, they found the air stale and a bit musty smelling. CeeCee had asked Rab to set the furnace just high enough to keep the pipes from freezing, so the place felt chilly as well. She wandered into the kitchen, not looking for anything in particular. As she was about to open the door to the cellar, she heard Dottie's voice calling her excitedly from the direction of the living room.

"For the love of heaven, would ya look at this now! Isn't this a sight!" Dottie exclaimed as CeeCee joined her.

They stood together looking at the Christmas tree. Its needles, or what was left of them on the tree, had turned a shade of silvery beige. Evidently a spider had taken up housekeeping and decorated the branches with dozens of gossamer webs, making the tree look like some kind of ghostly figure standing silently between the draped windows.

"Oh, blast!" CeeCee said in a loud voice, making some lingering needles fall to the floor. "Forgot all about it. Golly, it looks simply hideous, doesn't it. We'll have to drag it outside. Can't leave it like this, it's a real fire hazard."

"Looks like somethin' out of one of them horror movies," agreed Dottie, who secretly adored scary things.

Christmas itself had been a hideous time, as far as CeeCee was concerned. Celebrating, if you could call it that, with the Kibbidges. Trying to enter into the spirit of the season and failing miserably, CeeCee wished she could have spent the whole of Christmas Day in bed and let the Jolly Season pass her by. But the Kibbidges had been so kind and understanding, she didn't have the heart to let them see how she really felt. She didn't want to spoil their fun. They had a beat-up old piano in the tiny room off the kitchen they called the parler. Dottie banged away at the yellowed keys. She played entirely by ear with a great deal of gusto and accompanied Rab who had gotten out his violin, or fiddle as he called it and stomped his boot in time, making the dishes on the oak sideboard rattle. Up until then, CeeCee hadn't known they were at all musical, but they told her that everyone played something or other and sang at the drop of a hat Back East. Second nature, Dottie called it. The two of them sang and played their way through a whole series of Christmas carols, including some that were new to CeeCee.

Several times she had to leave the room. The old familiar tunes made her choke up and she was glad she had her own room where she could have a good cry until she felt better. She'd been extra careful not to drink too much that day, especially when the dinner was put on the table and the sight of the turkey in all its glory brought another flood of memories. The girls had called earlier to say the four of them were flying Down South for the holiday week. They thought they might just as well get some sun since they couldn't persuade their mother to come into the City, and, well, they *certainly* weren't going to traipse away out there, what with all the holiday traffic and the uncertain weather and the state of the roads. CeeCee didn't blame them. But she had no desire to join them.

"Well," said Dottie, after they had disposed of the tree's skeleton and swept up the fallen needles, "where do ya want to start?"

"Oh well, I guess with Hink's things. His clothes and stuff. Oh Dottie, can't tell you how much I'm dreading this."

"Tell ya what," said Dottie, when they'd climbed the stairs and opened the doors to the enormous double closets in the bedroom, "I'll make a start on this stuff and ya get back down and look for some boxes or bags or somethin' to put it in."

"Good idea," said CeeCee, who escaped back down the stairs, through the kitchen and down into the cellar.

Dottie started pulling the clothes out of what had been Hink's closet and heaping them on the bed. *My, he did have a lot of stuff,* she said to herself, as she detached at least half a dozen pairs of beige pants, all exactly the same style, from their hangers and dumped them on top of a large pile of sports shirts in shades of green and brown. *I suppose these could go to that second hand shop up to Cooley's, they're hardly worn at all, some poor soul will be awful glad of them,* she thought as she got to the last pair with only a few coins and a clean handkerchief to show for her efforts.

Mr Denton sure was neat in his habits. Not like her brothers and her father. You never knew what all you were going to find in their pockets when you turned them out before throwing them in the wash. Half-empty packets of matches, flattened cigarettes, well-used handkerchiefs, bits of string. And always lots of spare change. Once she even found a five dollar bill, which each brother insisted was his, but which she turned over to her mother, putting a quick end to the bickering. "Wait a minute," she said out loud, "what's this?" From the last pocket of the last pair, she withdrew a piece of stiff blue paper that had been folded into a small square. Carefully unfolding it, she saw there was something on it written in pencil. The words were hard to make out, so she took it over to the window and held it up against the light.

H — Need to meet with you ASAP down at The L

Thurs 2 pm okay? maybe I can explain then – F

This looks like somethin' that young Gussie woman ought to see, Dottie said to herself, carefully laying the note down on one of the dressers just as CeeCee came into the room with a bunch of empty cardboard boxes.

26

ELIZA'S MYSTERIOUS VISITORS

About the same time CeeCee and Dottie were occupied with the difficult and, for CeeCee, agonizing task of sorting over Hink's possessions, Syd was making his usual weekly call to Gussie to see if she had anything new to add to his 'On the Bickerton Beat' column.

"Sho shorry. Mishter Shpilsb'ry. Snot in," the nasal voice of Myrna the receptionist informed him, after the phone had rung about ten times. "Kin I givver a mishidge?"

"Do you, uh, know when she'll be back?" asked Syd, puzzled at the odd response. What was going on over there? "I really need to talk to her. By tonight," he added.

"We-e-ell now, jes' a minute, lemme shee, could be anytime shoon," the voice continued lazily. It sounded like Myrna had her mouth full of something. Chocolate creams, no doubt. He knew she had a weakness for them. They didn't do much for her figure, though. She could barely squeeze her enormous bulk in behind her desk. She had a pretty face, which was deceptive when you first came in and saw her sitting down. But if she happened to stand up while you were still there, well ...

"Do you know where she went, then, Myrna?" Syd persisted. He was rapidly losing patience with the woman. He wondered if she reacted the same way in an emergency. It would be awfully frustrating for the person who was calling in for help. Impossible in fact. But since she was a daughter of one of the many sisters of the old constable, Gerald, there was no use complaining. They were Bickertons after all.

"Couldn't shay. But sh'did mention umpthin er other 'bout goin' over Dunhampton way."

By now, Syd was thoroughly fed up.

"Myrna!" he said sternly, "have you been drinking?"

"We-e-ell, no-o-o. Why d'y'ask?"

"Because I can hardly understand a thing you're saying!"

"We-e-ell, it could be theesh dee-lish-us choc'lates my new boyfren' gimme. Yuh know, Eldon Shtimp-, ah, Shtimpshon? Kinda bald? Got 'imshelf a job at Shpilsb'rys las' week. Eldon, now, he tol' me they're ex, exsh-pair, uh, ex-shpair-um -."

"Experimental!" Syd said explosively, not being able to wait any longer for Myrna to get out the word. "What in the world do you mean by 'experimental'?"

"Thersh um, uh, some new taste in 'em, think ish called, uh, 'hint-o-rum 'n then thersh 'gin-dandy', um, that one zreal good. Nice 'n gooey, jes' the way I like 'em 'n then thersh — jes' a minute. Tryin' t' read th' label. Oh yesh, 'dam-brewie' 'n—"

It's Drambuie, you idiot, Syd wanted to shout, but instead he told Myrna she better get some strong coffee into her right away and to tell her boyfriend the Spilsbury company ought to try again. Experimental indeed.

It was more than two hours later when he finally heard from Gussie.

"Syd, oh Syd! You'll never believe what I just found out!" said Gussie excitedly. "I just got back from that nursing home over in Dunhampton, you know, Our Happy Home? What a name for a place like that! Anyway, I wanted to visit Mrs. Roxton, Eliza Roxton. I heard, oh never mind what I heard. Anyway, you remember the old lady? The one who was always calling Dad to complain about cars turning around in her driveway? She used to live in that big rockpile of a place? Up on the hill?"

"How could I forget her," said Syd. "She was always phoning my Dad to complain about something in the *Bugler*. She was after him all the time, told him he ought to put more in the paper about the Roxtons. All the wonderful things they'd done for the town. Why them I could never figure out, since she wasn't really a Roxton, only married to one. Wasn't she a Gaffield or something?"

"Not a Gaffield, that was her first husband. No, she was from another branch of that awful family, the Watsons. Have you forgotten? Everyone said she slept her way into big money. What an awful thing to say. Anyway, they told me over there she'd been without any visitors for ages. For at least five years they said. Until last fall, that is. In October or November or something. Two men who said they were her nephews came in to see her late one afternoon." Gussie paused for breath.

"Nephews?" said Syd into the gap. "I thought the only relatives she had left around here were George and Sherry."

"Well, the people I talked to at the Home said that's what these two guys told them. You have to sign in every time you go in there as a visitor. And sign out too. They put their names down as Jake and Charlie whatever. The last name was impossible to make out. I got them to show me the register book. It looked like someone had smudged the ink while it was still wet. Run a thumb over it, looked like. Whether they did it on purpose, you couldn't tell," Gussie barely paused for breath.

"Anyway, the Home has a real strict policy when someone unknown to them comes in to visit for the first time. One of the staff has to accompany them and stay with them for as long as they're there. It was busy that day, they said. Some of the rooms down one wing were being renovated, so there were all kinds of people, workmen, you know, in and out all day. Three of the regular staff were off sick with some kind of virus, so they were short handed.

"The only person around at the time was one of the young nurses they were training in how to deal with old people, so they got her to escort these two guys to Eliza's room. It's in the nicer part on the second floor, real pretty view from up there, not that she looks at it. Seems to stay in her bed most days. Not long after the three of them had gone up, about five minutes or so, I think, something happened in the room next door to Eliza's. One of the guests, that's how they refer to their residents, they never call them patients, I think it was a man, fell out of bed or lost his footing in the bathroom or something like that and started calling for help, so the nurse left the two guys alone with Eliza for a few minutes and went next door to see what was going on."

Syd didn't need to ask any questions or probe for information. Gussie was on a very unaccustomed roll.

"When she got back, the old lady was in a fit of hysterics, crying and screaming for them to get out and the nurse had to ask the two guys to leave. They had to give Eliza a strong dose of some kind of medicine to calm her down. The receptionist on duty that day doesn't work there any more, but the manager said he remembered she reported that before they left, the two guys told her Eliza got upset because she hadn't seen them for such a long time. The manager said he thought that was kind of funny. He thought she would have been real glad to see some of her relations.

"By the time they figured out that something wasn't quite right, the two guys were gone. No one had seen them drive into the parking lot so they've no idea what kind of a car they came in. The manager said they don't bother with a parking attendant because they have so few visitors. He said he told the receptionist if the two ever came back, they were not to be allowed in and she should let him know right away. But they've never shown up again."

While she'd been talking, Syd noticed she hadn't repeated herself. Not once. Maybe it was because she was so excited she hadn't had a chance to think about it.

"Wow! Did the two guys put up an argument when they got kicked out?"

"It didn't sound like it, but they left so fast they never signed the OUT column in the register."

"What happened then?" asked Syd. His newsman's curiosity was really aroused now. "Did you get any kind of description of these two characters?"

"Yeah, I got lucky on that score. I got a hold of the receptionist who said she remembered them real well. She said one was tall, over six feet she figured. Dark hair, real black, she said. A real good looker was how she put it. The other was short and heavy-set. Also dark, but acting real nervous. The tall one did all the talking, the other one kept looking around, made her feel jumpy, she said. Still makes her feel weird when she thinks about it. She said if they were brothers, they sure fooled her. They didn't look anything at all alike. She said they stuck in her mind because of the way they were dressed. The tall one was all in black, pants, coat, the works. Very soo-wave was the way she described him. The shorter one was done up like a hunter, a sandy beige or a light grey or some such colour, she said. From head to toe. That's why she remembered them so well. They were such a contrast to each other. And not the usual kind of visitors they get over there either."

"You haven't said, but did you manage to get in to see Eliza after all that?"

"No. They said she hadn't been too well lately and they thought it would be too much for her, seeing as how I was in uniform. They told me to come back in a week or so and wear ordinary clothes, and to let on I was an old friend of George's. She *might* remember him, but it comes and goes. Her memory, I mean. They weren't too hopeful I'd be able to get anywhere with her. They said she's gotten so forgetful since Christmas, the whole thing might be a total waste of time."

"Still might be worth trying again. You never know. So what else have you been doing?"

"Well, I did manage to get up to Cooley's, to the gym you know, and put in a half hour or so on the weights and you'll never guess who I bumped into, doing the same thing. The elusive Mr. Fearnley! I got a call from his neighbour to say he'd come home, but when I phoned him, no answer. So I went down there, but he'd gone out again. He didn't try to avoid me or anything, he told me he just got back from taking some birdwatchers around Costa Rica or Costa del Sol or someplace like that. Then they went from there to some other place. He really has been gone since the neighbour said he was. He said he didn't know about Hink Denton and seemed real shocked when I told him, was speechless, in fact. Then he said he was real sorry to hear it, the Dentons seemed like nice people, not like some of the newcomers we've been getting. When I asked him what he thought of Mr. Denton, he said he found him real boring at first, but then he realized the guy was a serious birder, just a touch over-enthusiastic, is how he put it. But then he said there are lots of novice birders like that and you have to have lots of patience with them and so when he could see Hink was really into it, he passed on a lot of tips about where were the best places to go and what birds he might find there."

"That's great, Gus. That you finally caught up with the guy, I mean. I guess that takes him off the list. Sounds like you've had a busy day. Have you eaten yet? I've really got to see you, it's important."

They arranged to meet at the Cosy Corner for a late snack. Gussie was exhausted, as she seemed to be most days lately. *Must be the spring coming,* she thought as she ran a comb through her hair before leaving the office. *There I go again, blaming the weather for everything.* Scrutinizing her face in the mirror, she thought in spite of being so tired, Maybelle's ministrations sure had made a difference to the look of her skin. Well worth going there for more than her hair. Maybe detective work was as simple as that. Getting people to tell her things without them realizing it was a lot easier when you weren't in uniform.

Grabbing her jacket, she locked the door of her office behind her. She found herself looking forward to eating out with Syd. Like a date almost. *Don't be ridiculous,* she said to herself as she set off down the street towards the restaurant. *It doesn't mean a thing.* She went over their conversation in her head. She'd been so excited that things looked as though they were finally breaking on the case, she'd skipped over the part about needing to see her. *What was that all about? And if Syd thinks Mr. Nick Fearnley's off my list, well, I've got news for him. Or rather, I don't, since I can't show my hand. Not just yet.*

In the last few steps before she reached the entrance to the Cosy Corner, she experienced the strongest flash of intuition she'd had since she started on this case. She hadn't really had a chance to think too much about it at the time, but now she found herself wondering if by any chance the mysterious visitors to Eliza Roxton that day in late October might have been the handsome Pete Wychwood. And maybe, just maybe, the guy dressed like a hunter had been Hinchcliffe Denton.

Since deceased, killed by a person or persons unknown.

27

WINTER DRAGS ON, BUT...

After what Gussie learned when she followed up an urgent call from CeeCee Denton and made a flying visit over to East Thorne, she decided she would have to have it out with Mac. She was beginning to suspect Hink Denton's death might have involved more than one person. But just exactly who — or more importantly why — were questions for which answers still eluded her.

Why was Mac being so close-mouthed about his relationship with Hink Denton? He'd always prided himself on knowing everyone and everything that went on in Bickerton and wasn't at all shy about letting the whole world know it. Especially her. Maybe if she went the long way around and started with what he knew about Eliza Roxton or maybe about the Roxtons in general, she could lead him up to the other things she had questions about without giving anything away.

She also needed to see Ferd Otterley as soon as possible. She'd heard from CeeCee that the Otterleys were planning to go away for a few weeks. Just when they were leaving was uncertain. Francy hadn't been too well since the end of January so it could be they were waiting until she was well enough to travel. CeeCee told her Francy hinted at the upcoming trip when she called to see if they might get together for lunch again. CeeCee said Francy sounded awful. She had a head cold and a terrible cough with the beginnings of laryngitis, she said. CeeCee was afraid her friend might be coming down with pneumonia. She was still confined to her bed. Ferd wouldn't let her get up until she stopped running a temperature. Francy said she was bored silly and would have loved to go out with CeeCee again. She said she and Ferd were getting on each other's nerves. Don't they call it cabin fever, she'd asked CeeCee and CeeCee had said yes, it's common when you've been cooped up in your house for a long time. Had it lots of times. When she heard that, Gussie thought she wouldn't mind being cooped up in *her* house for a while. There were days when she felt utterly worn out. It would be heaven to shut the world out for a while.

The situation with young Jesse Woodcock was also disturbing. Before she went to see Mac, Gussie thought she'd better pay another visit to the little cottage down by the Junior School and see just exactly what was going on. For the umpteenth time, she wished she hadn't taken the boy into the woods with her that day. It was obvious he was still suffering from the after-effects of his horrible experience. She'd talked to Kitty Woodcock on the phone twice and was relieved to hear Jesse's Pop had been in touch with them at long last. Apart from that piece of good news, the rest of what Kitty had to say wasn't so good. She was becoming increasingly worried about her son's moodiness. He changed the subject every time she tried to find out what was bothering him. Or shut up like a clam and went up to his room. Kitty said she was sure the incident in the woods was at the root of it all.

Kitty went on to relay the complaints she'd had from Lettice Snelgrove about his behaviour in class. She said she was ashamed to admit she'd gotten into an argument with the teacher over the subject of Jesse failing to complete his homework on time. She told the teacher in her opinion far too much was being made out of something she didn't believe in — piles of homework for young kids. It was okay to give them the odd assignment now and then. A nature project or maybe a book report or two. Miss

Snelgrove hadn't been at all happy with Kitty's criticism on how she ran her class and the result was that Jesse's term mark was the lowest he'd ever had. Added to that was the report from Dottie on the conversation she'd had with Sherry Roxton about Jesse asking for books on murders done with bows and arrows. Something was going to have to be done about young Jesse Woodcock. And soon. But not being a parent herself, and at this stage she wasn't even sure she wanted any kids in spite of Mac's burning desire to be a grampa, Gussie had no definite idea on how to go about remedying a situation that seemed to spiralling out of control where Jesse was concerned.

During their weekly conversation, which had now become a regular meal together, she asked Syd if he had any ideas.

"Does CeeCee Denton know it was Jesse who found the body, I mean know it for sure? Or is she just guessing?" he asked when they were at the coffee stage of their meal.

"I'd have thought she would have figured it out by now. I didn't want to tell her for sure until I have Kitty Woodcock's permission. Kitty was pretty upset with me, I mean upset with me for taking her son in the first place, you know. And Jesse has to agree too, that's for sure," Gussie said, putting her elbows on the table and wishing she could order some dessert. She decided it was getting late and anyway it was all so good-tasting at the Cosy Corner whatever she chose would be too rich and keep her awake. It was Jennie Brant's fault. She made the most tempting pies and cakes, all heaped with whipped cream or slathered in some kind of divine sauce.

"What about getting the two of them together? CeeCee and Jesse, I mean. With his mother present, of course. It might help the kid if he could meet the person whose life was most affected by what he found in the woods. And it might help CeeCee as well. Do you think she's faced up all the way to her husband being gone yet?"

"No. No, I don't. It's far too soon for that. Anyway, she always seems so calm when I talk to her. Too calm I think. She's escaped to the care of the Kibbidges. Those two took her in and now you'd think they're closer to her than her family. They certainly look after her better than her girls. The only good sign is that she's started to clear out the house. It'll take her ages, I mean ages, they have so much stuff. She told me it was mostly her husband's doing, the paintings, the books and all the rest of it. I wish you could have seen the clothes the man had. She and Dottie are sending all the cartons up to Cooley's. You know? That second-hand store called ReRuns? There were tons of them, and that was only his clothes! She says there's still a room in the basement that's chock full of stuff, I mean chock full. He never threw anything away if he could help it," Gussie said, trying to imagine what it would be like to have that much money to spend on clothes. "It's a great idea, Syd, what you just said. Putting the two together. Formally, I mean. It might solve part of the problem the kid is having. His mother says she can't get him to talk about it, his teacher says he's withdrawn and rude at school, George Roxton says he's had the kid in his office a couple of times. For a friendly little chat as he put it. Says he could see the kid's disturbed about something, but he wouldn't open up to him either."

"You said before you thought Jesse liked you. Maybe if you talked to him first before saying anything to his mother, you'd be able to get somewhere." Syd was pleased that he'd been able to help Gussie out, if only a little bit. Gussie said she'd have to think about that.

Later on, before she said goodnight, Gussie reached up and gave Syd a quick hug and kiss.

"Thanks for the suggestion, about having young Jesse and CeeCee meet. It might just work out at that, for both of them," she said, as they went out to where his truck was parked. When he opened the passenger door for her, she shook her head.

"Thanks anyway, but I'll walk back, I need to think." And she was gone, leaving a surprised Syd with a goofy grin on his face.

Maybe there was still hope for them after all.

28

MORE WEATHER PROBLEMS

Before Gussie could put any of the plans she had discussed with Syd into action, everything changed. After the long dreary weeks of winter, when it seemed the snow would go on falling forever, one night in mid-March, a southwest wind began to blow like billy-o as Mac would have put it, causing a rapid rise in air temperature. Those who lived close to the water were kept awake by the constant cracking and snapping of the ice, sounding like distant gunfire. When morning came, the wind continued its relentless sweep over the landscape and a sun, no longer butter pale, shone hotly orange from a cloudless sky.

In no time at all it seemed, the snowy mountains dominating the landscape around Bickerton flattened into hills, then mere hummocks, then were gone as if by magic. Old-timers who'd seen the phenomenon before said it was just another of Mother Nature's tricks. It meant the snow was so old, it was porous. Full of air, they said. Nothing to it.

And then there was another sudden change. The wind swung around and began blowing from the east, bringing heavy clouds with it. It started to rain. And rain. And rain. When this happened, the old-timers shook their heads and said they'd never seen anything quite like *this*, although they recalled their grandfathers' tales of strange weather when they were young. The heavy downpour caused streams, which had been stifled for

months under layers of ice to emerge and evolve into noisy tor-
rents, tumbling down to meld with the Lake. Fishermen who'd
ventured out on the ice just one day more, in a last push to add
to their catch, found themselves stranded on the rapidly softening ice, which the wind began to break apart and push far down
the lake shore. More than one had to be rescued by Perce who,
along with a couple of his more intrepid buddies, had been com-
mandeered to serve as an Emergency Rescue Squad. Butch's wife
refused to let him go with them. Said it was Bickerton's problem
and why should he risk his life for some pig-headed fishermen
who should know better. Butch was terribly disappointed to be
missing out on all the excitement. He was beginning to think
he'd married his mother.

Mac fumed when he heard about the trouble out on the Lake.

"Shouda called a halt to the ice fishing season by end of
February like I told the Council must be all of four years ago. Slap
a nice big fat fine on anyone staying into March. Stupid waste
of taxpayers' money having to rescue those young hotheads," he
complained to Gussie, when he caught her between emergencies.

"Not now, Dad. Please. Not now. Save it 'til later. I've got to
deal with things as they are right now, I mean, as they are right
now," Gussie said crossly, annoyed at this interruption when she
had all she could do to keep on top of things.

There would be much worse to come if the weather stayed
warm and the thaw continued at this hectic pace. Higher up in
the hills north of the town, there were dozens of old earthen
dams constructed years ago to create ponds along the courses of
smaller creeks, dams that couldn't be trusted to stand up under
the pressure of all that water arriving at once.

Gussie's biggest worry was the school kids. She knew they
couldn't resist fast flowing water any more than moths can
resist flame. She sent a flurry of urgent messages to the nearest
radio station, urging people to keep their children away from
the rivers and creeks where the banks were unstable. She also

warned of the dangers along the back roads, which were now becoming slick with water, their ditches filling up so high that in places it was hard to tell where road ended and ditch began. Especially after dark.

Before, there had been too much snow everywhere. Now there was too much water. Over in East Thorne, those who had chosen to live out their remaining years beside the Old Barge Canal were spending anxious hours, biting their nails, watching the rising water surge and boil between retaining walls whose construction dated back to an earlier century. For once, Francy Otterley had to admit Ferd had been right to insist they look for a house without a proper basement. Some of the older houses bordering the Canal had been built long before the advent of floor drains. At the time, Ferd said those kind of basements were unheated for the most part, and had such low ceilings it was impossible for most people to stand erect. Especially in this day and age, when people were taller than their ancestors. Anyway, he said, that space had been intended for storing preserves and coal and not much else. Damp musty places some of them were too. Full of spiders and other creepy-crawly things. The way he went on about it made Francy's skin feel all crawly. Ferd kept saying he wished he'd bought that sweet little old flat-bottomed punt he'd admired at last year's Boat Show in the City. Could have taken them out of there if it got any worse, he said. This did little to reassure the ailing Francy, who was longing to get well enough to go far far away from the cold and damp. Much farther than any old punt could take them. Even if it was just for a couple of weeks. Although lately she'd been having serious doubts about how smart they were to consider abandoning the old house with all this uncertainty.

As the snow and ice receded and the water rose, Ferd began staying up later and later at night, closing himself in his study and pacing the floor. Francy had to shut the door of the spare room, which she now considered her bedroom. It didn't help all that much, since the study was located directly under her. She could still hear him shuffling back and forth and carrying on one-sided conversations with himself. She lay huddled in bed under a heap of wool blankets and comforters, feeling like death warmed over, as she told CeeCee on the phone, listening nervously to the roar of the madly rushing water so close to them, scarcely fifty feet from the front porch. For the first time since they'd left the City, she was frightened. Not so much because of the threat of flooding, but because of what might be causing her husband's distress.

Meanwhile, CeeCee and Dottie were kept hopping in Rab's little grocery store. Whoever built the place had had the sense to locate it on a rise a good distance away from the Canal. People living in the lower lying areas were starting to worry about being flooded out. A trickle at first, their numbers soon became a steady stream of families anxious to add as much as they could carry of food staples and other supplies. Grabbing boxes and tins off the shelves, they compared notes on their situations, asked if anyone had a spare dinghy and where in the heck could you go to escape the rising water if, God forbid, it came to a flood. CeeCee was kept so busy she lost track of time, while Dottie regaled everyone within earshot with stories of storms she'd experienced as a child Back East. Of rugged coastlines where the unforgiving waves were often so high no ships dared try making port. Of winds so strong that houses lost their roofs and dories were smashed to pieces on the rocks. Of getting soaked to the skin in spite of waterproof jackets and sou'westers, those enormous hats worn by seagoing fishermen that make them look like top-heavy schooners.

"I mind the time my Grampa's big old wooden house was flung about so bad in the gale the cables holdin' it down to the rock snapped and it went right off into the bay. And they was steel cables too, as thick as my arm they were," Dottie told CeeCee one lunchtime when there was a lull in the spate of customers and they were enjoying a plate of oatcakes and some kind of cheese with a pleasant nutty flavour to it. When she asked what kind it was, Dottie said Rab got it from some monks up in the hills north of Cooley's Mills.

"Lucky no one was livin' in the place," Dottie went on, helping herself to another generous piece of cheese. "We moved out the summer before, gone to live with my Gram in town or we'd 've gone into the bay with it. And got drownded like my cousin Wully. Him and my two uncles, Henry and Gib, that was, was out fishin' one time 'n got caught in a storm. Never saw hide nor hair of 'em again. My Mam near cried her eyes out. Wully was her favourite nephew. Oh, them were some scary, those times. Want another slice of this cheese?"

"Oh Dottie, must you go on? You're scaring me half to death. No, no more cheese. Beginning to feel like a mouse. Was good though. Lost the rest of my appetite, listening to you," CeeCee said, getting wearily to her feet. "Come on, Dot. Lunchtime's over. Got to unpack those cartons Rab brought in this morning or they'll be in the road."

Dottie noticed with amusement that CeeCee was picking up the local expressions without realizing it. She made a quick tour. The shelves certainly needed restocking. Rab said they were selling the stuff faster than anything had moved out of the place since he took it over. He was afraid if the roads were flooded any worse, he'd have some fun getting any more stock in. So far, so good, he'd said that morning when they were having an early breakfast before opening up for another day of hard work.

"Course we was used to it, it happened every year, special in springtime. The stormin', I mean. But ya never get used to the drownins," Dottie went on, putting up the wooden stepladder she used to reach the higher shelves. "Hand me up a couple of those boxes of oatmeal, will ya, lovey, there's a hole up here needs fillin'." She'd shinnied up the ladder like a monkey and was leaning away from it at a precarious angle. She wore a pair of ancient running shoes, cast-offs of Rab's. They were too large for her and gaped horribly at the sides, but as she said to CeeCee, remembering the elegant shoes that she'd seen in the big closet at the Dentons', 'taint no glamour job, lovey. Anyways, I don't know why but I feel safer with these old things on than me own slippers.'

Just as she was wedging the outsize cereal boxes into the offending space, the bell over the door tinkled and someone they didn't recognize came into the shop, letting in a strong draft that set Dottie's skirts fluttering. The figure marched straight up to the counter, threw back the hood of its silvery rain slicker and the beautiful profile of Maggie Wychwood emerged. *What's that one doin' way over here, slummin' I betcha*, was Dottie's first thought.

Aloud she said, "It's Miz Wychwood, is it? From over to Bickerton? What can I do ya for?" She hitched up her skirts and clambered back down the ladder. "How's things over your way? Oh, I forgot, your place's high and dry, ain't it?"

Maggie shook out her hair, carelessly scattering drops of water over the stand of City newspapers next to the counter.

"I don't need anything," she said in frosty tones, ignoring CeeCee, who was painfully conscious of her own dusty appearance. *Probably makes everyone feel dowdy.* Dottie rubbed her nose with the back of her hand leaving a grey smudge behind and came over to lean on the counter. *What the heck does she want, anyways? Nosey creature that she is.*

Maggie fiddled with the enormous silver button at her throat and shook her hair again.

"Have you seen my husband Peter today? He said he was coming over here, but that was hours ago. We have an appointment and I need to find him," she said in an accusing tone, as if it was Dottie's fault Pete hadn't come home.

My husband Peter, she says! I feel like askin' her if she has more than one husband. Dottie shook herself mentally. *Now, now, Dorothy, my girl, mustn't be rude to the customers.*

"How do ya like this weather?" Dottie asked conversationally. "Stuck it out all winter, didn't ya. We figured ya'd have gone south. With the birdies an' all." She stood with her hands braced on the counter and waited.

A look of scorn directed straight at Dottie came over Maggie's lovely face.

"I *never* expose my skin to the sun," she said, tersely. "You haven't answered my question." *I repeat. Have you seen my husband today or not?*

Aha! Struck a nerve there, didn't I. Dottie had to bite hard into her lower lip to keep from crowing.

"Come to think on it," she said after a short pause. "Mister Wychwood *was* in here, but it was a good while ago. Somethin' 'bout business with Rab, but that one's off to help an old friend. Fool left his pickup too close to the water over by The Landin' and couldn't get it started. Thinks it'll be swamped if he can't get it moved."

"That's nothing to do with *me* ," Maggie said impatiently, with another shake of her head, sending more drops of water over the newspapers. "Did Peter happen to say where he was going from here?" she asked, moving closer to the counter. As she did so, Dottie straightened up to her full height, which was easily a head shorter than Maggie, and said no, he didn't. CeeCee watched in fascination as the two women looked as if they were about to get into a catfight. But the moment passed. Maggie pulled her hood back up over her head, turned and abruptly left the shop, nearly colliding with two people who were coming up the front steps. They heard a car door slam and the roar of a powerful engine start up and fade away.

"Well," said CeeCee, in a low whisper, "what was all that about? Dottie, you know perfectly well Rab was here when Mr.

Wychwood came by. Why did you make up that story about the pickup?" she demanded, keeping a weather eye on the newcomers, not wanting to get into a discussion in front of them that might look like an argument.

"Wouldn't give that woman the satisfaction. The poor guy can't go anywheres without her having to know where he is. He's been here before, ya know. Lots of times," Dottie said, coming around the counter and feeling the damp newspapers to see if they were still saleable.

"Him and Rab get along real good," she added, smugly.

CeeCee opened her mouth as a question popped into her head, but shut it again as more customers came into the shop. This was an interesting new side to her friend, a side that she hadn't caught even so much as a glimpse of before.

Until now.

29

GUSSIE'S LIST

It was the calm after the storm, as Dottie put it. Only she pronounced it to rhyme with ham. After more than forty-eight hours of heavy downpour, the rain finally slackened off and the sun began to tentatively show its face again, 'as it always does do,' Dottie said to CeeCee and Rab at breakfast, 'only there's some as has no faith', and to shine down on the bleak and sodden fields. The winter's accumulation of ice on the Lake had been blown far away to the west and the chunks left high and dry on land wouldn't last much longer under the strengthening sun. Slowly the frighteningly high water level in the Canal and in the creeks and streams draining into the Lake began to drop. People who only a little while ago had been worried sick about being flooded out, went out to take a look at the slower moving currents and told each other the danger had passed and it was safe to think about getting things back to normal. Some of them could, that is. For others, things would never be normal again.

Gussie was one of those. At the height of the flood scare, Mac who was just nicely over a bad dose of 'flu decided he'd better check up on a few things around his property. Having dozed off in his chair after a late lunch, he was in a hurry to get outside before what was left of the daylight was gone. Still feeling weak and dizzy, he decided to go down to the boathouse. Pulling on his raincoat and an old pair of boots, he took a stout cane from the umbrella stand in the back kitchen and made his way cautiously down the narrow path leading to the edge of the Lake. He hadn't been able to get down there since that first unexpected snowfall and congratulated himself he'd been good and ready when the sudden arrival of winter put an abrupt end to the pleasures of life on the open water. Most years, like so many other boaters he knew, he'd put off storing his boat until the last possible moment. There was always the off chance the weather would stay good until Christmas. This year, for some reason he couldn't quite recall, he'd stowed everything away early. Up until the day of the Big Thaw, as it would come to be known locally, the snow on the path to the Lake had been hip high, putting the boathouse out of bounds for the winter. He was anxious to see if there had been any damage from the ice that the fierce south west winds had driven over the jagged rocks bordering the shore.

The air was thick with moisture. Several times he had to stop and wipe off his glasses. The path twisted and turned between clumps of silver birch and enormous boulders as it sloped down towards the Lake. Several times he slipped, nearly losing his footing and had to stop for breath. Funny. He couldn't remember it ever taking him this long to get down before. Just beyond the corner of the old boathouse, which loomed at him out of the fading light, he could see enormous slabs of ice piled up on top of each other, looking like so many bloated bodies of beached whales. This was easily the most ice he could ever recall seeing along the shore. Usually it had been broken up into small chunks before it got this far.

After a few more slips and stumbles, he was relieved to reach the wall of the sagging grey structure his grandfather had put up years ago. Another step and then Mac was startled to see that instead of being locked up tight the way he'd left it, the side door was wedged open with an enormous chunk of what looked like pink granite. He stopped in dismay. *Now who in the heck, what kind of tomfoolery is this? The place'll be in a mess, all kinds of snow'll've gotten in, never mind 'coons, leaves, dirt, whatever else. How in heck did that happen?* Using his cane as a crowbar, he prodded at the offending rock, but it refused to yield. Giving up on the cane, he hunkered down and tried to move it out of the way with both hands. A sudden shooting pain in one arm made him wince. He must have pulled a muscle. Happened a couple of times before. Forgetting about the rock, he grasped the door-frame and eased himself over the sill.

But a pulled muscle it wasn't. That evening, just as Gussie had gotten in the door of her house and was taking off her coat, the phone rang.

"Think. I've done it. This time. Gus," Mac's voice croaked, sending a chill through her.

"Dad! What happened? Are you all right? I can hardly hear you! Dad? Dad!"

There was a pause. Then the raspy voice started up again.

"Terrible pain. In my chest. Hurts to breathe. And. It's gone. The boat. It's not. Can you—?"

"Hold on, Dad!" Gussie shouted into the phone, "I'll be there as quick as I can. Just sit tight now, I'm coming!" She broke the connection and called over to Dunhampton Hospital for an ambulance. No luck. All she got was a busy signal. With a shaky finger, she dialed the doctor's number. Luckily, Bill Blair had just come in from another call and said he'd head straight down to Mac's and meet her there.

"Sounds like he might be having a heart attack," he said laconically just before the phone went dead, throwing Gussie for a loop. *That was kind of a dumb thing to say, he hasn't even seen Dad yet,* she fumed. Fighting down panic, she struggled back into her coat and ran back out to her car, driving as fast as she dared through the pouring rain down the slippery road past The Landing to the old house.

And a mild attack it wasn't. Mac was rushed off to the hospital over in Dunhampton in Doc Blair's car with Gussie leading the way, Mac groaning, her own heart pounding. Before they left, she just had time to make a couple of calls. First to Syd. No answer. Where could he be tonight, she thought frantically, then remembered the regular Town Council meeting had been called earlier than usual to make sure all their emergency plans were ready to be activated. Then to the station. Thank God she got through right away. She left a message with Myrna to keep on trying to reach Syd and tell him what had happened and would he please meet her at the hospital. She was counting on him to follow his usual routine and go back to the *Bugler* office after the meeting. Finally, a quick call to the faithful Perce, where she was told he was out on a call down past The Landing. That was odd. She hadn't noticed anything going on there on her way down. The girl at the Cooley's station didn't say what it was about, said they'd tried to reach her, but something was wrong with the phone lines between them. Everything was happening at once, it seemed.

On the way over to Dunhampton, Gussie decided she had to face it. This job was too much for one person. The Town Council would have to be convinced it was high time they antéd up and hired a deputy. It might mean she'd have to take a cut in pay. So be it. She couldn't go on like this. Lately, she'd been so exhausted she couldn't do the job properly. Just that morning alone, she'd had a whole series of minor emergencies to deal with: a stalled delivery van blocking Main Street with several very irate drivers held up on either side (she managed to get everyone calmed down and the van towed away before there was a fistfight); a woman up near the highway being threatened by her teenaged daughter (the girl's mother accused her of taking money from her purse and the girl had gotten a knife from the kitchen, which she might have used only Gussie was alerted by a neighbour and got there in time to sort it out); and, a report of a ten-year-old boy missing since the evening before (he'd gone home with a friend and stayed the night without letting his parents

know). All this, added to the usual complaints that had to be followed up.

There was tension everywhere. Easy to blame the miserable
weather that seemed to have no end. On top of everything else,
she was getting complaints from Head Office in Dunhampton
that she was miles behind in her paperwork again and hadn't she
made any further progress on the Denton case. And she hadn't
been getting much sleep lately from a persistent cough left over
from the cold she'd had months ago.

Maybe she should tell the Big Brass in Dunhampton she was
throwing in the towel on the Denton case. She didn't seem to be
getting anywhere with it. But then, if she did that and someone
else took over at this stage, she would be letting CeeCee and her
family down. Not to speak of herself. As a woman, she felt under
constant pressure to prove she was up to the job. After all, as
Mac was constantly reminding her, good old Constable Gerald
had coped just fine on his own. She'd given up reminding him
there were a lot more people living in the area than when good
old Constable Gerald was in charge.

Doctor Blair had a rush call to go back to in Bickerton and
left, promising to check with her later. The hospital waiting
room was almost empty. A young couple huddled in one corner
looking grim and whispering to each other were the only other
occupants. Taking a seat on a dull brown sofa that looked like it
had seen better days, Gussie reached for one of the dog-eared
magazines on the coffee table, then drew back. Waste of time.
These magazines looked like they'd been there since the Second
World War. Hoping she wouldn't have too long a wait before the
attending doctor came out to tell her what was going on with
Mac, she hauled out her notebook and reviewed what she'd
learned about the people who might have been involved in Hink
Denton's death.

Let's see. First there was Nick Fearnley. He claimed he'd
been out of town when Hink died, but she had only his word

and the word of his neighbour to go on. She'd have to contact the people he said he'd been guiding on a birding expedition at the time. Nick said after he left them, they'd gone on some kind of extended tour farther south and weren't due back home to Cooley's Mills until sometime in early April.

Then there was Ferd Otterley. According to CeeCee Denton, his wife Francy said his behaviour had changed drastically over the last little while. *Was he afraid that once the snow was gone, the woods that had been so inaccessible all winter could be searched?* CeeCee also said Francy seemed to think Ferd had considered Hink Denton a close friend. She said that ever since they met, the two men had been competing with each other when it came to bird lists. Surely that was harmless enough in itself. But what was upsetting her husband so much that she complained about his behaviour more than once to CeeCee, who felt it important enough to pass on?

Pete Wychwood, now. Getting drunk was totally out of character for him. First, at New Year's. Well, lots of people do that. But then, at the Snake Pit? It's the sort of place where younger people hang out, not men of Pete's standing in town. And why was Tom Bartlett with him? Or had someone else called Tom to take Pete home? And another puzzle. Had it been Pete at the Our Happy Home that day back in the fall? Or had she just been guessing from the description she got from the receptionist? Maggie Wychwood said she didn't keep track of every move her husband made, that he wasn't fastenened to her apron strings. *As if a woman like her would be caught dead in something as unglamorous as an apron.* That statement contradicted what Dottie Kibbidge said about Maggie coming in to Rab's little grocery store looking for him. Why did she want to know his whereabouts on that particular day? According to Dottie, Pete had complained to Rab that his wife didn't care what he did. And, if it turned out it was Pete visiting that day at the Our Happy Home, what was his interest in old Eliza Roxton? Other than her house, which Maybelle said Maggie longed so desperately to own?

Tom Bartlett. He was a good friend of Pete's. Gussie thought it was kind of curious he'd taken a sudden interest in Lettice Snelgrove after all these years. Poor Lettice. Everyone in town knew how badly he'd once treated her. They also knew she was still carrying a torch for him. Why was he seen taking her to the best places around? Did he need her for an alibi for some reason? Or was he just feeling nostalgic? Could it be their renewed relationship was just a coincidence? But Gussie, like most people in law enforcement, didn't believe in coincidences.

CeeCee Denton herself. No. That was ridiculous. From everything she'd heard, the Dentons seemed to have been reasonably happy, as happy as you'd expect an old married couple to be. As far as she could determine, Hink didn't have a reputation for playing around or gambling or any of the other vices that men who retire when they're not quite ready to have been known to get mixed up in. When they're suffering from a loss of status. Or a fear of aging. Or not having some place to go every day and a pay cheque every two weeks to show for it. All the things Mac had once told her can happen when you retire when he was wondering if he'd given up his store too soon. And had to rely on being re-elected every three years. Anyway, from what she'd seen of CeeCee, the woman certainly didn't seem the type who would get rid of her husband in order to get her hands on the money quicker. If anything, Hink was the extravagant one of the pair. Or rather, had been. CeeCee seemed content with a simpler way of living, or she wouldn't have stayed so long with the Kibbidges.

Everything Gussie had come across in her reading about the suspicious death of a husband or wife said you had to check out the spouse before anyone else. But Gussie could still remember the stricken look on CeeCee's face when she was told her husband's body had been found. Those were no crocodile tears she'd shed, especially when she had to identify the body. She'd come close to collapsing in the doctor's office, if the staunchly loyal Dottie hadn't been supporting her. Unless the woman was one heck of an actress, Gussie was sure CeeCee Denton had been genuinely overcome with grief.

Gussie had done her best to find out if Hink Denton had made any enemies in the City. But nothing she learned about him had been of any use. The calls she'd made to the places where he'd been employed, and there were only three, all told her the same story. Hinchcliffe Denton had been a sober, reliable, honest, hardworking employee. His presence had left no lasting mark. Oh sure, his former managers were very sorry to hear that he was gone. And without much time to enjoy his retirement, either. But she thought they said it only out of politeness. Recalling what CeeCee Denton had told her, Gussie thought Hink must have undergone a complete change in personality after retiring and taking up a vastly different life in a basically rural community that some might call the backwoods, far removed from the one he'd led in the City. She'd had to choke back the urge to tell his former employers their unremarkable and colourless employee had been buried wearing flashy orange socks.

Something kept niggling at her as she sat in the dreary waiting room, something that had occurred to her while she mulled over what few facts she'd assembled on the case. *What the heck could it have been? Have I really covered everyone?* While she was puzzling over it, she thought it kind of odd that no one else had come into the waiting room in all that time. It must have been a quiet night for emergencies in Dunhampton. But then they hadn't had the rain to the same extent as Bickerton. It was amazing how much difference a distance of fifty-seven miles could make to the weather. Then she remembered what it was. Maybe that hadn't been Hink Denton with Pete Wychwood that day at the Our Happy Home. Maybe, just maybe, it had been someone else. Who else had she talked to who might have seemed a bit scary looking to the receptionist at the nursing home?

The only other person was that Joe Gaffield who ran the Quick Bite. If you thought about it, the guy *could* be called scary looking, with his heavy jowls and massive hairy hands. Could he have been hiding something from her, know more about what happened than he let on? He seemed jumpy enough the day she'd gone in to talk to him. But she thought it was because he was worried about the pot of chili he had cooking in that smelly kitchen of his. He must have known that Nick Fearnley was back, but he never called her. Even though he knew she was looking for the elusive birding guide. Nick spent so much time at Joe's, it was probably one of the first places he'd gone when he got home. Joe must have told him about Hink Denton's death and yet. And yet that day up in the gym at Cooley's, Nick acted like it was the first he'd heard about it. She'd have to go back down to The Landing and talk to both of them again.

Wait. There was someone she'd left off her list. Mac. No. Not Mac. Her mind kept veering away from that possibility. But what if, as she had long suspected, what if Mac knew more about what had happened than he was telling her. Every time she brought up the subject of Hink Denton, Mac left her with the distinct feeling he was holding something back. She'd have to face up to it. Her beloved Dad, who prided himself on knowing everything about everyone, hadn't been straight with her. And now, with his having a heart attack, what chance would she have of finding out just what he did know?

30

MAC'S CONSCIENCE GETS
THE BETTER OF HIM

By the time the specialist from the cardiac ward finally showed up, Syd had arrived. He and Gussie were sitting close together deep in conversation and scrambled to their feet when the doctor appeared.

"Constable Spilsbury? Your father's resting quite comfortably now, but he's going to have to stay put here for a while." The doctor cleared his throat and blinked. He had a round baby face and a nervous smile. *This guy can't be a specialist, he looks like he's fresh out of medical school,* was Gussie's first thought, as she stood looking down on him.

"He's had a bad time of it with his heart, I'm afraid. The prognosis is not too good" he added, answering Gussie's question before she had a chance to ask it. Gussie burst into tears and turned back to Syd, who held her close, making comforting sounds.

"Can we see him now?" he asked, over her shoulder, fishing awkwardly in his jacket pocket for the large handkerchief he always carried. He handed it to Gussie, who took it gratefully and mopped at her eyes.

"I'm sorry, Doctor," Gussie said trying not to sniffle. "I don't usually get this emotional. I can't afford to. Not in this job, I mean not in this job. That would have been my next question.

Can we go in and see him?" she asked, giving her nose a good blow in the hankie and stuffing it in her back pocket. "I'll be all right now, it's just the shock, I mean just the shock. Syd was just telling me Dad thought he might have a problem, but he made Syd promise not to tell me. I'm in the middle of a really difficult case right now and he thought it would just worry me if I knew."

The doctor looked from one to the other.

"Are you a relative?" he said to Syd.

"He's my husband," Gussie said, quickly taking a hold of Syd's hand again.

"That's okay then," said the doctor, with another nervous smile. "Right through this door. But only for a very few minutes. He's very weak."

Gussie was horrified when she saw Mac in the oxygen tent. He looked smaller somehow, shrunken almost. His normally ruddy cheeks, even his nose with its network of broken blood vessels, looked ashen and his eyes were shut. They thought he was asleep, but as soon as he felt Gussie touch his hand, he opened them. Without turning his head, he rasped, "Sorry, Gus. Shouda said."

"Hush, Dad. It's okay. It's going to be okay," Gussie said, trying to convince herself that it would be. "Don't try to talk. Just rest now."

"That's right, just take it easy," was Syd's contribution. He was still reeling from Gussie saying he was her husband. Did that mean ....

"Denton," said Mac distinctly. Then, "Letter. Desk." He closed his eyes again from the effort. "Find letter."

"I'm afraid that's long enough," the doctor's voice came as if from far away. "If you'll just step outside for a few minutes, I can—"

At Mac's words, Gussie had straightened up from where she'd been leaning over her father.

"Did you hear that?" she turned to Syd, who'd moved in behind her.

"Sure did," he said in a low voice. "Sure did. Let's get out of here."

Gussie gave his hand another squeeze and told him they'd be back as soon as they were allowed and to be good now and do what the doctor told him. Mac kept his eyes shut, but through the tent they could see a little colour was slowly creeping back into his face.

He thinks we're back together, Gussie said to herself. Well ...

"Are we?" she said to Syd as they reached the hospital parking lot.

"Are we what?"

"Back together. Dad thinks we are. Didn't you see his face?"

Syd took both her hands in his and turned her to face him.

"I'm game if you are," he said slowly. "I was a fool to leave in the first place. It was all because of the *Bugler*. I really hate the thing. I wish I could close the door on it and never go back."

"But, but you said -"

"Never mind what I said. I was wrong." He held her close in the warmest hug he'd ever given her. They stood for a moment, enjoying each other's proximity. Then Gussie pulled back.

"The letter. What Dad was trying to tell us. I've got to know. Coming with me?"

Back in the hospital, Mac lay half in and out of consciousness. He didn't know whether he was talking out loud or if it was all in his head.

Told her. Shoulda done it. Ages ago. Wonder what she'll think? Wonder...

31
AN INTERESTING EVENING

On their way back to Mac's house from Dunhampton Hospital, Gussie and Syd ran into more rain. Their already tired eyes were soon burning from having to peer through water sheeting off their windshields in spite of running the wipers at high speed. Gradually it became a struggle to keep their respective vehicles on the highway as the rainfall steadily increased until it was a solid downpour.

What have we done that the weather gods are treating us like this? First all that snow and now all this rain ran through Gussie's head as the rain pelted down. *I'd feel better if Syd and I were in the same vehicle. Good thing there's so little traffic tonight. God, this is awful!*

Syd gritted his teeth as he followed along behind Gussie, trying to maintain a safe distance yet keep her in sight. Soon they were forced to slow down to a crawl. More than once, Syd found himself wishing Gussie would pull over and stop, but he had to remind himself how stubborn she could be. That was one of the things he'd always loved about her. She was no quitter.

To add to their misery, as they got closer to the Lake they were enveloped in a thick, swirling fog. It seemed an eternity before the entrance to Mac's little narrow lane with its rusty mailbox, marked M. S. NOBLE in broken letters, finally appeared in their headlights. No sooner had they parked and stumbled into the welcome shelter of Mac's house than the phone in the kitchen started to ring. It was Myrna, still on duty after more than eleven hours.

"There's-a-problem-down-near-The-Landing-Perce-needs-you-nothing-else-has-happened-I-stayed-here-until-I-could-get-a-hold-of-you-can-I-go-home-now?" Myrna's squeaky voice came over the line in such a rush Gussie had to ask her to slow down and start again. She leaned against the wall trying to concentrate in spite of her fatigue, as Myrna went on to explain there was some kind of emergency she didn't know exactly what. She paused long enough to ask about Mac, genuine concern in her voice. She'd always had a soft spot for Gussie's Dad who liked to trade jokes with her whenever he dropped into the station.

"How soon can you make it? Down to The Landing, I mean." Myrna's voice still sounded several octaves above normal.

"Mac's doing great, thanks," Gussie told her, trying to be positive. "Sorry, Myrna. I left my beeper behind in the rush. Still not used to it, I guess. Right away. If Perce calls again, tell him I'm leaving right away." She hung up and struggled back into her wet coat for the second time that night.

Syd chuckled to himself. So. He was right. It took a real emergency to fire up the normally sluggish receptionist. He didn't think she'd last long as a regular dispatcher in a bigger town, though. It would be too much for someone with her temperament.

"No. No. Not this time. I'm too pooped," Syd said before Gussie could ask him if he was coming with her. "I had to get up at some ungodly hour this morning. I know I should be on the scene, but honestly I can't do another thing today. Guess I'm not much of a newshawk, am I? I'll stay put right here and wait for you. Maybe rustle us up something to eat. I'm starving, I don't know about you." We should really have stopped for something back in Dunhampton, he wanted to add. But he knew Gussie was in a tearing hurry to get back and look for the letter Mac had been so anxious to tell her about. The secretive old coot! What had he been keeping from them all these months? He hoped it was something useful to do with the Denton case. Gussie was going to make herself sick over it if some solid clue or a fresh piece of evidence didn't turn up pretty soon.

"Wish like heck I didn't have to go out again," Gussie sighed. "Don't know that you'll find much," she said, giving him a quick hug and kiss goodbye. "Mac's not one for keeping a lot of stuff on hand. A can of soup. If we're lucky. He used to stash biscuits in a tin on the back shelf of the pantry. Other than that..." she shrugged. Secretly, she was thrilled Syd had decided to stay for the night. Maybe, just maybe they'd get a chance to talk about the unexpected turn their relationship was taking. "Be back as soon as I can." And she was gone, back out into the wet night, leaving Syd to ponder where she got the energy to keep going. Her job was more exciting than his, *that* was for sure. But he'd be the first to admit the hours were far worse.

He still couldn't get over her calling him her husband. Was that because she was under a strain and forgot momentarily that they were divorced? Or did she still think of them as married? He knew *he* did. *The biggest mistake of my life, walking out on Gussie. I must have been crazy. But maybe there's still a chance.*

Inside of an hour she was back. As soon as he heard the car door slam, Syd hurried to meet her at the door, pleased with himself he'd refrained from looking for the letter while she was gone. He started to tell her about it, but she waved him away.

"I'm dying to talk, just give me a chance to get out of these wet clothes. Gosh, what a night! Even my slicker couldn't handle it, lining's soaked through," she exclaimed, draping said coat over the back of the kitchen chair next to the wood stove, which was giving off a good steady heat since Syd had gotten a good fire going. Plumping herself down in the same chair, she wrenched off her boots, dropping them on the floor with a clunk, and peeled off her sodden socks.

"Mmmm, the house feels nice and toasty. It's worse than ever out there." She stood up, stretched and yawned. "Think I'll go straight up and take a hot bath. I don't want to catch another cold."

Noticing for the first time that Syd was wearing one of Mac's old pullovers and his usually smooth hair was standing on end, she said wearily, "I see you already took one. Right after I left, I hope. The old boiler isn't much good for tons of hot water, you know."

"Yeah, I didn't forget. The minute you were out the door. And I found some vegetable soup and some crackers and a jar of peanut butter," he said, "and we have applesauce for dessert. *And I made tea! What do you think of that?*" He beamed like a kid who'd been on a treasure hunt.

"Sounds good to me," Gussie said over her shoulder as she went up the stairs. "I could eat almost anything at this point. Tell you all about what happened when I come down ..." her voice trailed off as she disappeared into the bathroom.

Syd went back to the kitchen and resumed looking through some old magazines he'd found piled on the counter. They were even older than the ones in the hospital waiting room and that was saying something. As he idly flipped through the pages, he could hear the water running into the cast iron tub above his head. Poor old Mac. He'd never gotten around to installing a shower. Said they used too much water. Said he'd rather sink into a nice warm tub than stand shivering under water raining on his head while the rest of him was freezing. Not until tonight had Syd realized how badly his former father-in-law had let the old place go since Gussie left. He'd only been in the place once or twice since he and Gussie split up. He and Mac usually met up in town.

The old farm kitchen with its wood stove was the most comfortable room in the place. The rest of the house was damp and drafty. The furnace was on its last legs, while the plumbing was noisy and unreliable. The pipes made an awful racket when you first turned on the taps and you could never be sure if what came out would run nice and clear or be a rusty brown. Gussie once told him she used to have to wait for a sunny day to do the laundry. The white things had to be spread out on the lawn because Mac wouldn't let her use bleach. When Syd asked what they did in winter, Gussie said the sheets and towels and especially their underclothes were often an interesting shade of yellow by the time the spring came.

He was just finishing an article on some of the newer gadgets being developed for boaters when he heard the water gurgling down the drainpipe inside the kitchen wall, then footsteps coming lightly down the stairs and Gussie was back, swathed in Mac's worn plaid bathrobe, her hair bound up in a towel. She looked delectable, her face glowing rosy and clean in the dim light of the kitchen and he had to resist putting his arms around her then and there. But his practical side asserted itself. Food first and then maybe...

Between mouthfuls of the scant meal Syd had scraped together, Gussie told him about her trip over past The Landing.

"There was a report somebody saw a body. Floating. Out off that long stretch of beach. You know the one?"

Syd nodded and spread a generous dollop of peanut butter on another biscuit.

"Past The Landing," Gussie continued. "Over closer to the mouth of the Old Barge Canal."

"The Canal again!" said Syd in surprise. "What in heck is going on over there? I've heard back in the old days when they hauled lumber down from the North Woods on those big old barges there used to be some wild goings-on. Fights and stuff. Sometimes a knifing. But now? Well? *Was* there a body?"

"Well, that's just the trouble," Gussie said, swallowing the last of her tea which had a slightly musty taste. "Ugh." She made a face. "Why did Dad let things get into such a state, I mean into such a state? I guess I should have paid more attention to what he was doing. But I've been so busy. And this, this Denton thing's got me down. I just don't know."

"You're trying to do too much as usual, Gus," Syd said more in sympathy than in criticism. "Go on. What happened?"

"Look who's talking," Gussie replied, equally sympathetic. "Do you suppose our fathers worked this hard? We never have time for ourselves any more. Only work. Oh, for the good old days!"

"Phooey on the good old days," Syd said impatiently. "Whoever said they were all that great? No cars, no phones. Go on, woman, you're keeping me in suspense." He ran his fingers through his still damp hair, smoothing it down and making him look more like himself again.

"Well," said Gussie again, trying not to look at him. He looked just the same as when they first started going together. Not one day older. "That's just it. By the time Perce got there, it was raining so hard he couldn't find anything. But the person who called it in, a young fellow by the name of Davey Crumb, swore up and down he'd seen a body floating out a ways. Just off shore like I said."

"Crumb. Crumb. I've heard that name before. Wasn't his father the one—?"

"You've got it," said Gussie, "the one who assaulted his wife and took off before we could charge him. Yes, well—"

"What was young Master Crumb doing down by the Lake after dark? And why did he think it was a body he saw?"

"Not so young any more. Seems he's been away at school in the City and couldn't wait to get back down to the Lake. When we asked him what he was doing down there in such terrible weather, he said he missed the Lake so much when he was away from it, he didn't care what the weather was doing. He had a flashlight with him, said it glinted off something when he shone it out over the water. Said it was a square shape, like something made of metal. Well, we couldn't find any body. Maybe it was just a piece of wood or something floating in such a way that it looked like a body. Anyway it means I'll have to get back down there as soon as it's light, I mean as soon as it's light. But, we *did* find something else." Gussie paused. "Are there any more of those biscuits?" She was gone in a flash to the pantry. Syd leaned back in his chair, absentmindedly digging peanut butter out of the jar and eating it off the knife. He felt guilty that he hadn't gone with her. Another body?

In no time she returned, a look of triumph on her face. "Nope. No more biscuits. But guess what *I* found?" And she waved a bottle under his nose. "Brandy! The good stuff! Dad had it hidden behind some empty jars!"

"Gussie Spilsbury, you're making me crazy! Finish the story, why don't you. What did you find?" Syd asked, scraping off his knife over the edge of the peanut butter jar and replacing the lid.

Gussie opened the cupboard over the sink where Mac kept the mugs and glassware. She plumped two glasses and the bottle of brandy down on the table.

"Dad's boat! The name jumped out at me when I shone my flashlight on it. The GUS E. DUP. Such a goofy name. It was up against some rocks, wedged between two boulders, actually. It was pretty beat up, paint's all scratched. Dad said it was missing when he went down to check on the boathouse, but I didn't take it in at the time, I was so worried about him. Now, all I have to do is figure out how it got there. It must have been there all winter, I mean all winter. Under all that ice and snow." She gave the cap of the brandy bottle a good twist and poured them each a generous dose.

"His *boat* ? How do you think it got there?" Syd said in surprise, scratching hard at the side of his nose. Mac had always been so fussy about his beloved boat. He never just pulled it up on shore when he landed somewhere, but was always careful to tie it to a tree stump or a rock. He had no use for careless boaters. Said they made things harder for the serious ones.

"Don't do that," Gussie cautioned. "You're making it all red. It's such a nice nose." She blushed, feeling awkward all at once. Pulling herself together, she went on. "Haven't a clue how it got there. Something else I'll have to check out tomorrow. Ask around and see if anyone saw it. Or anything. And find out if anyone's been reported missing."

They clinked their glasses together and took a good swig of the fine old brandy, relishing its warmth as it coursed its way down. Feeling a hundred per cent better, they decided to look for the letter Mac had struggled to tell them about. Desk, he had whispered. Desk?

The only piece of furniture that could remotely be described as a desk was an old table with a small drawer under one side, which refused to budge when they tried to pull it all the way out, so Gussie had to be content with reaching in. At first, the only things she brought out besides clumps of dust were an old scribbler, some pencil stubs, a tiny box of ancient postage stamps, a handful of rusty paper clips and a broken ruler. But wedged in at the back, Gussie's thin fingers encountered the corner of what felt like an envelope. She managed to get it out without tearing it. It was addressed to *Constable Augusta Spilsbury* and contained three sheets of lined paper. Gussie recognized the handwriting immediately. Half afraid of what she was going to find out, she unfolded the pages and spread them out on the table.

A few long minutes later, she and Syd were still sitting at the old table staring at each other, Gussie, in true daughterly fashion, in a state of shock and Syd, in true newspaperman's style, wondering how much of what he had just read could be safely used in the *Bickerton Bugler* .

32
TOGETHERNESS?

"Well," said Gussie, letting out her breath after a long pause. She sat erect, the last page of the letter hanging limply from between two fingers. "You can see what I have to do now, can't you? No way around it, I mean no way. I don't believe it. I just don't believe it." And she put her head down on the table, her shoulders shaking.

Syd was just as shocked as she, but came to himself more quickly. He let her cry for a few minutes to let the tension be released, the tension she'd been under for so many months. Then putting his hand gently under her chin and lifting her head up, he said firmly, "Gus. Look at me. It's late and we're both exhausted. We've had a terrible day. Let's go to bed. We'll figure out what to do in the morning. There's nothing more we can do tonight. We need sleep. Come on, atta good girl," and he helped her up out of the chair. As if in a trance, they turned out the lights and went slowly up the stairs side by side.

Sometime later, Syd woke up and for a few seconds he wasn't sure where he was. Then he heard soft familiar breathing and realized he was in Gussie's old bed. Upstairs in Mac's house. With Gussie. *With Gussie!* He lay back and thought about that for a minute. Then he started to wonder what had made him wake up after being so dog-tired.

The rain was still beating a tattoo on the roof above them, one of those grooved metal roofs that transfer every sound to the inhabitants below. *Brings you closer to nature.* He could hear Mac's voice in his head. But it had been raining like that when they went to bed. That wasn't it. Then he realized it was the lack of sound. That steady low rumbling noise from below. The furnace must have quit. Oh well, nothing he could do about that now. He turned over and snuggled closer to Gussie, pulling the patchwork quilt she'd left behind when she married him up around his chin.

He slept.

33
NIGHTMARE!

When Syd woke up the second time, he was alone. Above his head, the rain was beating in a syncopated rhythm, RA-tata-TAT-ta-RA-tata-TAT-ta-RA-tata-TAT like a snare drum in a jazz band, the same rhythm that had rocked him back to sleep when he'd been wakened in the night. A pearly light that was trying to pass itself off as sunshine shimmered behind the pale blue curtain covering the only window in the room. He lay there for a few minutes, fragments of a nightmare lingering around the edges of his consciousness.

> *He and Gussie are out on the Lake ... in the GUS E. DUP ... facing the shore ... looking back ... at Mac's house. As they watch ... unable to move ... the water swells up over the shoreline ... until the dock ... and then the boathouse ... disappear ... leaving Mac's old house an island. They hear loud groaning sounds ... coming from the house ... and then it detaches itself from its foundations ... spins slowly around ... and begins moving ... slowly and majestically ... out into the Lake ... like an ocean liner ... straight at them. They can see a figure ... that looks like Mac clinging to the top of the chimney ... waving frantically and calling out to them ... but they can't make out what it's trying to tell them ...*

Syd opened his eyes wide, then squeezed them shut in an attempt to erase the sickening image. When that failed, he sat up abruptly, swung his legs over the side and left the warmth of the bed. Making his way slowly down the narrow stairs to the kitchen, he was happy to hear a welcome fire crackling and snapping in the old wood stove. Gussie couldn't have been gone for too long. Her heavy yellow rain slicker and boots were gone, but the soggy socks were still draped over the chair back. She must have dug out a pair of Mac's socks. Shuffling in his bare feet across the worn linoleum and listening to the comforting sound of the fire, he wondered if by any chance Mac had squirreled away any coffee in the back pantry, when his eye was drawn to something white on the kitchen table. A scrap of paper was sticking out from under the empty peanut butter jar. In Gussie's slanted writing, it said:

> *Sorry to leave, but you know why. Can you come to the hospital with me tonight? Leave me a message at the station.*
>
> *Love, G*

Still not fully awake, he sat down at the table to read the note again. Something lumpy was on the seat of the chair. He pulled a pair of work socks out from under him. Good old Gus. She'd thought of him before she left.

The note read exactly the same as it had the first time. Wow. That brandy Gussie found must have been strong stuff. *Funny. She drank just as much as I did. How come she could get up so early and get out of the house so quietly? I didn't even hear her car leave. Better get a move on and get up to town. Find out what the heck's going on. Wow, I'm going to be really late today!*

Then he remembered Mac's letter. It wasn't on the table where they'd left it last night. Or was that early this morning? Gus must have taken it with her. She'd have to keep that little time bomb in a safe place, that was for certain sure. What a mess! Who would have believed it? It read worse than a cheap novel. But he was more than relieved for Gussie's sake that something was happening at last. As Gus herself would have put it, the case was beginning to crack. Even though it was at the expense of Mac's heart. If it hadn't been for his attack and his subsequent revelation, she probably would have had to get some outside help to solve the Denton mystery. That would have been an awful blow to her professional pride. Especially after she'd worked so hard for so long. But. There was always a but. But it would have been ten times worse if Mac had died. Poor Gus. He wondered how she was feeling this morning, knowing the father she adored, who'd encouraged her to go into police work in the first place, was now himself involved in a crime. One of the very worst kind of crimes. And would have to be arrested and questioned. By his own daughter.

For a minute, Syd wondered if he'd dreamt the whole thing. But the bewildered look on Gussie's face while she was reading the letter had been no dream. And the parts of the letter he'd seen, in spite of the hazy effects of the brandy, had etched themselves into his brain.

Don't hate me, Gussie girl ... got out of hand ... couldn't stop them ... Hink Denton went crazy when he found out ... swore he was going to report us ... something about Pete. Oh yes. *Pete said his wife's been hounding him day and night* . Syd shook his head at the recollection. Just shows you never can tell about people, what they're really like, what kind of troubles they have. Everyone in town thought Pete's wife was the best looking woman around. Who'd have guessed she was a nagging witch. What else? Oh yeah *Nick backed out at the last minute ... said he didn't want any part of it...* Wasn't that Otterley character from over to East Thorne in there somewhere? Oh yeah *Ferd said he didn't care what happened ... already in trouble with the law in the City...* And the last part? Think, Spilsbury, *think* . Something about Joe.

He sat there, staring at the table, feeling a headache coming on. He could really use some coffee. Strong coffee. What *was* it about Joe? And which Joe? There were several in town. Pressing the tips of his fingers hard against his throbbing temples, it struck him. Most likely Joe Gaffield. That was the only Joe that Syd could remember Mac talking about. Wait a minute. Wasn't he some kind of distant cousin to Mac's late wife? All Syd knew about the Gaffields was that they had a reputation for getting involved in deals that were on the slightly shady side. At least the old-timers in and around town had always said so. Old man Gaffield was a regular old rip, he remembered his Dad saying. But the Gaffields had never done anything to put them behind bars. At least, not so far as he could recall. Just enough to make themselves a few dollars. Scary stuff, Syd remembered thinking when he was a kid and overheard his Dad talking to his Mom about it. There were even rumours the Gaffield ancestors were the brains behind the liquor smuggling that used to go on in the old days. Ran the stuff right across the Lake to The Other Side, bold as brass. Until their fastest boat disappeared after a storm.

Years later, pieces of the boat were found washed up on one of the islands that dotted the Lake. But never a trace of the men thought to be aboard her. It was said all five of them were Gaffields. One way or another. But no one knew for sure. No one wanted to talk about those things any more. Best forgotten, they said, if the subject came up. Like so many other unsavoury goings-on in the good old days.

Probably everyone and his brother was into smuggling back then. When he'd first heard stories about what used to go on in Bickerton way back when, Syd asked his Dad about their ancestral Spilsburys. His Dad just laughed and said, oh no son, no, never in a million years, the Spilsburys were too God fearing to get mixed up in those kind of shenanigans. Syd knew that his great grandfather Enoch Spilsbury was a preacher. His Dad had told him about being scared to death when the old man used to shout about hellfire, damnation and evilry, as he called it, and make threatening gestures at his congregation with one fist while pounding the pulpit with the other, making it wobble and shake so violently he was sure it would break.

When his Dad grew up and left home, he refused to go to church. Made him too nervous, he said. Said he had to catch up on his rest and wasn't that what Sunday was for? A day of rest? Syd's Mom had to settle for taking Syd and her sister with her. Mac had written *it was Joe ... Joe's the one. It was all Joe.* Something about some land somewhere. He'd added a postscript for Syd. *Check into the Roxton land. It's all in the old books. Down in the vault under the Town Hall. Make a first-class story for your readers, son.*

The Roxton land? Syd had always heard the Roxtons had piles of money. But land? Other than Hill House and an old fishing lodge somewhere Up North, he didn't know where, he had never heard of anything else. Certainly no land of any great importance. At the very least, nothing worth committing murder over.

Syd was fully awake now. He put on the work socks and went back upstairs to retrieve his clothes. High time he got home, got back to the newspaper office and then got over to the Town Hall. Maybe even find time to check out the newspaper morgue where his Dad had stored all the old issues. Maybe find out what land Mac had been referring to. *Looks like it's shaping up to be a busy day.*

Busy for him as well as for Gussie.

34

THE BODY IN THE LAKE

It was almost over. Almost. But not quite.

Early in the morning of the day after Mac's heart attack, Gussie headed over to the beach area past The Landing where Mrs. Crumb's Davey claimed to have seen a body floating in the Lake. It was raining lightly and a bit foggy. She was still in a state of shock from last night's revelations. But her innate professionalism and a kind of toughness she hadn't known she possessed seemed to be carrying her through. It had been quite a while since anything this challenging had happened to her on the job. Only the experience with the Watson twins came anywhere close. And when she thought about that horrendous event, she figured it was only sheer ignorance of the danger she faced and a stubborn determination to take care of a bad situation, a situation that had the whole town up in arms for months, that kept her going.

Shock she could deal with. It seemed to act on her adrenal glands, sending a charge of the stuff pumping through her system, giving her the energy she was certainly going to need to get her through the next phase of the investigation. Time enough later on to worry about Mac's possible involvement. Anyway, his heart attack had left him too weak for her to question closely at this stage. She'd have to hie herself over to the hospital and see how he was making out. But that too would have to wait. First things first.

The ever-faithful Perce, who'd stayed overnight in East Thorne with an old school friend, promised to be on the scene when she got there. He was really quite incredible. She'd have to find the right moment to ask if he'd ever considered police work as a full time career. More than once he'd proved he had what it took. And without question she could give him top marks for reliability and dedication. What Mac would call good old fashioned stick-to-it-iveness. Characteristics she hadn't seen demonstrated in any of the Auxiliaries she'd had up until now. Besides, if things worked out the way she hoped, she might be lucky enough to get him for her deputy. So far, they'd worked extremely well together.

She'd been a bit apprehensive when she slid into the front seat of the venerable cruiser and turned the key in the ignition. But the old bus started up without a hitch. Sometimes it balked from the dampness, especially after it had been sitting outside all night. It was so old, it had to be babied along or it would quit on her. *Note to the Town Council: Constable Spilsbury needs a new cruiser.* But today it was cooperating nicely, warm air from the heater swirling around her legs even before she got as far as the turnoff to The Landing. To the east through gaps in the trees, she could see bits of sky the colour of smoked pearl. A few spirals of mist rose lazily from the water-filled ditches on either side of the road. As she crossed the rickety wooden bridge spanning a creek, the pungent smell of skunk wafted in through the air intake.

No one seemed to be up and about in any of the few houses scattered along the back roads around The Landing. All were in darkness. Not a single car on the road either. *I could be alone in the world,* she thought as the cruiser bumped and splashed its way along. She kept wondering if what happened last night had been her imagination. Or did she and Syd ... did they really ... but then, she'd been so utterly exhausted she couldn't even remember going up the stairs.

Seeing Syd lying there in her old bed so peacefully asleep, so familiar, so dear, as if the last few years had never happened, she hadn't had the heart to waken him to say goodbye before she left. But knowing him as she did, she was sure he'd understand. He always had in the past. And then, his life was just about as hectic as hers. Maybe that had been the trouble when they'd been together. No real time for each other. Or anything else but work, for that matter.

As they'd arranged the night before, Perce was to wait for her on an uninhabited side road that served as a shortcut to the Lake. This way they could easily get down where they needed to go unobserved. True to his word, there he was, bareheaded in the misty air, wearing what looked like some kind of rubberized suit and leaning against the hood of his pickup, enjoying his first cigarette of the day. When he spotted the cruiser lurching towards him through the overflowing potholes that decorated the SUMMER USE ONLY road, he stubbed out his cigarette and reaching in through the open cab window, hauled out a sack containing a large thermos of coffee and a couple of freshly baked bran muffins his friend's wife had thoughtfully provided. After greeting each other — good morning, good morning yourself, gee Perce you sure know my weakness for muffins, another lousy day wouldn't you know it, weather's supposed to clear up later on — they demolished muffins and coffee in a companionable silence. Then, undeterred by the weather, they followed each other down the road, which quickly deteriorated into two deep and muddy ruts to where it ended at a concrete barrier erected to keep people from driving their cars directly onto the beach.

Parking their vehicles to one side, they climbed out and skirting the barrier began picking their way across the broad stretch of sand to the water's edge. Through the rain, Gussie could just barely make out a squat figure that looked like a fat yellow mushroom standing beside an outboard motorboat pulled up on the beach. When they got closer, the mushroom turned and waved and Gussie saw to her surprise it was none other than Rab Kibbidge, wearing an enormous sou'wester, the kind she'd only ever seen in pictures of fishermen.

"Least I could do to help. All Perce's doin'," Rab said in his modest way, a shrug his only acknowledgement of Gussie's thanks.

After they'd climbed aboard and taken the seats Rab indicated, he poled them skilfully off with an oar. With her policewoman's eye, Gussie made a quick scan of the boat and spotted two odd-sized buckets sitting on top of some coils of rope near the stern. At her questioning look, Rab explained that one was for bailin', t'other for lookin'. He picked up the larger bucket and held it so she could see that its bottom was solid glass.

"Somethin' we usta use back home for huntin' for things under water," he said, then turned and yanked hard on the pull cord to start the motor.

Spasmodic gusts of wind were throwing up waves, which slapped against the sides of the boat as they headed out along the shore, where only a few hours ago they'd been groping around in the dark. Gussie sat next to Perce, hoping and praying she wouldn't disgrace herself by throwing up the muffins and coffee. She'd never been too keen on boats, even though Mac loved to take her out with him in his old boat the WHOLLY MACKRELLE when she was a kid. No matter what Mac said, she never could get used to the idea that it was quite safe. Even though there was only a thin layer of wood separating her from all that water.

Mac used to tease her and call her his little landlubber. And besides, this particular morning she was still under the influence of the brandy she'd indulged in the night before. It wasn't long before she became aware that Rab was watching her closely. She smiled weakly at him, trying to put a brave face on it, wishing with all her heart for nothing more than to be back on solid ground. Rab winked at her, making her blush, and adding to her embarrassment. Reaching into his back pocket, he withdrew a small brown bottle and passed it over to her.

"Stummick bitters," he shouted over the sound of the motor. "Good for settlin' things down some. Go ahead, girl. Bottoms up!"

Gussie did as she was told and almost immediately felt much better. She nudged Perce's elbow and offered him the bottle, but he just shook his head and went back to watching the shore. Rab motioned her to hang on to the bottle which she stowed in the inside pocket of her slicker, smiling her thanks.

The mist was beginning to dissipate as they bumped along. Gussie could see they were fast approaching the spot where Davey Crumb had led them the night before. Through the pouring rain. With only a flashlight to show the way. She remembered seeing the light bouncing off the huge chunk of bleached driftwood, which served to mark the end of the sand beach. From there on, the shoreline was littered with sharp rocks. Clumps of silver birch interspersed with the elephant-grey trunks of other trees stood nakedly against the sky. It was hard to believe in a few short weeks they'd be cloaked in a glorious spring green. Somewhere farther along the shore, the GUS E. DUP was resting, caught helplessly between two boulders.

The sky was much lighter now and the islands farther out in the Lake were beginning to resume their familiar shapes after being mere smudges on the horizon. Perce leaned forward and shouted "Okay, Rab. Here oughtta do her". Rab brought the bow around, cut the motor to a crawl and they began working their way back, parallel with and closer to the shore. Rab took the glass-bottomed bucket and showed Perce how to use it, lowering it part way into the water and looking through it. This meant leaning out over the side, which Gussie wasn't at all anxious to do.

They travelled back and forth over the area, edging the boat closer in to shore with each pass. Eventually Gussie's natural curiosity was aroused enough that she took a short turn with the bucket, the bottom of which acted like a huge magnifying glass. It was amazing how clear things looked when you didn't have the fragmented surface of the water to contend with. In places you could even see the Lake bottom, with here and there the odd clam shell and clusters of rocks festooned with long trailing weeds, looking like green water snakes. Some places it was shallow enough for her to worry that the boat might run aground, but Rab seemed to have an unerring instinct for where those places were, probably from his years as a kid with a fisherman for a father. He must have spent hours out on the ocean.

After an hour or so, when Gussie was starting to feel a bit disoriented in spite of liberal doses of Rab's bitters and thinking maybe they should give up the search and get someone to drag the area, Perce let out a shout and plunked the bucket back into the boat. Rab immediately shut off the motor and dropped a rope, with a chunk of rusty iron tied on one end, over the side.

"There's something down there," Perce said excitedly, pointing up past the bow. "I just caught a glint of something shiny. Lotta branches on the bottom here, looks like a whole tree. Think I'll go check," and before Gussie could stop him, he was over the side. She was relieved to see he landed with his head still above water. That meant the Lake at this point couldn't have been much deeper than five feet.

"Don't you think maybe -" but Gussie's query was cut off as Perce suddenly ducked under the water's dimpled surface. In a moment, he heaved himself back up and asked Rab to pass him a rope. Then he was gone under again. After what seemed like a lifetime to Gussie, he popped up, panting, something black and shapeless rising to the surface beside him.

"It was caught in some branches," Perce said, coughing and breathing hard from the effort. He eased the mass over to the side of the boat and secured the rope to one of the cleats. Then he hoisted himself carefully back into the boat.

Rab leaned over to take a look. "Mother o' God! It's a body right enough!"

"It was the belt buckle the kid saw all right. That square metal thing. *And* the metal buttons," said Perce, who'd recovered his breath.

"Got anything stronger than those bitters?" he asked Rab, who grinned and reached into another of his many pockets. A larger bottle appeared and was gratefully seized by Perce, who twisted off the cap and took a long draft. *Omigod, not another body,* was all Gussie could think. She wished he'd offer her the bottle, but thought she'd better keep her head clear, now that she finally had it that way.

"Bit cold in there," he said to Gussie and Rab, who hadn't been able to take their eyes off the black shape floating beside them. Gussie moved up closer to the bow and leaned cautiously out over the side, hoping the others wouldn't notice how nervous she was. She gasped as the black mass swung around on its rope and she caught a glimpse of the face. Fishbelly white. And swollen. The eyes wide open, staring sightlessly at the sky, heedless of the water that was washing over them.

"I'm not just sure who this is," she said shakily. "Hard to make out. Perce, *you* take a look."

After another swallow from the bottle, Perce obliged.

"Nope," he said, after a moment. "Sorry, boss. Don't know him."

Rab said, "Let me give her a go." He moved into the bow and tugged on the rope until the body swung around again. He took a good long look at the distorted features, then at the hands, the fingers of which were beginning to bloat, then scrambled back onto the stern seat.

"Mother o' God," he said again. "I don't know but what it looks like that Wychwood fellow." He scratched the back of his neck under the sou'wester making it bobble in a comical way and took another long pull from his bottle. "Blessed if it don't look like him. Was in to see me just the other day. What he wanted though I never did find out."

He took a square piece of cloth out of his sleeve and blew his nose. "Too busy with unloadin' supplies for them, as feared o' floodin' as I was. He usta come in to the store off'n on. He liked to sit and gab. Just sit and gab. Didn't seem to care if I gave a listen or not. Having a mite of trouble at home, I reckon." He cleared his throat and continued, "Dottie said that wife o' his come by the store lookin' for him. Said she and CeeCee were that surprised to see her. She never come in before. "

"When was that?" Gussie asked. "Yesterday?"

"No, no, let me see now. Day before. Or maybe 'twas the day before that. I kinda lost track what with bein' so busy an' all. Come to think on it, must have been the day before yesterday."

"Did Dottie say what Mrs. Wychwood wanted him for?"

"Somethin' about an appointment they had. Seemed real put out they didn't know where he'd got to."

There was silence for a moment. The boat gently rocking to and fro. The body swinging idly back and forth at the end of its tether. Perce squinted up at the sky. It was almost full daylight. He noted the wind had dropped and the trails of mist were slackening off. At long last. Gussie was too busy thinking to pay attention to what the weather was doing.

"Well now," she said at last with a sigh, "I guess I've got a lot more questions to ask, I mean a lot more."

35
ON WITH THE JOB

The body proved to be decidedly uncooperative when they tried to bring it aboard Rab's boat. It required teamwork skilfully directed by Rab, who said they wouldn't like to hear how much experience he'd had in such matters. And to keep the boat from tipping all of them into the Lake. As they edged their way back around the concrete barrier with their pathetic burden, its arms dangling, water streaming off the tips of its sleek black boots, they agreed it felt like they'd already done a full day's work. It was barely nine o'clock in the morning. It took their combined efforts to carry the body the whole distance without needing to put it down. Perce said that he guessed that was what was meant by a dead weight.

Away from the Lake with its faint odour of long dead fish, the air was rank with the early spring smell of rotting vegetation. Rab remarked that the way the weather was lookin', it didn't hold out much chance of gettin' some better quick. A glomish kinda day, to be sure. Gussie said she figured she'd be so busy, she wouldn't care what the weather did.

After mulling it over for a few minutes, she decided not to start searching the body for identification with the clothing being so wet. Any papers that might be in the pockets would likely disintegrate. She'd wait until she got it back up to town and carry out the search under better conditions. Finally they reached their vehicles and eased their burden slowly to the ground. While Perce was busy with a cigarette, Gussie asked Rab if he'd come over to Bickerton later on that day. Under such circumstances, it was more than likely he'd be needed as a witness. His response reminded her of the breathless way his sister sometimes talked.

"Anythin' to help, Missus Constable, anythin' a'tall, CeeCee 'n Dottie now, they don't know where I be, I sneaked out real early, see, 'n Dottie gets right peeved when I miss my breakfast, says I be needin' it to keep up my strength, don't know what she thought I did afore she got here anyhow. When might you be wantin' me, Missus, after lunch like?"

Suppressing a smile, since the quaint little man with the crinkly eyes had been so quiet up until then, Gussie said that would be about right. She reminded him to keep their early morning excursion, and their find, to himself until the coroner had done the preliminaries. Then, if they were half way sure it was Mr. Wychwood, she'd have to get Mrs. Wychwood in to identify the body.

"As the next of kin, she should be told right away before Bickerton's overworked grapevine gets a hold of it," she cautioned him.

Rab nodded, "Sure thing, Missus, whatever you say, I know my sister, she'd be tellin' every soul as so much stuck their nose in the store, and with poor CeeCee just gettin' herself right again, well, she don't need more upset."

Gussie sighed. This meant another call to Len Perry for his hearse. She'd have to find a phone somewhere in one of the houses further back on the road. She asked Rab if he minded staying with the body until she could make the call. She didn't want to ask him to do it. That was her job. Rab said quickly, you bet, Missus. Anythin' to help. He went back to the barrier and perched himself on the edge of it, whistling softly through his teeth. Perce polished off another cigarette and said he had to take off right away back up to Cooley's Mills.

He was long overdue to have his teeth looked at. One of them had been giving him a lot of trouble lately. His wife had made him an appointment with the local dentist for just before lunch, he said apologetically. But if Gussie needed him, he'd come right back down to Bickerton as soon as that ordeal was over. He'd been laid off his regular job at the mill for the winter months and was looking forward to getting back to work at the end of the week. Gussie said she was sorry to hear about his sore tooth and of course he should get on home and get it fixed up. Now was not the best time to bring up the subject of police work with him, although she figured the way things had been going lately, she could almost guarantee him full time work as her deputy.

When Perce had roared off in his truck, the stillness that descended on the lonely road seemed to vibrate in Gussie's ears as loudly as any sound would have. Before leaving, she scanned the roadside and the woods. She'd suddenly remembered someone having reported seeing a black bear down somewhere down here. Was it a bit early for bears? No, none that she could see or smell, thank goodness. She was anxious to get back up to town once the hearse arrived and get this latest mess sorted out as quickly as possible.

Grasping the cruiser's steering wheel firmly, Gussie drove carefully back over the ruts and the potholes up to the road to where the houses had ended. *If this is another homicide, which I hope to goodness it isn't, it'll set some kind of record. Oh well, whatever it is, I've got one less suspect to interview. Augusta Spilsbury, are you by any chance getting callous? How could you even think such a thing. The poor soul, what on earth could have happened to him? And what in heck was he doing down at the Lake anyway? I wonder if that stuck-up wife of his knows anything. If Rab's right and it turns out to be Pete Wychwood, that Maggie's a widow woman now.*

Probably not for long though, knowing what kind of man-eater she is. Honestly, Gussie, what unkind thoughts you do have.

After spotting a house where the lights were on, she pulled into the driveway and went around to the back door. The woman who answered was surprised to see her so early, but after being assured that her family wasn't involved in whatever it was, she said, sure go ahead, the phone's over there on the wall.

Len answered right away and said he'd be down as soon as he could pick up the necessary forms. He was astute enough not to make any comments about the possibility of a second murder and for that Gussie was grateful.

When Gussie drove back down the road minutes later, Rab was still sitting on the barrier and couldn't resist making a joke.

"He never moved a muscle while you was gone," he said and winked. Gussie didn't respond but she didn't blame him. It had been a tough morning.

A few minutes later Len's hearse appeared, moving cautiously so he'd splash as little mud as possible on its gleaming black sides. He'd brought an assistant with him and the body was stowed quickly and expertly. Rab said he'd be off now, see you later, and walked back to the shore and his boat.

As Gussie finally turned onto the main road back to town, she suppressed the urge to switch on the siren. That would wake everyone up if they weren't up already. That was a sound they didn't get to hear very often. Too bad. The whine of the siren might have helped to block out her thoughts momentarily. For a while there, out on the Lake, her nerves were so frayed she'd felt like screaming when the body popped up beside Perce. She could have let the old cruiser's siren do the screaming for her. But the thoughts stayed firmly lodged where they were. *How in the world did Pete Wychwood end up in the Lake? I can't figure out what he could have been doing down there in all that rain last night. He was a handsome son of a gun, all right. Always wore black, even in the summer. Always looked like a million bucks. Not so wonderful looking now is he, with his face all bloated. That is, if it is him. How the heck am I going to figure this one out when I haven't sorted the Denton case out all the way yet? What if they're connected? What if it really is another homicide? That'll make two in less than a year. In Bickerton! Who'd a thunk it? Omigod this whole thing is turning into a bloody nightmare.*

Abruptly shutting off the thoughts that were plaguing her, as soon as she came to the familiar BICKERTON sign, she drove straight up to the station. She didn't want to alarm the doctor's patients by showing up unannounced at his office in the cruiser. She'd better let that starchy sounding nurse know she was coming. People get nervous when they see a police car pull up. They stop talking, look furtively at each other, trying to guess which of them she might be after, wondering if maybe it's the doctor who's in some kind of trouble. Well, Nursie could take care of it.

Myrna was at her desk, looking tired, but talking, as usual, to someone on the phone. She rang off when she saw Gussie.

"Your ex, umm, I mean, Mister Spilsbury was here. Just a few minutes ago. He left a big parcel of, uh, something in your office." Gussie could see that Myrna was dying of curiosity. At least the girl knew enough not to ask straight off what had happened with Perce the night before or to ask Gussie where she'd been all morning. She'll find out soon enough, Gussie thought. Besides, if it was something real nasty, with blood and everything, she knew Myrna would rather not know.

When Gussie asked if there had been a report of anyone missing, the receptionist shook her head, making her streaky hair, which she wore in a topknot, wobble in a comical way.

"No, thank goodness," she drawled in her lazy way. "Not unless you count dogs. Two different calls about missing pooches. Just the usual stuff so far. New lady, a Mrs. Nesselroad, some name like that. You know? Bought the, uh, dress shop down the road? Locked herself out and came in here all upset, so I sent that young guy down at the hardware store over to see if he could help. You know. The cute one wears the tight jeans? That ought to make her feel better." Myrna snorted at her own wit. Gussie smiled, but didn't linger to hear more.

When she opened the door to her office, the pungent scent of fresh cut flowers was unmistakable. An enormous bouquet of satiny pink and white tulips, accompanied by feathery ferns and arranged in a silver vase, occupied most of her desk. The folded note tucked in with them read:

> *Sent a bunch just like this one over to Mac in Dunhampton. Thought that gloomy old room he's stuck in needed some brightening up. Will pick you up tonight whenever you say so we can go over together this time.*
>
> *Till later, love S.*
>
> *PS What happened this a.m.? Anything interesting?*
>
> *CALL ME*

The sight and smell of the flowers and the thought behind them almost made her forget what she had to do next. Moving the vase to one side, she dialled the doctor's office. His nurse, as starchy as ever, said 'he's busy with a patient, you'll have to call back later, miss.' When Gussie tried to impress on her that 'this is an urgent call, this is police business' the woman still hesitated, until Gussie, trying not to lose her patience, said in her sternest voice,

"This is Constable Spilsbury from the Bickerton Police calling, maybe you didn't hear me the first time? I've got to speak to him. *Right now.*" Darn the woman anyway.

No apology was forthcoming, but Gussie heard a click and the doctor's voice came booming over the line, so loudly she had to hold the receiver away from her ear.

"Hey, gorgeous, what can I do for you so early in the morning?" This was followed by a chuckle.

"Sorry to interrupt you, Bill, but I've got another one for you!" she said keeping her voice low and ignoring the familiarity.

"That's right, believe it or not. *Another body.*"

36

AT THE WOODCOCKS'

Kitty was in her kitchen putting the finishing touches to a cake she'd set to cool on the sideboard. This wasn't just any old cake, but a special double-fudge-chocolate-chip-triple-layer cake she'd made from scratch and put together with a rich date filling, the whole concoction swathed in a whipped chocolate mocha frosting and topped off with toasted coconut. A feast fit for the gods, Albie had pronounced it when he'd come into the kitchen unexpectedly and caught her in the middle of the crucial mixing stage when she was helpless to get rid of him. She'd wanted it to be a surprise. Albie just laughed off her chagrin and said he was too old for surprises. Kitty seldom got around to baking anything other than a few crumbly peanut butter cookies. And then only after Jesse coaxed and flattered her into it. You make the best peanut butter cookies in the world, Mom, honest you do, he'd say. Who could hold out after that kind of compliment?

She didn't know why, but she'd never felt really at home in the kitchen. Her mind was constantly occupied with something she'd been reading. Or she'd be daydreaming about what it would be like to live somewhere else, somewhere other than this unfriendly little town. She'd forget all about the oven and then the casserole or the cookies or whatever else she was trying to make would be burnt to a crisp. Or she'd let things boil over, leaving her with an awful mess to clean up. The neighbourhood squirrels and chipmunks had often been the beneficiaries of what she laughingly called her culinary disasters. Sometimes she felt like crying instead. She was no cook, that was for sure. But she swore that this time, in honour of the occasion, things were going to be different. This time she'd forced herself to concentrate on the job at hand. So far her efforts looked, and smelled, like they'd be paying off.

Every few minutes she glanced out the window overlooking the tiny backyard to see how her men were getting on. From the sound of things, her men were doing just fine, thank you. Jesse's high-pitched soprano, interspersed with Albie's booming bass, penetrated the house even with all the windows closed. In spite of a twinge of envy she tried in vain to squelch, it was a joy to watch father and son together as they worked to refill the dozen or so bird feeders that had hung neglected from the trees for the long months Albie'd been gone. This was the first chance they'd had to get outside and check over the feeder situation, what with the terrible weather of the last few weeks. This morning, the sunshine was hinting at warmer things to come. Kitty couldn't help noting that the change in the weather coincided with the change in Jesse. Winter suddenly turning into spring when his beloved Pop showed up at long last, late one night. But not so late there wasn't time for a bedtime story for his adoring son.

As she was sprinkling on the last of the coconut and congratulating herself for having resisted the urge to lick her fingers, there was a sharp rap at the front door. Clapping her hands together to get rid of the last few shreds of coconut, she was surprised to find the tall lean figure of the young Town Constable on the porch.

"Sorry I didn't call first, just took a chance you might be home," said Gussie matter of factly after Kitty had ushered her into the small living room. "I just heard your husband came back home, when was it? Day before last? And I wanted to say how glad I am to hear he's okay and, oh dear! Am I interrupting something?" Clusters of red and blue balloons were bobbing gently in the air currents stirred up by the opened door. A blaze of bright red tulips in a squat blue vase on the dining room table caught her eye. The house was redolent of fried onions and garlic overlaid with something sweet. Kitty herself seemed a bit flustered. Instead of her usual jeans and sweatshirt, she wore a flowered apron over a pale pink dress with puffed sleeves and her long yellow braid was interwoven with pink and white striped ribbon. Traces of something powdery, which looked suspiciously like flour, decorated her face and arms.

"Oh no! At least, not yet," Kitty replied brightly. Seeing Gussie's look, she took a swipe at her cheeks with the back of her hand, leaving a smear of chocolate mocha frosting behind. *I must look a fright! She always looks so neat and trim. How does she do it with that job of hers, I wonder. Must be messy sometimes though, hauling bodies through the woods.* Aloud she said, "We're having a combination Welcome Home and Happy Birthday party for Albie tonight. Though it's not really his birthday. He had that when he was still away from us. Won't you sit down for a minute?"

"I won't stay long," Gussie assured her, looking around for some place to sit. The sofa was piled high with newspapers and magazines, while the only other seat in the room was a well-worn and legless chair. Stepping carefully over a jumble of toy cars and a half completed jigsaw puzzle, which was taking up most of the floor, Gussie reached the chair and eased her long body down onto it.

"I had another reason for wanting to see you, I mean another reason," she began. "I've been wondering how Jesse's been getting along. I heard there was some trouble over at the school. With his teacher, I mean. You know how it is in this town. Everybody talks about everything," she added by way of explanation.

"Well, now that his Pop is back, I hope that'll all change," Kitty said, perching awkwardly on one arm of the sofa and making no attempt to apologize for the clutter. "His teacher, that Miss Snelgrove, told me in no uncertain terms, in fact she was real sharp about it, his marks are so bad he might not pass in June."

"That's what I'm here about," said Gussie. "First I want to apologize again for taking him over to the woods with me that day. I shouldn't have done it. It wasn't a good idea for a kid his age to be exposed to something like, well, anyway, I shouldn't have done it. But I want you, and him too of course, to know that if I hadn't, Mr. Denton might not have been found until spring came and then poor Mrs. Denton ..."

"I know what you mean. I know exactly what you mean. How dreadful she would have been feeling all this time, not knowing. I mean, well, you can see how it was with us, not knowing all these months where Albie, well, poor Jess was in a pretty bad way, I can tell you." Kitty sighed and began fiddling with her hair ribbons.

"That's the other thing I wanted to talk to you about," continued Gussie, clasping her hands around her knees, which, from the lowness of the chair, were forced upwards at a steep angle. She was beginning to wish Kitty had taken her into the kitchen where the chairs, old and beat up as they were, might have been a lot more comfortable. "I've done some checking with different people about kids in his situation and I wondered, that is, with your permission, that is, you and his father together of course, if you both agree, if you think it might be a good idea for him to get together with Mrs. Denton."

"As far as I know, at least from what Miss Kibbidge tells me, Mrs. Denton still hasn't a clue who it was that found her husband. I think, well, it might help Jesse if he knew what a difference it made to her that he happened to go into the woods that day. With all that snow we had, and the wild dogs around here, well..." She gestured with both hands and returned them to their position around her stiffening knees. "And besides, I don't want Mrs. Denton to go on thinking *I* was the one who found him, that I did it all by myself, I mean, all by myself. And ..." she shifted her hands to her lap and crossed her ankles, "I think it might help the situation at school if his teacher could be told just exactly what's been bothering him." She leaned forward, anticipating Kitty's reaction.

Kitty's eyes widened. "You mean she *still* doesn't know? Mrs. Denton I mean? I can't believe, well, with all the gossip in this town I would have thought that—"

Gussie shook her head. "The fellows who work for me are real good at keeping things to themselves. I don't think even their families have the least idea, I mean the least idea what was going on. And then of course everyone got distracted when that first big blizzard hit us so unexpectedly."

"Mmmm, that's true. Awful, wasn't it. I was so worried about Albie that night. Well, all that's over with, thank goodness." Kitty looked thoughtful for a moment. Then she stopped fiddling with the ribbons and leaned towards Gussie. "What you said before, about having Jess meet Mrs. Denton. Do you really think it would help? I was hoping he'd forget all about it. Well, most of it anyway. But I've seen this kind of strange faraway look come over his face every once in a while, and I don't think he, well, he's never talked about it, not to me anyway. But he sometimes cries out in his sleep. Real loud. So loud sometimes that it wakes me up. I'll have to ask Albie what he thinks," she said firmly, sitting erect again. "He hasn't been home long enough to hear the whole story. At least, I don't think—"

"Did you find out where he was all this time?" Gussie broke in. "We put a tracer out on him when you first told me about it, but it didn't turn up a thing."

"Oh, yes! I guess it's safe to tell you. But it mustn't go any further. Promise me you'll keep it to yourself, won't you? I mean, if you weren't a cop ..."

When Gussie nodded in agreement, Kitty leaned forward again and said in a low voice, "Undercover work. For the government. There was talk over at the Reserve the Indians were unhappy about some land deal going on they thought was going to affect them and Albie was sent in to—"

"Don't tell me any more. I can guess. And of course they ordered him not to say anything about where he was or what he was doing. Even to his wife. Too bad. That kind of thing is always so hard on the rest of the family. Not knowing. I remember Mac telling me once—"

"Something else I guess I should have told you at the time." It was Kitty's turn to interrupt. "I mean, before you took Jess with you. But I was too scared. I'd been getting these strange phone calls for Albie. Late at night. At the time, I thought it might have something to do with, well anyway, turns out it was just an old buddy of Albie's trying to get in touch with him. I don't know why the man wouldn't give me his name. Probably he's in the same line of work, maybe some other secret stuff for the government. Albie hasn't said. Anyway, between Jess and those phone calls ..."

"That's too bad," Gussie said again. "You've had a lot on your plate haven't you? What did your husband do before—"?

There was a noise from the back door and heavy footsteps could be heard coming into the kitchen. The footsteps stopped, then muffled giggles were followed by whispers, then deep exclamations, followed by more giggling.

"Hands off that cake, you two," Kitty called out. "Come in here. We've got company."

The noises in the kitchen stopped abruptly, then Jesse poked his head around the doorframe. When he saw who it was, he came bounding into the room, trailed by the big dark man that was his father.

"Hey Pop, this is the lady I was just telling you about. Remember? That day when — but I didn't tell him everything, I, I, I..." Jesse sputtered to a stop and looked anxiously from one woman to the other. But his mother had a smile on her face. And the lady cop, who was also smiling at him, stood up. Wow. Jesse could see she was a whole lot taller than his Pop. Wow. He'd always thought Pop was big.

Albie stepped forward to shake Gussie's hand.

"Some funny goings on, I hear," he said in his deep, rich voice. "Look what happens when I'm not here for a while," he said, looking down at Jesse with a twinkle in his eye.

"It wasn't a while, it was for a long, long, *long* time," countered Jesse, snuggling up close and rubbing his chin on Albie's arm like a friendly pup.

"Happy to meet you at last, Mr. Woodcock." Gussie extricated her hand from Albie's grasp. And she'd always thought Mac's handshake was firm. "I just dropped by to say I was glad to hear you were back safe and sound, I mean safe and sound. But I'll be getting out of your way now so you can get on with your celebrating," Gussie said, stepping back over the clutter on the floor. "I'll be in touch in a day or two," she said to Kitty who was still perched on the sofa arm, staring at her husband and son and thinking she'd been right about one thing. Albie *was* the most important person in Jesse's life. Oh well, maybe she should think about having another baby. Maybe. Or then again, maybe not.

"Pop says I might be able to get a dog!" Jesse grabbed at his mother's apron.

"Did he really?" said Kitty in surprise. "Well, we'll see. We'll see how things go with your schoolwork." *Trust Albie to go behind my back. Oh well, maybe that's what the kid needs after all he's been through. Something cute and cuddly to call his own.*

"How's your father coming along?" she asked Gussie when they'd reached the front door. "We heard he was pretty sick. Is he still in the hospital or ...?"

"Not much longer, thank goodness. I got him into that new little nursing home up in Cooley's. I wasn't impressed with what

Dunhampton had to offer." Gussie replied, remembering the Our Happy Home incident.

"That's good. In a smaller place, he'll be sure to get more attention. And Cooley's is a lot closer, that's for sure," agreed Kitty.

"Yeah, it should be a lot easier to get up to visit him. He's going to be there for quite a while, they tell me. Thanks for asking," Gussie said as she went down the steps to her car.

On the short drive back to the station, she wondered which land the Indians were worried about. Surely it couldn't have been ... well, when she could find a spare minute, she'd have to look into this a bit further.

37
ALMOST THERE!

"And then! And then — oh Syd! You can't imagine how *awful* it was! There she was, that gorgeous creature, dressed to the nines as usual with the make-up and jewellery to match. There she was — faced with a dead body! Doc Blair has this little room way down at the far end of the hall he keeps for, well, you probably know for what," Gussie paused to untangle her legs, one of which had developed a painful cramp from sitting too long.

She and Syd were on their way back from a tour of the nursing home up in Cooley's Mills. It was that in-between time called twilight, when the visibility can make driving a little tricky and hard on the eyes. The light's almost gone, but it's not really dark. Syd kept his eyes firmly fixed on the road. He was a little worried about his truck. Something funny was going on with the engine. It had been making odd pinging sounds and had a tendency to cut out when he least expected it. He'd been too busy all day to take it in to Aikins Car Repair: *We're Just Aikin to Fix Your Wagon.* He'd been so anxious to see Gussie again, he took a chance and offered to take her up. He decided the best thing he could do was to concentrate on nursing the old bus along and give Gussie her head. Even though he'd been itching to ask her if she'd gone through with the arrests. But he knew her well enough to figure she wouldn't feel much like talking about any of it until after she'd checked out the place where Mac would be recuperating from his heart attack. The little convalescent home in Cooley's had just opened the month before. Mac would be one of their first patients.

"Awful!" repeated Gussie vigorously massaging the offending leg. "I mean, there he was, flat on his back, draped in a horrible yellow rubber sheet. His face was all we could see of him. And it was bloated," she gave a shudder, then went on, "and, and, uh, well it looked absolutely *ghastly!*" This last came out in a squawk as she squirmed around in her seat, finally turning slightly towards him in an effort to get comfortable. "I mean, this wasn't the first time I've seen a dead body, but somehow this one, well, you know how handsome he was. Those dark eyes. That killer smile. Always dressed from head to foot in black. Slick as a Mississippi river boat gambler."

Syd nodded, remembering how often in the past he'd envied the man for being such a sharp dresser. Always so sure of himself, living in that house up on the hill with the most stunning woman in town for a wife. Well, he sure didn't envy him now.

Then, when he realized Gussie had fallen silent, Syd asked, "Well? What did she do? Burst into tears? Faint? What?"

"That's what was so awful," Gussie said after another vain attempt to get some relief from the cramp. "She just stood there. No loud shrieks and no gasps. No tears. Not even a change of expression. Not one shred of emotion. Nothing, nothing at all like poor CeeCee Denton. She was like, like ice." Gussie broke off and attacked the offending calf again. "Gosh, I'm glad we don't have too much farther to go. My leg is just about killing me." And she told him about her visit to the Woodcocks'.

"Go on about the ice maiden. What happened then?"

"Well, she just stood there, I mean just stood there. Stock-still like a beautiful statue. Staring down at him. Then she turned and headed for the door. We couldn't stop her, I mean, we didn't want to have to chase after her. Past all those people in the waiting room? Can you imagine? It's too bad there isn't a separate door to that part of the building. Well, I shouldn't say that. Maybe there is, but she wouldn't have known or even cared at that point where it was. Anyway, when she was asked directly by the doc was it her husband Peter Wychwood or not, she said through her teeth, 'it's him all right, the fool'. And then she broke away from us. She didn't look left or right, just marched right through the waiting room and was gone! Can you believe it? Doc Blair said he's seen odd reactions before, but never—"

"So much for all those good looks. She sounds like a real—" Syd stifled a snort. "I'd better not say it."

"I know, I know. You're just being polite. Well anyway, right after that I went over to East Thorne to pick up Ferd Otterley. I struck it lucky there. They were just on their way out the door. Just finishing loading up their car. If I'd gotten there a few minutes later, well ... Francy Otterley looks terrible, pale as a ghost. I hear she's been sick most of the winter. Bronchial pneumonia or something, CeeCee said. And Ferd? Well, he knew the jig was up as soon as he saw me. He kept saying over and over, 'it was an accident, I tell you, it wasn't supposed to happen, it was an accident'. Francy started crying and threw her arms around him and I had to pry her away and tell her to get back in the house. I told her she better call someone to come out and stay with her. I don't know, maybe I should have done something for her, helped her with her suitcases or -"

"I know," interrupted Syd. "You were afraid old Ferd would cut and run."

"Yeah, but he didn't. He just stood there, with his eyes closed. Francy probably called CeeCee Denton to come over and stay with her, I mean, who else is there? CeeCee told me Francy's always complaining she can never get a hold of her daughter. She lives in some kind of commune in the City. What a family! Anyway, as soon as she disappeared back into the house, I put Ferd in the back of the cruiser. He came quietly enough. If I didn't know any better, I'd say he seemed real relieved, I mean real relieved."

"Did you find out what he'd done back in the City? The trouble Mac mentioned in his letter?"

"Nope, not so far. I hope I'll be able to tomorrow though. There's this cop I know who can find out for me. Anyway, as soon as we got going, our Mister Otterley clammed up and stayed that way. All the way over to Dunhampton. He had this strange look on his face, like he was somewhere else. In a world of his own, I mean. You know, I've been thinking maybe he's not quite right in the head. Early senility or something. They called me from the jail just before you picked me up. He still hasn't said anything. Not one word, other than wanting a lawyer, that is."

"Good for you, Gus. That's two down anyway. Or should I say three. Then what? What about that Nick Fearnley? Word is, he's off somewhere again."

"Yeah, well, when I found *that* out, I made a quick call to the police down in Texas. Our innocent-acting Mister Fearnley's with a bunch of birders, somewhere in the Rio Grande area. I got that little tidbit from his neighbour down at The Landing. She told me Nick didn't make a secret of where he was going. He must think we're awfully stupid or something. The sheriff I talked to said they'd track him down and ship him back here. Under escort of course. I already got the paperwork done. It shouldn't take too long. I hear those Texas cops are pretty good."

"That just leaves ...?"

"Yeah, well ..."

That left two, but Syd didn't dare say it, knowing she was thinking about Mac. That arrest was going to be the hardest.

"Yeah. Joe Gaffield. I didn't want to handle that one alone so I waited 'til Perce could come along for backup. I couldn't be too sure how old Joe'd react. He's kind of a tough customer, I mean a tough customer. You never know what a guy like that'll do."

"A typical Gaffield, I'd say. Although there is quite a bit of Bartlett blood in there. You'd think maybe—"

"You never can tell, can you? I remember what you said before, about the Gaffields, I mean. Anyway, as I was saying, good old reliable Perce showed up mid afternoon. Poor guy. One side of his face was all swollen out to here from having been at the dentist's, but he insisted on coming down anyway. I was kind of afraid Joe would try to make a run for it before we could get there. I guess with Pete dead, Nick away and Ferd already picked up, there was no one to warn him. Well, we drove the cruiser right up to the front door of the Quick Bite, and there he was, looking out the window. So he saw us coming. He tried to get out the back way, but good old Perce took care of that all right. Joe put up a struggle, gave Perce a hard time for a couple of minutes, but I managed to persuade him it would be for his own good if he came with us. Maybe I've got Mac's gift of the gab after all!" Gussie burst out laughing so loudly she startled Syd, who couldn't help laughing with her.

"Thank God I had Perce with me," she went on, suddenly turning serious again. "That Joe character scares me. After we hauled him over to Dunhampton, we went straight back down to the Quick Bite to have a good look around."

Syd could tell that Gussie was feeling pretty good. And she was. It had been a rough day, but she'd managed to do what had to be done with a minimum of fuss. And help. They were almost back in Bickerton now. Up ahead they could see the streetlights stretching around the last curve before the town proper. Syd half considered asking Gussie to come home with him, then thought better of it. His place was a mess. And anyway, if he wanted her to think seriously about them getting back together, he'd better take it nice and slow, one step at a time. After all, last night could have been a fluke. But Gussie was ahead of him.

"Want to come over for a bite of something? I can finish telling you the rest of it. What I found at Joe's place. And a few other things."

"What an inducement! And what a story this'll make for the good old *Bugler*. It'll give the town something to talk about, for sure. And, I haven't told you what I found out this morning. About the Roxton land, I mean. Let's just hope this old crate doesn't conk out before we get there."

It was really late by the time they'd finished eating and Syd told Gussie she still made the best spaghetti he'd ever tasted and Gussie said that was good to hear, she didn't have much time to cook these days. But, as she modestly put it, a good bottle of red wine can turn any meal into a banquet. After the spaghetti and tossed salad, she got out an apple pie she'd picked up from the Cosy Corner that morning, cut two big wedges and added a scoop of vanilla ice cream to each. They polished that off in short order.

Gussie topped up their wineglasses and then settled in to tell Syd about the rest of her day. About searching the ramshackle shed behind the Quick Bite and finding a small car tucked away in at the back behind a huge pile of junk, old chairs and crates of empty pop bottles and tubs of rancid grease. Stuff like that. A real fire trap, she said it was. And about Perce climbing on top of the car and finding a well-used bow, the kind he remembered his Dad using to hunt wild turkeys, stashed in the rafters up on top of a stack of newspapers. An empty quiver was with it. No arrows though. Just the bow with a broken string dangling from one end. Gussie was sure there must be an arrow or two around somewhere. They'd have to go back again and look around some more. Before leaving, she made sure the stove was turned off and the café was locked up tight. The last thing she did was stick the SORRY WE'RE CLOSED. PLEASE COME AGAIN sign in the window. Perce thought stringing some yellow police ribbon around the shed might be a good idea, but Gussie didn't want to draw attention to it at this stage.

"I know what you're going to say," Gussie said as she cleared their plates away. "There's still Dad. How in the dickens am I going to handle that? I need to talk to him, but the doc says he's still too weak. Have to wait a little longer, he said. A few more days, maybe. I can't leave it much longer than that. But I sure don't want him to have another attack, I mean another attack. He's looking much better today by the way. I dropped by the hospital after delivering our Mister Gaffield." She sighed and sat down again. "I still can't believe it. Dad. Of all people."

"What a tough break," Syd agreed as he swallowed the last of his wine, "and he might be the only one of the bunch you'll get the whole story from. How they did it. Or better still, why. Although we might have part of the answer to that already. I've had a busy day too, you know. I got into the Bickerton Archives. Down in the vault under the Town Hall just like Mac said. Funny I don't remember Dad ever mentioning anything about them."

"Maybe there's something in there he didn't want you to know about. After all, everyone has a skeleton or two hidden away."

"It could be you're right. I'll have to go back down there again when I have more time and see what I can dig up."

"Don't dig too deep," Gussie teased. "Did you have any trouble getting in there?"

"Nope, none at all. Old Jack Bickerton looks after all that stuff. Says anyone can look at them. I just had to sign his book. The same one they use for anyone visiting the building. Jack said the last time anyone was down in there was over ten years ago. Everything was coated in dust. Anyway, there they were. Boxes and bags of 'em. Shelves full of mouldy old registers. 'Births, Deaths and Marriages.' Stacks of land transactions, transfers, deeds. All kinds of musty old papers, going back for years and years, right back to when they first started keeping records after the first settlers decided to stay put and keep track of stuff.

Some of the old books just fell to pieces when I touched them. It's just too bad they're in such a sorry state. It made for some pretty interesting reading, I can tell you."

He stretched and yawned. "Tell me something, Gus. Why does everything have to happen at once? It's a bit hard to handle, isn't it. No real excitement around here for a long time. No murders for a donkey's age. And now we don't just have one. It looks like we might have two!" He chuckled. "And people around here think this sort of thing only happens in the City."

Gussie laughed. "You're right. Not in our nice little town. Well? What do they say? It never rains but it pours? I don't know about you, but I've had enough rain, and snow, and bodies to last me a lifetime. But I've got to tell you something, and keep this under your hat, will you, until we know for sure? I don't think Pete Wychwood was murdered. What I think is, since Doc Blair said from his preliminary examination of the body that Pete's lungs were full of water, what I think is our handsome Mister Wychwood went down to the Lake to see if he could find Dad's boat. By himself. After dark. He must have been the one to leave it there. Maybe he got caught out in that first big blizzard. He must have had to abandon it. Maybe he figured with all the snow melting so fast, the boat would show up and someone would be sure to find it. Everyone knows Dad's boat and how fussy he is with it. Maybe Pete had some wild idea of getting it back over to Dad's before it was spotted. With those fancy boots of his, he could have slipped on the rocks. Hit his head and fallen in. And drowned. Just like that. And only a couple of yards away from the GUS E. DUP."

"Do you really think they used Mac's boat somehow, without him knowing? But they must have. Why else would Pete have been so anxious to find it? Was that how Hink Denton's body got way over by the Old Barge Canal?"

"That's what I still have to figure out. Dad swears he locked up the boathouse. It was the only thing he had strength enough to say just before I left him. He's terribly upset his boat's not where it should be. More than somewhat, I think. That's why I figure he didn't even know it had been used. And then there's that note Dottie found in Hink Denton's pocket. Oh, there's still a lot more work to do to put it all together. To make a proper case, I mean."

"Do you think they could have killed Denton somewhere else and then hauled him over to the Old Barge Canal and then into the woods?" Syd couldn't let go of the idea. "That must have taken some doing. Taking a chance like that. Hoping and praying nobody would see them."

"It could be. That would explain the GUS E. DUP thing. But I've got to have proof. It's no good just speculating." Gussie sighed again. "I'm sure Dad knows exactly what happened. I just hope I can get it out of him before the powers that be over at Dunhampton decide to lock him up along with his cronies Ferd and Joe. And Nick Fearnley when he's been hauled back from his birding expedition. After all, just because Mac's my father doesn't let him off the hook."

"Yeah. Too bad for him. And for you too of course," Syd said, reaching across the table and taking both her hands in his. "It's going to be rough, Gus."

They sat quietly for a minute, still holding hands. Then Syd said, "I didn't finish telling you about the stuff I found in the archives. It took me most of the morning. I was about ready to quit when I finally came across a reference to some property down past The Landing. A big chunk of land that's Roxton land. Right smack dab on the waterfront. It belongs to old Eliza for as long as she lives and then goes to her heirs. It has to stay in Roxton hands. That'd be George or Sherry, I guess. Or both. Unless there's more Roxtons kicking around somewhere we don't know about. Probably they'll start coming out of the woodwork as soon as old Eliza's gone. I wonder if that's why those two — Pete and you think maybe it was Joe — showed up at the Our Happy Home that day. Something to do with that property."

"But why? What interest could they possibly have had? And what did they hope to gain by terrorizing the old gal? That's the question I've got to find the answer to. And how in the world does Hink Denton fit into all this?" Gussie stood up. "Well, we aren't going to sort it out tonight, are we. Besides, I'm too tired to think about it any more."

Syd stood up at the same time, still holding one of Gussie's hands. "Does that mean you want me to stay over? I'd love it if you did. I've got so much to tell you. About the *Bugler* and—"

"We can talk upstairs," said Gussie, giving his fingers a gentle squeeze. "I've got some things to say to you too."

38

THE WISDOM OF
DOROTHY KIBBIDGE

"My!" said Dottie, "my, oh my! Oh dearie me, I need to sit down. Right now!" and she plumped the canvas bag she'd been carrying down in the middle of the old pine table in CeeCee's kitchen and herself onto one of the chairs. "This is some strange story. This bears thinkin' about, that's for certain sure."

"Know it's unbelievable," CeeCee, who'd already collapsed onto another chair, was quick to agree. "Couldn't hardly accept it myself at first. Glad to find out at long last what really happened. Even if it sounds like some kind of wild tale taken out of, well, one of those cheap paperbacks with the awful covers." She wrinkled her nose.

Surrounded by the debris of moving house, the two friends had just come back from a quick trip to the City. Boxes and bags of discards were stacked by the kitchen door, waiting for Rab to take them to the dump. Through the open doorway across the hall, the once opulent living room looked sad and abandoned. The oil paintings in gilded frames Maggie had secretly appraised the day she and Pete dropped in, had left their mark on the walls in the form of bleached shapes and empty hooks. They'd already been sent over to Dunhampton to be auctioned off.

Some said CeeCee might have done better on them if they'd been taken in to the City, but after an exploratory drive around the residential neighbourhood, she figured there was lots of money in the County town. The man from Dunhampton's House of Auctions had come over to pick up the paintings the day after she phoned. If she'd tried one of those bigger places in the City, it could have taken them weeks to send someone out as far as a little place like Bickerton and then they would have charged for their time on the road. And anyway, as she told Dottie, she didn't want to have to look at those pictures any longer than she had to.

The green velvet sofa with its coordinating chairs and the carpets so admired by Dottie had been gone for weeks. Sold to the nice young couple who were buying Bewyching Wood. After the death of her husband, the glamorous Maggie Wychwood had decided to move on. Any hope of her acquiring Hill House had vanished with the revelations in the *Bugler* that were still making the town buzz with rumours and speculation. No one seemed to know where she'd gone, but as some said, well, that one was like a cat, sure to land on her feet.

As she'd half expected, CeeCee's daughters were appalled when they found out about the paintings. Especially Janette. Mother, how could you, Dad took years to collect them, you've practically given them away. CeeCee worried when she heard this last. Had she raised a Maggie Wychwood without realizing it? No, it must have come from her son-in-law. Surely no daughter of hers could be so covetous.

The things that CeeCee really valued – her books, a few photographs, her collection of crystal figurines and some things of her mother's – were already gone, over to the Kibbidges'. The only things still waiting to be moved were the old pine table and the chairs they were sitting on. Old and scratched up they might be, but they were the only pieces of furniture she wanted to keep.

Dottie and Rab had told her repeatedly she could stay with them as long as she liked. Forever, if she wanted to. At the moment, she was grateful for the offer, but thought it best to get rid of the house first and let some time go by before deciding what to do next. She might even buy another house. In town, this time. Or in the village. Even though everyone knew who she was by now, notorious as it might seem, it was still preferable to the anonymity of the City where no one cared much if you lived or died or what your family name was. It didn't seem to matter now whether she fit in or not. Or that she wasn't related to half the people in the County. She'd gotten used to the charm and the tranquility of the town and its surroundings. Especially over in the Village of East Thorne. Not a bad place to end her days.

But that event could be years away. Right now, she had plenty of life left in her. The rush trip they'd just made to the City was for CeeCee to see a lawyer. Not that there wasn't a lawyer in Bickerton. She just felt she wanted to keep her affairs as private as possible. Hink's will was finally being probated. In a few more days, she'd learn what her financial status would be. Then and only then could she think about making any solid plans. Maybe do some traveling if she could afford it. She remembered reading somewhere that widows should wait at least a year before making any major decisions. She didn't think it would take her that long to adjust. CeeCee didn't know it, but the astute Dottie had already noticed how much her friend was enjoying her new-found freedom.

It had been a long and tiring day. The drive back home passed in relative silence, with the two women content to admire the way the brown of the fields was gradually yielding to the freshness of green and to welcome the lift that spring's arrival always gives to those who have to suffer through long winters. Back once more at her former home, while they were waiting for an agent from Countryside Real Estate to come and give an estimate on the house, CeeCee related the rest of what she'd found out about Hink's death from Constable Spilsbury. Dottie was right. It *was* a strange story. CeeCee still wasn't quite sure if she understood it all properly.

"Anyway," she told Dottie, who was sitting across from her, goggle-eyed and speechless, a rare state for her. Dottie was shocked, but at the same time, thrilled to hear what nasty things some people she knew had been up to. "Anyway, seems there was some kind of get-rich-quick scheme cooked up among the whole bunch of them. Francy's husband, can you believe? Ferd Otterley, that pompous little so-and-so?" Dottie nodded, but kept quiet. She was dying to hear the rest of it and was afraid if she made a comment, CeeCee would clam up.

"That Ferd, making her life miserable all winter and her so sick and everything." CeeCee paused to clear her throat and then took up the story again. "And then there was that smartass, pardon my French, that birding guide Nick, Nick Fearnley. When I think of how he made fun of Hink's socks that day and all the time he, well, I won't say it. Won't make me any better than him. And Pete Wychwood, rest his soul. And that awful Joe Gaffield. You know? The owner of that little café? More of a greasy spoon I'd call it, down near The Landing. And the worst of all? Gussie's Dad, Mac Noble. Imagine! Poor Gussie. Her own father mixed up in something like this. Felt sorry for her when she told me. Said Mac tried to stop them. That's what started his heart acting up."

CeeCee got up to see if anyone had come up the lane unheard, then came back and sat down again. She leaned across the table and lowered her voice. "They say he isn't doing too well, might not make it. And Gussie's hoping to put him in a nursing home Up North, but ..."

She sat back in her chair, wondering if it was too late to have one of those glazed doughnuts and decided it was. "Anyway, as I was saying, all five of them were in on it. Gussie said there might even be more, but anyway, my Hink got in their way. Seems the bunch of them thought they could make a killing if they could get their hands on a certain piece of land up past The Landing. No, no," CeeCee added before Dottie could say anything, "not near the beach where they found poor Pete Wychwood's body.

Up the other way, where there's a lot of trees that come right down to the water. Place is lousy with birds. Remember Hink talking about it one time after he'd been out with Ferd. Didn't pay much attention at the time. He was always going on about this place or that. Sure was good birding in there, he'd say. It always got so involved. What they saw and where they saw it. Guess I just stopped listening."

"What kind of a killin'?" Dottie asked, expertly stripping the skin off a ripe banana she'd taken out of the bag. She was glad to get a word in edgewise. "And what do you mean by a killin' ?"

"Making a pile of money. At least that's what they thought. Don't know which one of them it was heard there was some big shot down from the City nosing around. Looking for a place to put in a marina and this spot has a natural harbour without all the—"

"A marina? In Bickerton? What next!" Dottie shook her head. She broke off a large piece of banana. "Go on," she said as she popped it in her mouth. This was better than a mystery book. It was almost like living in the middle of it.

"Know it sounds odd," replied CeeCee, reaching into the bag for a banana and coming up with an orange instead. "Not enough people around here with big boats. Or boats of any kind, except those little outboards. At least, not yet there isn't," she said, neatly slicing through the thick peel with her thumbnail. "Maybe the man, whoever he is, knows something we don't."

"Come to think on it," Dottie said, getting ready to finish off the rest of the banana, "Miz Crumb told me yesterday when I popped over to see her, she said her Davey, ya know the young fella, well anyways, he saw somethin' in a newspaper that said City people are startin' to look for places more quiet. Maybe like yous did. Or even them Otterleys. Somewheres to get away from all them crowds and noise. And dirt. Maybe this big shot, like ya said, figures to get in on the ground floor and be ready for 'em."

"Well, the Otterleys were looking for more than peace and quiet. Tell you that story some day. Not now, though. Could be you're right about the rest of it, though. Heard the man who's thinking of buying Tom Bartlett's house has a big boat. Rab told me he called the other day to ask where's a good place to keep it. Got his name from Gussie. Didn't he tell you about it?"

"Half the time he forgets to tell me if he's comin' in for dinner. He prob'ly forgot, what with all that's been goin' on." Dottie rummaged around in her purse for something to wipe her sticky hands on. "Ya know, CeeCee," she went on, after discovering an old hankie down near the bottom, "that killin' business? That's the trouble with some people. Never have enough, it seems. Always wantin' more. Gettin' greedier every minute. Never satisfied, are they, poor things. Never learn, do they. Money," she snorted, "money don't buy you happiness. Never has, never will. Why is Tom sellin' his house?"

"Something to do with his lady friend. That teacher, Miss Snelgrove," CeeCee said, unfazed by Dottie's abrupt change of subject. "Anyway, as I was saying, somehow one of them found out that piece of land was Roxton property. You know? Poor old Eliza, whose big house is up next to the Wychwood place up on the hill? Anyway, they got the idea to go over to that Our Happy Home place where Eliza's been for the last few years and talk to the old lady. See if they could persuade her to sign over the property to them. Don't know for the life of me how they found out she owned it. Maybe Gussie's Dad thought that, anyway, Gussie said they told the people over at the Home they were relatives. Gussie said at first she thought from their descriptions the two who showed up that day were Pete Wychwood and my Hink. Later on she found out it was Pete all right. But — and I could have told her this much — Hink being the honest guy that he was? The other fellow wasn't him. It was that awful Joe Gaffield. From the Quick Bite." She gave a little shudder. "Said she got that part of the story out of Nick. Joe hasn't admitted to a thing, at least, not so far."

CeeCee had divided her orange into sections and was carefully arranging them in a row on the tabletop.

"Gussie said they almost scared the life out of poor old Eliza," she went on, picking up a section of orange. "Turns out she couldn't have done anything. The Roxton property is only hers for as long as she lives. What they call a life interest in the property, Gussie said. Once she's gone, it automatically goes to the next oldest Roxton."

"What about that Tom Bartlett? Was he in on it? I heard he was a good friend of Pete Wychwood's." Dottie couldn't resist any longer and started in on the box of doughnuts she'd picked up in the City. "I better make us some tea," she added. "Good thing ya left the teakettle and some cups here."

"Can't be without our tea, can we, although a cup of coffee would go nicely with these", and CeeCee picked up a chocolate-coated doughnut. "Too bad all we've got is a tin of that old ropey tasting stuff Hink liked so much. Poor Hinky! He was always so straight. Bet he didn't want to see property spoiled for some development. With the trees all cut down, there'd be no more birding in there, for sure. Didn't finish telling you this last bit, did I? Nick said Hink threatened to go and see Syd Spilsbury and have him put something in the *Bugler* about it. Well, they put a stop to that happening, all right. You're so right, Dottie. Greedy fools. The whole darn bunch. Greed took my Hink's life."

"But what about Tom Bartlett?" persisted Dottie as she filled the teakettle. "Didn't Gussie mention him at all?"

"What makes you think *he's* involved?"

"Well, that day over at the library. Remember? When I was after gettin' more books for Miz Crumb and Sherry Roxton told me ... hmm ... I can't tell ya what she told me, well, at least not yet, uh, Sherry said Tom was the one who took Pete Wychwood home when he got drunk that time and everyone was talkin' bout Pete and why he was gettin' drunk in public. It could be Pete was so far gone, he let something slip to Tom and that's when—"

"How on earth did that subject come up? Must say I'm surprised at you, Dottie. Thought you were there to get books, not to catch up on all the gossip," CeeCee said with a sniff of disapproval.

"Tisn't gossip if it's true. Leastwise that's what my Mam always told us," said Dottie defensively. She'd nearly said too much. CeeCee still didn't know about young Jesse. She ought to be told, but Dottie didn't think she should be the one to tell her.

"How did Tom's name come into it? Come on, Dottie. All ears here. How?" CeeCee wasn't giving in on this one.

"Well," Dottie began. She was interrupted by the rumble of a car coming up the lane. Talk about letting something slip. And she hadn't had a drop to drink. Not even tea. She hurried to finish what she'd been saying before the real estate agent reached the door. "Don't think Tom Bartlett had a thing to do with it. That's what that nice lady cop told me anyhow. He remembered Pete's folks. From when he lived here before. His Dad and Pete's were good friends. He just wanted to help Pete, is all."

They heard a car door slam, followed by the sound of footsteps on the porch and then a brisk rap at the door. CeeCee got to her feet and went out into the front hall. She had mixed emotions about selling the place. This had been their dream home, well, Hink's anyway. That was all over now, wasn't it. With him gone, it was time for her to make a new start. She took a deep breath, squared her shoulders and with a welcoming smile on her face, opened the door wide.

ABOUT THE AUTHOR

Laura Haferkorn is a retired advertising copywriter and editor, currently living on the North Shore of Lake Ontario with her husband and two Dandie Dinmont terriers. A keen observer of human interaction, she is working on the next Gussie Spilsbury mystery. Her other writings can be found at her website: www.laura-haferkorn.com.